Al & Rose,
T.

eing
zunch
!
bt

Praise for *Behind My E*

MW00423547

"Jessica Holt has delivered an intriguing book which captures the reader's attention and holds it firmly. Following two young women from different worlds as each of their journeys eventually leads them into the life of the other, the story is captivating and ultimately satisfying. Hard to put down. An impressive work from a first-time author."

-Carl E. Beck, Executive Editor, Retired
Herald-Journal, Spartanburg, SC

"A captivating story of two women from opposite worlds and equal affliction, *Behind My Eyes* is a must read for everyone! The narrative is both unique and engaging and Jessica Holt does a fantastic job bringing the emotion of each character's perspective to life. This book is sure to have you invested and turning page after page as you follow the story of Juliet and Jasmine."

-Meredith Higgins, Copyeditor

"Jessica Holt's book is a compelling story, well done and with the possibility of a film version. I look forward to seeing *Behind My Eyes* as a film someday!"

-Ed Y. Hall, Author
Brigadier General, Retired
United States Army

Behind My Eyes

Jessica Holt

Behind My Eyes

Copyright © 2015 by Jessica Holt
Cover Art © 2015 by Joe Locke

No part of this book may be used or reproduced in any manner whatsoever without the prior written permission of the copyright owner, except in the case of brief quotations embodied in critical articles and reviews.

This is a work of fiction. Any references to historical events or real locales are used fictitiously. Other names, characters, places, and incidents are the product of the author's imagination. Any resemblance to actual events, locales, or persons, living or dead, is entirely coincidental.

ISBN-13: 978-0692562833
ISBN-10: 0692562834

www.jessicaholtwrites.com

For my mom and dad, most of all

Behind My Eyes

Part I

A Beginning
at Every Ending

CHAPTER 1

COOPER

South Carolina

1922

THE MEMORY FEELS LIKE a thousand bees stinging my skin, but while it was happening, I felt nothing. I had to get my wife out of the bathtub. Her face was above the water, but her lips were blue and specks of ice glistened on her eyelashes.

I plunged my arms into the frigid water and lifted Liza's limp body. Her wet skin slid through my arms like a block of ice as I rushed her to the bed. Remembering what I'd been taught about body heat being the best warmth, I stripped off my clothes and lay down beside her. I wrapped her in a cocoon of bed covers and body parts and waited for any sign of life.

My own heartbeat pounded out the tips of my toes, but Liza's pulse was so faint that I had to press my palm into her breastbone just to feel a tap against my fingers. I held my other hand to her nostrils until a weak stream of warmth let me know she was alive.

I vigorously rubbed Liza's arms and legs, thinking if I could just get her blood flowing again, her heart would find its beat, her lungs would demand air, and she would wake up with rosy cheeks. One day we would laugh about the day her knight—in overalls rather than shining armor—saved her from the wintry bathtub. But no amount of rubbing seemed to warm her, much less wake her.

Suddenly Liza's body stiffened, and a faint moan emerged from the depths of her unconsciousness. I'd never been around a laboring woman, but I had assisted enough deliveries on the farm to know the baby was on its way.

My brain flat-out refused to put a single thought together as to how to help Liza. A minute passed with me helpless to my failing mind and her helpless to her failing body. The moaning stopped as abruptly as it started, Liza's stomach softened, her limbs relaxed, and she melted back into the mattress.

I threw on my pants and ran shirtless into the frozen night. The crisp air shocked my brain out of its stupor, and I spent the entire trip cursing myself for going into town and leaving Liza alone all day.

What was worse, I had insisted that Liza's mama ride with me and go visit a friend while I did my business. She hadn't let Liza be for over a week, and neither had her daddy and me. Every time Liza moved, we all scrambled as though the baby might fall right out of her.

I thought I was doing a nice thing for Liza by giving her a little peace and quiet before the baby came, and she had seemed eager to have it, assuring us she felt fine as she waved us up the driveway.

I called for Liza's mama as I ran, the icy remnants of a light dusting of snow crunching beneath my feet and slowing my progress through the pasture.

I was still a good hundred feet away when a lantern appeared on the porch, bounced down the steps, and glided effortlessly across the field in front of me, the owner of the hand that held it determined to reach her daughter.

The light disappeared inside my house, and by the time I toppled through the doorway on legs that felt like they had turned to jelly, Mrs. Ford was already by Liza's side, taking hold of her feet and pushing her knees up to her ears.

"Was she like this when you got home?"

"Yes ma'am, except she was in the bathtub! I don't know how long she'd been there, but the water was ice-cold and her lips were blue and she wasn't awake and she hasn't woken up since, even during the pain! Can she get the baby out?!"

"We'll help her get the baby out," Liza's mama answered calmly. "And then we'll tend to Liza. Now come hold these legs in place, son, so the baby will have more room."

I moved to Liza's side and set one hand on each of her knees.

"Okay, you stay right where you are and don't let those legs come down. The next time there's a contraction, I'm gonna get ahold of the baby's head."

Liza's stomach tightened. Mrs. Ford gripped the baby's head with sure hands, grimacing as her daughter groaned.

"Pull them legs back," she grunted.

Liza showed no signs of discomfort aside from the muffled moan and a slight curl in one corner of her mouth, but as churned up as my insides were, hers must have been screaming in agony as my mother-in-law patiently delivered the baby's head.

"When the next contraction comes," she instructed, "we're gonna get this baby out. You pull Liza's legs back as far as you can, and as soon as you see the baby's feet, go get a string and a pair of scissors."

I pulled until Liza was in a fetal position herself. Mrs. Ford held the baby's head with one hand and pressed on Liza's stomach with the other. Gradually, the baby came into the world—shoulders, arms alongside the back, a bottom, two legs, and two tiny feet at the end.

For a few seconds I was overcome by the miraculous little life Liza and I had made together, but as quickly as the joy came, panic set back in. Across Mrs. Ford's palm lay a limp baby as blue as its mama.

"Why ain't the baby making a noise? And why's he so blue? Is he dead?"

"He ain't dead. Right now he's still living through his mama. You'll hear him as soon as we cut the cord."

I realized then that I was the reason the baby was still attached to Liza. I pulled the pocket knife from my pants and the lace from my shoe. Mrs. Ford set the baby on Liza's stomach while she tied off the cord and cut it.

She cleaned the baby with a towel, being no more gentle than she would be with a washboard. I had seen newborn calves receive the same treatment and come to life, but my baby didn't respond to being kneaded like a ball of dough.

Picking him up by the ankles, Mrs. Ford gave him one good smack on the bottom. He went from blue to purple to maroon and wailed with an anger I had never been so happy to hear coming from another human being.

With the baby breathing on his own, Mrs. Ford sent me for my father-in-law. He was already stomping through the frozen field, coming to see what was keeping his wife. I hollered for him to hurry and ran back inside.

Mrs. Ford had swaddled the baby during the few seconds I was gone and was tucking blankets around Liza and murmuring a prayer only God could decipher.

"We've gotta get her to the hospital," she yelled to Mr. Ford when she heard his footsteps inside the front door.

Liza's daddy sent me to Dupre Carrington's house to ask for the use of his car. Mr. Ford's flatbed would expose Liza and the new baby to the harsh night—a risk that would most likely not end well for either of them.

I sprinted as fast as the frozen ground would allow, yelling, "Dupre, Liza needs to go to the hospital!" again and again.

The car met me halfway down Dupre's so-long-it-had-a-name-on-the-town-map driveway. I jumped into the passenger seat and we lumbered to the house, sliding on snow that was quickly becoming a sheet of ice.

Dupre blew the horn as he turned into the driveway. Liza's daddy hurried out the door with his daughter in his arms, and her mama followed close behind with the baby. I moved to the back seat, and Mr. Ford draped Liza across my lap with her head resting in the crook of my elbow.

What should have been a twenty minute drive turned into a forty minute creep to the community hospital. Liza didn't move once, and nobody else made a sound aside from the occasional mewing of the new baby.

ʕ ʔ

THE DOCTOR said we were just waiting for Liza's body to stop working. The nurses warmed her up and gave her medicine to make her comfortable, but her organs were already failing when we got to the hospital and nothing could be done to fix her.

Liza's mama and daddy went in to say goodbye while I waited in the hallway with the baby. Alone with my thoughts, the events of the evening rushed through my mind. I noticed details I had been unaware of in the moment—like how the house was dark when I got home and Liza wasn't waiting at the door to greet me. I should have known something was wrong before I stepped inside, or at the very least when I saw the broom propped against the living room wall with the dust pan half full on the floor next to it. Or when a dirty breakfast plate was still sitting on the kitchen table. Or when the bed was unmade. Or when no fire was burning in the fireplace.

But I hadn't consciously noticed any of the warning signs. I had just been anxious to see Liza after being away from her all day. If only I had recognized something wasn't right and rushed to find her, I might have found her in time. Maybe I would be sitting outside a room waiting for news of the arrival of my new baby rather than the last breath of my bride.

I felt the first sting as I sat there thinking *what if*. The sensation was so real that I almost lost my grip on the baby. It only lasted a fraction of a second—long enough to reach into the water and save Liza—but then I felt it again and again. The sting of bad decisions. The sting of missed opportunities. The sting of losing the love of my life. The sting of raising a motherless child.

My thoughts continued to brand my arms until I could hardly stand it. Just when I thought I was going to have to set the baby down to keep from dropping him, Mrs. Ford appeared and took him without saying a word.

Rubbing my forearms and reminding myself to breathe, I walked toward the door Mr. Ford held open. His eyes stayed fixed on the ground as I slipped past him and stepped into the hospital room to see my wife alive for the last time.

Liza looked peaceful. A handful of sand-colored freckles dotted her flawless porcelain face. Her red hair flowed down the arms of her nightgown. She looked like she was simply sleeping, but rather than the slow, rhythmic rise and fall of deep sleep, her chest jumped with quick, sporadic breaths.

I sat down on the edge of the bed and took Liza's hand in mine. Tears choked my words, but I composed myself long enough to tell her goodbye.

"Liza, I guess we ain't gonna get a proper goodbye. But you gotta listen to me now, all right? You had a beautiful baby..."

I couldn't finish the sentence. I thought of the baby as a boy, but I had only seen his backside before Mrs. Ford wrapped him in a blanket. I kissed Liza's hand and promised her I would be right back before I hurried out of the room and found Mrs. Ford sitting on a bench at the end of the hall.

"Is the baby a boy or a girl?" I asked breathlessly when I was close enough to speak without shouting.

Liza's mama looked up, distress showing on her face for the first time since the night began. Rather than giving me an answer, she held out the bundle. "Why don't you and Liza find out together?"

I carried the baby to Liza's side and removed the blanket. Carefully unpinning the baby's diaper, my breath caught. "You had a baby girl, Liza."

As I fumbled to reassemble the cloth around the baby's bottom, I gave my wife the only glimpse she would ever get of her daughter. "She's perfect. She's got real light hair with just a little red in it. And her eyes are as blue-green as the most beautiful ocean in the world, just like you imagined. She's gonna be okay, you hear? I'm gonna take real good care of her. I'll give her all that I can, and she'll go to school all the way through, and she'll grow up to be something, Liza. I'll see to that. Don't you worry about her. And she'll know her mama. I'll tell her about you every day and show her your pictures and make sure she knows her grandparents, too."

With the diaper back in place, I slid my hand under Liza's and felt a gentle squeeze. "That's right, Liza. I'll be okay, too. I'll think of you always, but I'll be strong for the baby. Me and the baby, we'll take care of each other. I need her just as much as she needs me."

Liza's hand squeezed mine a little tighter. Her eyes were closed and her breaths were shallow, but I knew she was with me.

"I believe with all my heart, Liza, that you're gonna see God today, and when you can tear yourself away from all the glories of heaven, you'll be able to look down on us and see that we're doing all right."

I laid the baby across Liza's chest and ran her hand along the tiny body. "This is Jasmine Rose Fowler. She'll be called Jasmine, just like you wanted."

A whisper of a smile crossed Liza's face. She took in our little daughter with one last, lingering breath and gave my hand another squeeze, holding on to life as long as she could.

At the end of what was both the longest and shortest moment of my entire life, Liza's hand went limp, settling across the baby's back. And just like that, the love of my life and mother of my child was gone.

CHAPTER 2

JULIET

London

1922

IF ROMEO'S JULIET was right about the rose, I offer then, that which we call abandonment by any other name would feel as catastrophic.

My nanny called it an extended holiday.

Two days after my fifth birthday she woke me before dawn and placed me in the bath. She scrubbed me with such vigor that I was unsure whether her purpose was to make me shine or bleed. She explained that I, or she, or perhaps both of us, either separately or together, would be going away for a bit. She seemed unclear on who was going where or for how long, and the more flustered she became, the harder she scrubbed.

With the bathtub scouring complete, Nanny dressed me in a new white Mass dress, white stockings, and glossy black shoes. She released my black curls from their foam restraints and tied the ends of a white ribbon into a bow on top of my head.

She led me outside and helped me onto the back seat of the car where my mother waited. It was only when my nanny, the woman solely responsible for my having survived five years of life, closed the door between us that I realized, somewhat frantically, that I would not be taking my extended holiday with her.

My mother called it matriculation.

As we left London and entered the English countryside, she spoke more to the chauffeur than I had ever heard her speak to any of the help. She babbled excessively about matriculating me, nervously shifting her focus between the back of the driver's head and his reflection in the rearview mirror.

I watched the driver as my mother talked, hoping for a clue as to what her obvious anxiety meant for my immediate well-being, but his eyes did not leave the road as he acknowledged her with only a compulsory nod or *yes ma'am.*

The driver called it school.

The car passed through an iron gate and slowed to a stop in the shadow of a sprawling stone building. The driver held the door open while my mother and I exited the car. As I stepped past him, he said, "Enjoy your time at school, Miss Juliet."

Before I had the opportunity to question him, my mother ushered me up a dozen stone steps to two daunting wooden doors. As she lifted a fisted hand to knock on the right one, the left one began to open with the slowness its heaviness required.

The door lethargically revealed a stern-faced nun. With no time for pleasantries, she led us into a small office and showed us to two chairs before sitting down behind an oversized desk. Clasping her hands on its surface, she glared at me over the rim of her eyeglasses.

The nun called it relinquishment.

"I understand you wish to relinquish your daughter to our care," she said, turning her attention to my mother while one eye mysteriously remained on me.

My mother's poise did not waver as she began a seemingly well-rehearsed monologue. "Sister, Juliet's father and I wish for her to have a superb education, and we believe your school to be the best in all of England. We understand that you do not accept boarders before their sixth birthdays, but if you will allow me to explain our circumstances, we feel that you may be inclined to make an exception."

The nun lifted her hand to prevent my mother from explaining the aforementioned circumstances. "We received your records and have spoken with your husband. It is the desire of the convent to accept your daughter into our school at her present age."

My mother's eyes closed and she bowed her head, silently thanking God for a satisfactory answer to a prayer He had likely not been asked to weigh in on before that very moment.

"Juliet will be attending the nursery school program with the day students," the nun continued. "She will live with the other boarders, however, and will participate in all of their activities. I will show you to her dormitory now."

"That won't be necessary." My mother stood and gathered her handbag. "I trust Juliet will be properly cared for. The car is waiting outside, and I don't wish to delay the driver any longer."

I slid off my chair and attempted to connect my hand with my mother's. Feigning oblivion, she folded her arms across her chest and tucked her hands out of my reach.

"Very well." The nun rose from her chair and offered me her unnaturally long, bony fingers which looked more skeletal than healthy human. When I did not accept her waiting hand, she took it upon herself to grab my wrist and squeeze my knuckles just tightly enough that no amount of maneuvering set me free.

The nun was still in the process of heaving the door open when my mother slipped through the narrow space. I tried to follow, but the nun's firm grip held me in place.

"Mother!" I cried as she walked down the steps.

She turned around with a forced smile stretched across her face. "You're all right, darling. Don't be afraid. I shall come to visit you soon."

With no resemblance of a proper farewell, I peered through what remained of the door's opening and, being restrained by a woman I did not know, watched my mother fade away.

My father surely called it the next logical step in a child's rearing.

I didn't know what to call it. The concept of being separated from all I had known was so foreign to me that there was no word for it in my vocabulary.

Veronica Adams called it exactly what it was.

She was eight years old and in need of a roommate. Since I was apparently in need of a room, the gaunt nun dragged me down a long hall and deposited me into a small, drab room decorated only with creams and browns. The room contained two single beds with a bedside table between them, two bureaus, and two small desks. On one of the beds sat a girl with hair the color of a candied apple and more freckles than I knew one face was allowed.

"Veronica, this is Juliet. You will be sharing your room with her," was the only introduction we were given.

"Oh, I'm sure we'll be fast friends!" Veronica gleefully bounced off of the bed and took both of my hands in hers.

Seeing that I had been well-received, the nun dismissed herself from the room. With the click of the door, a look of absolute disgust swept across Veronica's face. She dropped my hands, scoffed, and returned to the doll on her bed.

I sat down on the edge of the unoccupied bed and stared out the small window, its view obstructed by bare branches scraping the glass. The twigs—not proper branches of sufficient size to aid an escape—clawed at the window, and I shuddered as I relived the sensation of the nun's cold, skeletal fingers against my flesh.

Veronica broke the silence once she had thoroughly planned her attack. "Your mummy and daddy wouldn't even accompany you to your room, huh? They abandoned you at the door. At least my parents made sure I had a suitable place to stay before they left me." Immense pleasure seeped through her mocking tone.

"Abandoned me?" I separated each syllable into its own question.

"Abandoned you," she repeated, exaggerating her lip movements. "Dumped you. Threw you out like the garbage."

Veronica gave me time to process her definition and then said, "What did you say your name was?"

"Juliet."

"Well, Juliet, you are no longer part of your parents' lives. They are at home right now, the home that was also yours just this morning, celebrating your absence. This is the moment they have waited for all your life. It's a glorious day for them and quite a dreadful one for you."

Veronica returned to her doll, and I returned to the window, its picture now blurred by my tears. From the hate-spewing mouth of a child came the truth. I had been abandoned.

ርჳ ৪০

SURROUNDED BY an audience of friends at the dinner table, Veronica sang, "Little baby Juli-ette, can't even write the alphabet," repeating the rhyme until everyone at the table was either laughing or singing along with her.

"My name is not Juli-ette," I murmured toward my plate. "It's *Ju*liet."

"What's that, baby Juli-ette? I can't hear you. You must speak up, darling," Veronica teased.

"That's enough, girls," a young nun announced sternly, her eyes on Veronica. Shifting her focus to me, her face softened and a smile brightened sparkling brown eyes. "You must be Juliet. I'm so glad to meet you. My name is Sister Ava. Won't you come have your dinner with me?"

I accepted her outstretched hand, and as we walked across the room, her warmth passed into my hand and settled in my core. *Maybe she's an angel*, I thought. *My angel.*

She certainly did not look like a nun. She was beautiful, and her beauty was not hidden behind a habit. Her clothing was that of a commoner—a white blouse, a knee-length black skirt, and flat black shoes.

"Don't mind those girls, Juliet. They're simply afraid you're going to get all the attention." Sister Ava pushed my chair to the table and sat down across from me. "Go ahead and eat, darling."

I took a bite of potatoes. "Are you my teacher?"

"I'm your friend."

I took another bite as Sister Ava continued her introduction.

"I'm the three-year-old teacher, so you won't be in my class. Have you been to school before?"

I shook my head.

"You have quite a new experience ahead of you, then! You must eat your dinner, wash, and go right to bed so you will be ready for tomorrow."

"I don't know how to wash myself," I admitted. "My nanny does it for me, and in the morning she combs my hair and helps me dress."

"I see." Sister Ava paused as if she were really contemplating the predicament. "What if I help you tonight? I'll make sure you're tucked into bed before I leave, and I'll help you dress in the morning."

I looked up from my plate and returned Sister Ava's smile. For the first time since my abandonment, I did not feel the urge to cry.

CHAPTER 3

COOPER

IT WAS TOO SOON for Liza to be nothing but a memory. I went to church and wished she was there. I passed the schoolhouse and thought of all the years we spent there together. I walked inside our house and felt the worst heartache of my life.

My daughter wouldn't get the life she deserved if we stayed on the farm. She'd have her family, but in Abbeville, Jasmine would always be that poor little girl with no mama.

My first thought was to go back to Charleston, where I was born. But in Charleston, if you weren't rich, you weren't much of anything. We would end up living on a farm, probably in old slave quarters, and I would spend my days out in the fields picking whatever crop that farm happened to grow while Jasmine was cared for by the housemaid until she was old enough to increase the farm's productivity. She might or might not go to school, but she almost certainly wouldn't go past the sixth grade.

I couldn't do that to Liza's child. I had promised to raise her right, and I intended to keep that promise.

After an exhaustive search through the want ads, moving to a more populated part of the Upstate was the most appealing option. Textile mills had sprung up all over Spartanburg County, and every man who was willing and able to work was given a sure job and an affordable house to rent. The pay wasn't great, but all Jasmine and I needed was a roof over our heads and enough money to get by.

So against the well-meaning advice of Liza's mama and daddy, I loaded up Dupre's car and he drove me and Jasmine eighty miles northeast on a chilly, gray afternoon. We turned into the mill village when the sun should have been setting, but the sun hadn't shown itself all day. Children halted their games and scattered to the sides of dirt streets as the car crept closer to the house number I had been assigned.

Dupre came to a stop in front of a pale yellow, box-shaped house situated on brick pilings. The dirt from the street turned into more dirt patched with brown grass. Four cement steps led to a wooden porch that stretched the width of the house. A weathered wooden door stood in the middle of a clapboard wall with an oversized window centered on either side.

I carried my sleeping baby girl across the yard and up the steps. The planks on the porch were quick to let me know that I shouldn't linger on any one board for too long. The front door opened into a living room furnished with a sofa, two cloth chairs, and a coffee table, all of which looked to have been used by the tenants before us and the tenants before them and so on.

The living room turned into the kitchen without so much as a divided wall for warning, and with halls apparently considered a waste of space by the builder, a door off of each room emptied directly into the bedrooms. The first room looked more like a storage shed than a functioning bedroom, with barely enough space for a set of bunk beds, a cradle, a mattress propped against the wall, and a chest of drawers. Crammed into the other room were a bed, a bedside table, a chest of drawers, and a dresser.

Nestled between the two rooms was a bathroom, complete with a toilet, sink, and bathtub. I turned the knob and watched in awe as rushing water pounded against the white enamel. How happy Liza would be to know her baby was going to grow up with indoor plumbing, a luxury she never had.

"This is gonna be your room, Sugar," I cooed to the baby as I laid her in the cradle. She fluttered her eyelids and stretched, quickly settling into her new bed.

As soon as my belongings were unloaded, Dupre headed home. I was still unpacking the first box when Jasmine's wails let me know it was long past her supper time.

The evening was already turning bitterly cold, but I took her out to the front steps to feed her. I needed the fresh air, just for a minute. Wrapped tightly in her blanket, Jasmine was perfectly content sucking on her bottle outside.

While she ate, I took in my new surroundings. Closely spaced houses lined both sides of the street. Most of the houses had space for a garden, but not much was growing in the dead of winter. Each house was a replica of the one beside it, and each row led to another row until my eyes could see only a dusky blur of yellows and tans and grays.

The mill itself towered over the blur, glaring down at everything around it. Lights shone through the windows and smoke billowed from the smokestack. A low hum floated through the air, which was at best nothing like being in the country where the only sounds were the ones God made and at worst a horrifying indication of what it must sound like inside.

As I forced my attention back to the street, I noticed a familiar sight. Certain that my eyes were deceiving me, I walked toward what appeared to be a cow roped to the side of a house. Sure enough, a milk cow was chained to the back porch like it was the family pet. A pig stuck its head out of a shed in the back yard and chickens pecked at the sparse ground. *If only I'd known,* I thought, *I would have brought a cow and a pig from home.* Gardening and tending farm animals was something I knew how to do.

I looked out at the sprawling brick building, wondering what I had gotten myself into. I had no business working in a mill. I only knew how to work the land, and there was little land here to work.

I stayed on the porch long after Jasmine finished her bottle, unaware of my flushed cheeks and numb nose until her cries reminded me it was too cold to be outside. I went into the house, strongly doubting my decision to move someplace where I knew no one. Who was I to think I could be a mill man? Back home, the advertisements made it look like an offer I couldn't refuse, but the ads had conveniently overlooked the gloominess hanging over the neighborhood like a storm cloud.

I moved Jasmine's cradle into my bedroom and crawled into bed, anxious and scared of what tomorrow might bring. Hearing the baby breathing beside me offered some comfort, but the dismal feeling lingered. Eventually I drifted off to sleep, but all too soon the morning came.

CB BO

I WAS to report to the mill at seven o'clock, two hours later than my day started on the farm. I put on my nicest button-up shirt and slacks, not knowing the attire for a worker but wanting to look my best. Jasmine refused to be roused from sleep, so I dressed her and fixed a bottle to take to the nursery.

I walked through the bone-chilling cold, a whipping wind fighting every step forward, in search of the nursery and finally found it tucked away in a far corner of the property. A long hallway stretched down the center of the building with doors lining each side. I stepped inside a door labeled *Infants*, assuming that was the place for Jasmine.

Cribs covered most of the room, situated side by side with enough space for an average-sized person to squeeze in between. Two rocking chairs sat on a pastel rug—the only color in the stark room. A middle-aged woman in a white nurse's outfit was changing a baby's diaper at one of the cribs. Four or five other babies were sleeping and one baby sat in a crib, chewing on a rattle.

I walked up behind the lady. "Excuse me, ma'am."

"Yes?" She didn't look up from the baby she was diapering.

"I have a one-month-old daughter. Is this the right place for her?"

"A one-month-old?" The lady spun around and eyed the bundle of blankets covering Jasmine. "She should be at home with her mama." She returned her attention to the baby in the crib, our conversation finished as far as she was concerned.

"Her mama's gone, ma'am. She passed away last month."

The caregiver's tone turned from scolding to pity. "Oh, I see. Let me put this one down and I'll take her." She set the newly changed baby in his crib and reached for Jasmine. "This is the youngest one we've had, I believe." She held Jasmine in the air, letting the blankets fall off of her so she could get a good look. "Yep, she's a tiny one."

Jasmine curled into that ball all newborns make, her head flopping forward against her chest. The lady twisted her in every direction like she had never seen the likes of such a small child.

"We'll take good care of her. You go on now," she said when I didn't leave on my own.

"Don't you wanna know her feeding and sleeping schedule?"

"We put the babies on our schedule. You're gonna be late if you don't go, Mister…"

"Fowler. Cooper Fowler. And that's Jasmine." I nodded toward the baby. "Thank you for watching her. I guess I'll see you this afternoon."

The lady nodded a farewell, but leaving Jasmine with a complete stranger was easier said than done. I pictured her in Liza's mama's arms, and then I pictured her in Liza's arms, and then just as my eyes filled with tears, the lady said, "I love them like they're my own, Mr. Fowler."

I forced a smile that probably looked sadder than if I'd not smiled at all and left the room. As I walked down the hall, I heard the lady say, "Hello there, Miss Jasmine. Welcome to your new home."

And just like that, my daughter's world became confined to a property line.

CHAPTER 4

JULIET

IN THE WEEKS FOLLOWING my abandonment, Sister Ava woke me each morning and walked me to school. In the afternoon, I waited in her classroom while she prepared lessons and met with attentive parents. We ate dinner at our table for two, and then she helped me with my bath and tucked me into bed.

I had been at the school for two weeks when, as Sister Ava bid me goodnight, I threw my arms around her neck.

"I love you, Sister Ava," I whispered, not quite as softly as I should have, judging by the snort coming from Veronica's bed.

Sister Ava kissed the tips of her fingers and touched them to my forehead. Turning to Veronica, she patted her back and told her goodnight. It had been explained to me that if Sister Ava was going to oversee my bedtime routine, it was only right that she do the same for Veronica.

The door clicked, and Sister Ava's footsteps trailed off down the hall. I closed my eyes, hoping to will myself to sleep before Veronica decided to say out loud whatever it was that was making her body shake.

As though reading my mind, she suddenly sat upright and exclaimed, "I love you, Sister Ava!"

She fell onto her back in a fit of laughter, and in my mind I told her exactly what I thought of her behavior as she continued to chuckle.

ଔ ଓ

THE SPRING HOLIDAY was the first true test of the authenticity of my abandonment. Until then, the school had remained open on the weekends, but the annual four day closure meant I was required to vacate the grounds one way or another.

I sat amongst the other girls on the front lawn with my bags packed and ready to go, genuinely believing that someone—my nanny, the chauffeur, perhaps my mother if she had liquored herself up a bit—would come for me.

The cars came for the girls one by one, until only Veronica and I were waiting outside. *I would wait until the last possible second to retrieve her also,* I thought.

Veronica was not so kind as to keep her thoughts to herself.

"Little baby Juli-ette, no one's come to get her yet! If no one wants her anymore, it's probably because she's such a bore!"

"You hush, Veronica Adams!" I threw myself on top of her. I had never felt so enraged, but I knew part of what she said was the truth. No one wanted me. No one had ever wanted me.

My mother was thirty-eight when I was born, my father forty-four. They had been happily married without children for sixteen years. Their lack of conception had convinced them they were unable to conceive, so they filled their days living among England's elite. Dinner parties, horse races, afternoon teas, and other social events occupied my parents' time.

Learning they were expecting me must have been the most dreadful news they could imagine. At least an illness would either run its course or kill them, but I'd be there always, a constant thorn in their sides.

The most time I spent with my mother was the nine months she carried me, and she didn't last a full nine months. I was born five weeks early, much to her delight, I'm sure. Two days after my birth, the hospital nurse passed me to my mother who immediately passed me to my nanny, and future encounters with her were infrequent.

So it came as no surprise when my mother left me at the convent without shedding a tear, but even she could not have meant to walk away forever.

Veronica quickly gained the dominant position amid the scuffle, and while it would have been easier to pull her off of me, Sister Ava grabbed my arms and scooted me out from under her, ignoring Veronica altogether.

"Juliet, what got into you?"

"Veronica's nasty to me all the time, and I'm sick of it! I hate her!"

Veronica smirked victoriously as Sister Ava sat me on the ground and knelt beside me. "Hate is a strong word, Juliet, and I don't want to hear you use it again. You shouldn't feel that way about anyone. Hate is a hurtful emotion, and it hurts the one whom it consumes the most."

In the midst of my scolding, a lone car pulled up the drive. Veronica's father emerged from the automobile and politely embraced his daughter.

"Goodbye, Sister Ava! See you on Monday! Bye-bye, baby Juli-ette!" Veronica called gleefully as the car door closed and separated us for four glorious days.

Sister Ava sat down beside me on the grass. When the car had passed through the gate and faded out of sight, I dug my fists into my hips and demanded an explanation as to why I had been singled out.

"Why did you not scold Veronica? She started it."

"And you finished it," Sister Ava answered bluntly. "I expect better from you."

"But not from her?"

Sister Ava looked out across the sprawling lawn. "I will always require better from Veronica, but I will never expect it. And unless you are in danger of bodily harm, you must not let someone like her dictate your behavior. When you retaliate, you are doing exactly as she wishes. Don't give her that satisfaction. Do you understand?"

I bobbed my head up and down as I watched the sun slowly set on the truth of my abandonment.

Sister Ava rose to meet the school secretary as she exited the building and officially locked the doors for the long weekend. An exchange of alternating arm gestures and hands on hips took place, and after both women glanced at the desolate road, one shared shake of the head sent Sister Ava back to me.

"How would you like to spend the holiday with me?"

"Won't my family be looking for me?"

Sister Ava glanced at the ground before returning her eyes to mine. "Your nanny phoned. She's fallen ill, and she's afraid she might be contagious, so she thinks it best if you stay here this weekend."

"Oh." I reached for a blade of grass and twirled it around my finger. The thought of spending four uninterrupted days with Sister Ava was pleasing, but the reason for her company was unsettling. Was I really such an unwanted inconvenience that neither my parents nor their staff were willing to put up with me for a few short days?

Sister Ava waited expectantly, as though she was not my sole alternative to sleeping outside.

"All right." I stood up and reached for her hand. As we walked across the school grounds, my heart began to hurt. I did not realize how desperately I wanted someone to come for me until no one did. I thought I simply wanted to prove to Veronica that I had not been abandoned, but I wanted to go home. I wanted to spend the night in my own bed, surrounded by my beloved stuffed animals. I wanted to wake up to the smell of sausage and coffee. I wanted to have a tea party with my dolls. I wanted to lick the bowls after the cook poured the cake batter.

Those were the hopes and dreams of my five-year-old self. Heavy tears slid down my cheeks as I realized I would most likely never experience those luxuries again.

As I swept my free hand across my face, Sister Ava noticed my tears and knelt in front of me much like she had after my outburst with Veronica, but this time she did not correct my behavior or teach me a lesson or even tell me everything was going to be all right. She said nothing at all, simply embracing me and drawing me to her until my tears stained her blouse.

With my arms still wrapped firmly around her neck and my face buried in her shoulder, Sister Ava stood and carried me the rest of the way to her small stone cottage at the edge of the property.

She gave a tour of the entire house with a sweep of her arm. After apologizing for not owning a second bed, she said, "The couch will fit you nicely, though, and I have plenty of blankets."

I nodded to acknowledge that I had been spoken to, but I was not yet over my heartache.

Sister Ava warmed a stew, and we ate at the small table in the center of the kitchen. The tinkling of spoons against china bowls was the only break in the silence.

"How would you like to go to the theater tomorrow?" Sister Ava asked as I attempted to maneuver my way around a piece of floating cabbage that seemed to find my spoon no matter where I placed it.

The theater? My mother and father attended the theater almost every Friday night. They left the house as proper, well-spoken, well-dressed, pleasant-smelling Brits. Upon their return hours later, my mother had turned into Eliza Doolittle, pre-refinement.

I liked, possibly even loved, this version of my mother, despite the stink of alcohol and cigarettes that filled the bedroom when she made her grand entrance. Her alcohol-fueled state led her to believe she was tiptoeing up the stairs, unlatching the door without a sound, and creeping to my bed, but the hard thud as she met each step was sure to wake me if her shrieking voice had not already done so.

Accomplishing the feat of reaching the bed, she would kneel beside me and run her fingers through my hair. Peppermint lingered on her breath—an unsuccessful attempt to cover the less pleasant smells of the theater.

Through unsavory breath and slurred speech I heard the only stories I was ever told. My mother recalled act for act, scene for scene, the details of the play she had attended. Few tales were child friendly. Shakespeare received her most animated retellings, while Moliere followed close behind.

I fought to stay awake and soak in this version of my mother—her hand willing to hold my hand, her lips willing to kiss my cheek, her eyes willing to look lovingly into mine. Sleep always won, and the next morning when I sat down at the breakfast table, my mother had returned to pristine condition, with not a hint of the previous night to be found.

The theater transformed its audience in profound ways. In my mother's case it was always for the better, but Sister Ava was already close to perfect, so it seemed the only direction she could go was down.

"I didn't know nuns were allowed to go to the theater."

"They are. And I'm not a nun," she quickly reminded me. "Never have been. Never will be."

"Have you been to the theater before?" I was certain she had not.

"Yes I have. Many times. Have you?"

"No."

"Well, tomorrow's the day then!"

Sister Ava left no room for argument, and I had no desire to disagree. I wanted nothing more than to experience the place that possessed the miraculous power of making my mother love me.

◌ ◌

I TOSSED and turned on the couch, anxious for Sister Ava to appear. After what felt like hours, the bedroom door opened and she stepped into the living room wearing a powder-blue, drop-waist dress. Her auburn hair fell to her chin beneath a cloche hat. It seemed as though the theater was already working its magic. Nun to flapper in one night.

Presenting me with a package, she said, "This was to be your Easter gift, but I want you to have it now."

I was unaware that it was common practice to give Easter gifts, but I thanked her and tore open the box. A coral-pink dress lay inside, along with a matching hair ribbon and shiny Mary

Janes. I stroked the dress like it was the most precious gift I had ever received and then threw my arms around Sister Ava's neck.

"Thank you, Sister Ava!"

"You're welcome, darling," she said, returning the hug. "I thought you would like the ruffles and lace. Now try it on, and let's see how you look."

The dress fit like it had been stitched around my body. I stood at the full-length mirror and admired myself. Sister Ava came into view beside me and I slipped my hand into hers, thinking, *this must be what it feels like to have a mother,* and smiling radiantly at the thought.

೮೮ ೮

THE GRAND MAJESTIC THEATRE lived up to its name. A man wearing a knee-length black overcoat and top hat greeted us at a wrought iron door.

"What a lovely young lady," he told Sister Ava as he tipped his hat and winked at me.

He thinks I belong to her.

"Yes she is," Sister Ava agreed, tightly gripping my hand so she wouldn't lose me in the crowd.

I do belong to her.

The man accepted our tickets and held the door open for us to enter the lobby. A crimson carpet led the way across a mahogany floor to a staircase almost as wide as the lobby itself. At the top of the stairs, a man in a black vest ushered us through an elaborate wooden door with an entire Asian village carved into it.

The man showed us to two seats on the front row of the balcony. Intricate designs brought life to ivory walls. Curved boxes, decorated in red and gold, jutted from the walls. Each box held a handful of exquisitely dressed patrons being served drinks by a man in a vest. I supposed my parents watched from a floating box complete with their very own vested server.

Oversized crystal chandeliers sparkled below a painting of the heavens on the ceiling. The rows ascended behind me until they reached the first strokes of the heavenly mural. A sea of people filled the room below. A dark hole spanned the width of a red curtain at the front of the auditorium.

The murmurings of the audience swirled around me. My anticipation grew as the orchestra filled the hole. A cacophony of tuning stringed instruments permeated the auditorium. The lights dimmed, and a braided gold rope drew back the red curtain to reveal more darkness.

A hush fell over the room, and for several seconds, twelve hundred people sat in silence. Then, in perfect synchrony, the lights illuminated the stage and music filled the air.

I watched in awe as Peter and the Darling children flew to Neverland. I was with them as they encountered the pirates and Captain Hook, the Indians and Tiger Lily, the Lost Boys and Tinkerbell.

When the curtain unexpectedly closed, harsh light forcing me back to reality, I whispered, "Is it over?"

"No dear, this is intermission. A time to stand and stretch your legs. Would you like to walk downstairs?"

I shook my head and returned my attention to the stage, sitting at the edge of my seat and waiting for the first sign that the curtain was about to open. After what felt like an eternity, the lights blinked and then went out completely. The curtain swung open, and I was back in Neverland.

The Darling children returned to London, the players took their final bows, and with the audience on its feet applauding, the curtain permanently separated me from my beloved Neverland.

The rows around us emptied, but I remained in my seat. I had lived the magic of the theater and was not ready to leave it behind.

Sister Ava sat quietly beside me until we were alone in the balcony. Standing up, she said, "We can't stay any longer, Juliet. There's another performance tonight, and the auditorium has to be cleaned before the audience arrives."

"Can't we stay and see it again?"

"You enjoyed yourself, did you?" Sister Ava smiled. "I promise I'll bring you again. Just not twice in one day."

That seemed like a fair compromise. I slowly walked to the aisle. Leaning over the railing, I looked below, above, and all around. *I will see you again soon, theater. It has been a pleasure.* I met Sister Ava at the top of the stairs and together we reentered the real world.

As the car left the city, I announced my desire to be Peter Pan.

"Not Wendy?"

"Peter," I said emphatically. "Wendy only visits Neverland. Peter lives there forever, and he never grows up. Wendy grows up. I don't want to be her."

"You want to be a child forever?"

"I don't want to be a Juliet child forever. I want to be a Peter child."

Sister Ava nodded. "You can be."

"I cannot be! I don't have any fairy dust!"

"You don't need fairy dust." Sister Ava seemed to be taking the conversation more seriously than would be expected from an adult.

"How would I get to Neverland then?"

"All you need is imagination."

"How do I get that?"

"You already have it. You just have to use it."

"How can I use it when I don't know where to find it?"

"You find it in there." Sister Ava set her hand on top of my head. Seeing that I was in need of further explanation, she said, "Do you have dolls?"

"I did when I lived with my mummy and daddy."

"Did you ever have a tea party with them?"

"With my mum and dad?"

Sister Ava smirked at my wrinkled nose. "With your dolls, silly."

"Oh, yes, with my dolls."

"Did they really drink the tea?"

"There was no tea to drink. I'm not allowed to make tea."

Sister Ava suppressed another smile. "But you set cups and plates down in front of them, yes?"

"Yes."

"That's imagination. An entire world exists inside your mind. Peter created his world and made it exactly as he wanted it to be."

"I can do that too?"

"Of course. Imagination is often what allows one to survive. Without it, one must spend all of his time in the real world, and the real world is not always a grand place to be."

Veronica's freckled face popped into my head. "So when Veronica's teasing me, I should pretend I'm somewhere else?"

"Yes, create your own Neverland behind your eyes, and go there whenever you wish."

"Behind my eyes?"

"Close your eyes," Sister Ava instructed, "and tell me what you see."

I scrunched my face around my eyes to keep my eyelids from fluttering. "I don't see anything."

"Think of something happy. Now what do you see?"

I smiled at the Peter Pan-esque exercise Sister Ava had me performing. *Think happy thoughts. Think happy thoughts.* "I see...a puppy."

"What does he look like?"

"He's small and black with a curly tail."

"What is he doing?"

"He's jumping on my legs and wagging his tail. He's waiting for me to throw a stick for him to fetch."

"Open your eyes."

The dog was replaced by Sister Ava's smiling face.

"You just went to Neverland."

"I did? I'm going to go again!" My puppy friend returned, this time with the stick in his mouth.

By the time Sister Ava and I arrived at her cottage, the theater had fully worked its magic. I was a changed little girl. No matter my circumstances, I could escape into my mind. I could live behind my eyes.

Part II
ও ৯
The End
of The Beginning

CHAPTER 5

JASMINE

South Carolina

1930

THE MILL crushed us long before the stock market tried to crash us. That's what my daddy said when I asked why the depression wasn't depressing us. Apparently we were already as depressed as we could be.

In the eight years since we moved to the mill hill, I had never been any farther than my own two feet could take me. Daddy luckily still worked full shifts, so during the summer I was my own babysitter. I thought myself a rather good one until the day my own two feet assisted a bicycle in taking me a little farther than I'd ever been. Two blistered bare feet and a trip to Popsicle jail later, the crash had caught me.

CB ∞

I WOKE UP sticky, twisted in sweat-soaked sheets. I peeled the sheets away from my bare skin and ran through the house in my underwear, hoping to air dry before dressing for the day.

I pulled on a pair of overalls, tied my strawberry-blond hair into a sloppy ponytail, and took off through the house again, with arms spread wide in an attempt to catch whatever breeze I could create. I swept my weekly chore nickel into my pocket as I passed the kitchen table and ran straight out the door into the so-hot-you-can-barely-breathe July morning.

By the time I reached the company store, I had mustered up enough sweat that my eyebrows couldn't hold back the salty flow. I slowed to a walk, passing casually in front of the old men sitting on the porch, trying not to look desperate to get to the relief waiting inside.

The door was propped open and the shop boy was helping a lady on the other side of the store, so I didn't have to worry about silencing the bells that would announce my presence. I skipped the charade of wandering around the non-perishables and made a beeline for the cooler.

I pried open its top and folded my upper half over the rim until my face hovered millimeters above a chunk of ice. Sweat beads reversed course and sank back into my skin.

I plunged my arm into the cooler and fished blindly for Popsicle packaging. My first attempt didn't produce a Popsicle. My second attempt resulted in a Popsicle, but it was root beer flavored. Fighting the urge to gag, I dropped it back into the cooler and tried again. Orange. A step in the right direction but still not worth the nickel I had worked for all week. When root beer showed up for a second time, I stuffed the repulsive ice pop into my pocket to get it out of the way.

I was still diving for a cherry Popsicle when I suddenly took flight, swooped off the ground by my overall straps. I dangled in the air with an arm turning me like I was the real-life version of a baby's mobile until I was face to face with a giant of a man.

"Whatchew doing?" His hoarse voice was too high-pitched for such a burly man.

"Looking for a Popsicle." I glared into his yellow eyes.

"Looks like ya already gotchew a Popsicle." He raised his eyebrows toward my pocket.

"That one's root beer." My overalls had worked their way up to places that made it uncomfortable to have a conversation about preferable Popsicle flavors.

"So?"

"Can you put me down, mister? Please?" He didn't deserve a please, but my pleases and thank yous had been smacked into me from an early age.

Ignoring my request, he cut his eyes at my pocket. "Were you planning to pay for that?"

"No, sir."

"At least you're honest." The man's belly laugh got caught in his throat, erupting as a gravelly cough.

I braced myself for a shower of spit, but as the cough spewed from his lips, his grip loosened and gravity sent me to the ground. I landed on all fours, lunging forward until I was up and running full speed toward home.

The man yelled as best he could for someone to stop me, telling the men on the porch that I stole from the store, but his voice didn't carry and those men were permanent fixtures on that porch, not willing to leave their chairs for anything short of a natural disaster.

My accuser lacked the lung capacity to catch me before I made it home, so as long as I was inside the house before he turned onto my street, he would have to knock on every door like a madman before he found me.

Four houses from the safety of my own home, a voice said, "Who you running from?"

Miles Carter and his little brother, Andrew, were standing in their front yard dousing each other with water from their mama's watering cans. I turned into the boys' yard and sprinted past them, pointing behind the house.

"Jazzy, what's wrong?" Miles called after me, concern now in his voice as he and Andrew followed me around back.

Firmly pressed against the clapboard and hidden from the street, I tried to explain, my lungs only allowing me to say two or three words without needing air again.

"I...I was...at the store...and...a man...big, giant man...pulled me...held me...said I stole..." I crumpled to the ground, heaving.

Miles and Andrew stared at me wide-eyed, unsure whether to fear for my safety or their own for being associated with me.

"Jazzy, you need to cool off."

Miles sent his brother for the watering cans and poured what was left onto my head, shaking the cans violently to get every last drop.

"At least your face don't look like it's about to explode no more. You looked like a tomato running through the yard a minute ago." Miles smiled. "I'd say you're closer to a strawberry now."

When I cooled to the color of whatever fruit Miles deemed normal for a face, he said, "My mama ain't gonna let us hang around with no thief."

"I ain't a thief." I stood up and shoved him as I passed.

"Where you going?"

"I gotta go pay for this disgusting Popsicle." I pulled the squishy remains from my pocket.

"You really think you should do that right now if some humongous man's after you?"

I shrugged. "I ain't scared of him."

"You sure was running fast not to be scared." Miles laughed and I shoved him again. Unfazed, he said, "Andy and I are going to the swimming hole. You wanna come? It'll keep you outta plain view, seeing as how you stole and all. Then you can right your wrong on the way back this afternoon."

"You mean the water next to the mill?"

"Naw, this ain't at the mill. My daddy takes us sometimes when he ain't working."

"I don't think I'm supposed to leave the neighborhood."

"Oh, it ain't far. I know exactly where it is. Lots of people from the hill go there to swim."

"My daddy probably doesn't want me doing that. We better do something else."

"Come on, Jazzy! It's so hot, and there ain't nothing here to cool us off. You can ride Andy's bike and he can ride with me." Miles folded his arms across his chest. "Andrew and I are going whether you go or not. You can just stay here and wait for somebody to knock on your door and haul you off, I guess."

Miles certainly was annoying to supposedly be my best friend. I mimicked his folded arm stance and rolled my eyes.

"Fine, I'll go. But if my daddy finds out about this, I'm gonna tell him to give you my spanking."

I pointed my finger at his face. He batted my hand away and ran into the shed, reappearing with two rusty bicycles, one smaller than the other. Turning the smaller one over to me, Miles hopped on the bigger one and looped around the house before stopping to pick up his brother.

My experience with bicycles was limited, but I could pedal and steer and stay upright for the most part. I mounted a seat much too small for me and attempted to pedal, my knees thumping my elbows with each rotation. After several swerves and tilts, I straightened up and headed down the street. Miles and Andrew followed, quickly taking the lead.

We avoided the company store, coasted down a hill at the back of the property, and darted into the covered bridge which I had passed through once to get into the mill village but had never passed through a second time to get out. A whole new world growing ever closer, I jammed my feet into the pedals and skidded to an abrupt stop halfway across the bridge.

Realizing I had fallen behind, Miles circled back. "Whatcha doing?"

"I don't think I can go. My daddy'll tan my hide if he catches me, and I already have to worry about him finding out what happened at the store. I'm just gonna go home and wait for that spanking rather than add another one to it."

"He ain't gonna catch you cause he ain't gonna know. You'll be dry and in your sleeping clothes before he gets home from work. And when he asks whatcha did today, you say you played with me and Andy in the water cause that's the truth. Only he don't have to know the water wasn't from the watering cans."

Miles made a convincing argument as the sweltering air inside the rotting bridge stifled my ability to think clearly. Inhaling a deep breath of stagnant air, I charged toward the great threshold and shot out the other side, my little legs pedaling as fast as they could go. Clean, odorless wind beat against my face as the songs of jubilant birds welcomed me to their world.

The combination of fresh air and songbird serenade gave my feet the oomph they needed to keep up with Miles. I followed him along the paved road and then, against my better judgment, onto a path of dirt and pine needles that disappeared into the woods.

We bumped along a maze of roots until a pond appeared in front of us. Miles's wheels were still turning when Andrew hopped off the back of the bike. He kicked off his overalls and made his way to the water's edge. Miles followed suit, and I watched them jump in while I straddled my bicycle from a safe distance, not wanting to allow even a drop of the forbidden water to touch my skin.

Miles waded toward where I stood, clearing the water from his eyes. "Whatcha waiting on?"

"I don't know how to swim. I think I better just watch."

"You didn't come all this way to watch! Plus, you ain't gotta be able to swim! Look, the water only comes up to here." He flattened his hand on the water's surface, moving it back and forth to show me that it hit below his belly button. "See? Andy, he can't really swim neither, but he jumped right in."

My face crumpled as I thought it over. The water did look refreshing, and I might never get the chance again. Plus, during the year I was seven, my boundaries had expanded from the house to the yard to Miles's house to the company store. I had yet to receive my eight-year-old expansion, so who was to say if I was really breaking a rule?

Daddy, that was who. But Daddy wasn't there right then to clarify, and I had already either disobeyed or not. The heat was making me delirious, and before I knew it I had stripped down to my underwear and was flinging my entire body into the water.

The cold water swallowed me, instantly cooling me to the bone. Human lungs forced me back to the surface when my chest started to burn.

"Don't it feel good?" Andrew asked as I swept my hair from my eyes.

"Sure does!" I splashed his face, and a splash war began. We splashed, jumped, and flopped until we were so worn out that we could hardly climb out of the water. The boys and I fell onto our backs in the overgrown grass.

"I can't believe you was scared, Jazzy," Miles chided. "I didn't think you was scared of nothing, but you been a chicken all day today."

"I ain't scared of nothing, except my daddy. And now I've got two things to worry about instead of one."

"Well, like I told you before, he ain't gonna find out unless you tell him, and I reckon your Popsicle was forgotten by the time it melted." Miles sat up and squinted at the sun. "We best be getting back, though. It's probably getting close to quitting time."

I reassembled my overalls and mounted the bike, struggling to pedal with bare feet that were sunburned and raw from the earlier ride. Grimacing, I pulled up next to the boys. "My feet are hurting real bad. I don't think I can pedal home."

I showed Miles the soles of my feet, and the look on his face assured me I wasn't simply being a baby.

"Andy can pedal back, and you can ride with me."

I hoisted myself onto the back of Miles's bike. He had to tell me more than once that I was squeezing his arms too tight, but after a shaky start he found his stride and we headed home.

The covered bridge grew ever closer, and I grew increasingly concerned with what awaited me on the other side. I was given more time to stew when Andrew hit a rock and toppled over the handlebars. Miles swerved to avoid hitting him, and I rolled off the bike, a consequence of having loosened my grip as instructed.

I landed on feet that no additional injury could worsen, but Andrew landed on his elbows. He held his arms bent against his chest, crying that he couldn't straighten them out.

"Jazzy, you're gonna have to take Andy's bike the rest of the way," Miles said, helping Andrew onto the back of his.

Knowing the end was in sight, be it good or bad, I mounted the bicycle and pedaled. I found that if I pedaled with the sides of my feet, I could only go half as fast, but I felt less pain.

We limped across the great threshold. By the looks of the deserted street, we'd made it home before the shift change which meant Daddy was still inside the mill and not out searching for me.

I was walking the bike up the hill and Miles was circling at the top, anxious to get Andrew to his mama, when the corner of my eye caught the movement of someone rising from his porch steps.

"Hey youngins, wait up!"

I knew that rasp. I turned my head and saw the goliath from the company store gaining ground. His body looked much more capable of catching me than it had earlier in the day.

"That's him!" I shrieked to Miles.

Miles's eyes grew wide. "Then hurry! Get on your bike and pedal, Jazzy!"

I stumbled to the top of the hill, threw a leg over the bicycle, and attempted to pedal without any forward momentum.

Miles pulled away. "Come on, Jazzy! He's gonna turn you in for some kinda reward!"

"Turn me in?!"

The bicycle tilted to the right and then to the left and then rolled backwards until I dragged my feet along the ground to keep it from delivering me to my accuser. The only direction it wouldn't go was straight ahead.

Miles looked back as he turned onto our street. "Jazzy, he's right behind you! Pedal!"

"I am!" I shouted. I was pedaling with all my might, but pain was overshadowing adrenaline.

"I'm gonna get your daddy!" Miles called, speeding away.

Before I got a chance to worry about the prospect of my daddy becoming involved, I was dangling in the air again, the bicycle crashing to its side below me. Instinct told me to fight. I kicked, hit, and screamed, but the man didn't let go or give in. He tossed me over his shoulder and restrained my legs, leaving me free to beat on his back and scream as loudly as I pleased.

Neighbors opened their doors or peered out their windows to see what the commotion was about, but it was no strange sight for children to be publicly punished by their parents, and I simply looked like an unruly child being escorted home with the knowledge that a whipping switch awaited her. Those who did take notice of my cries for help only shook their heads—at my outlandish behavior, not my captor's.

Our parade through the streets ended at a windowless brick building the size of my bedroom. The man carried me inside and plopped me onto a splintered wooden chair against the side wall. Wasting no time, I jumped up and scurried for the door.

"I don't think you should try that." My kidnapper calmly scooped me up with one arm and returned my backside to the chair. Meaty fingers dug into my chest to prevent a second escape attempt. "I ain't gonna hurtcha, kid. I just gotta get my due is all. If you cooperate and don't cause no trouble, as soon as the boss gets here, we'll all be on our way."

When my breathing slowed to a pace he no longer found threatening, the man removed his fleshy hand from the bib of my overalls. My eyes stayed fixed on his gargantuan body as it spread across the two chairs closest to the door. He looked more like a porch sitter than a mill worker, wearing a pair of overalls with no undershirt, and blubber spilling out in all directions. He leaned forward and propped his elbows on his knees, severely out of breath after lugging fifty extra pounds around the neighborhood.

"What if you walk home with me, and my daddy will give you a quarter, and the boss never has to find out?" The last person I wanted involved in this matter was my daddy, but I had a feeling that if I didn't prevent the boss's visit, Daddy might find himself dealing with more than one less quarter in his money can.

"I don't want your daddy's money, child. I want the boss man's." The man fell into a coughing fit, and I backed myself into a corner, as far from the spittle as possible.

I was about to make another run for it when a gray-haired man in a suit that looked like it had been dyed the exact shade of his hair appeared in the doorway.

"Mr. Marshall, how are you this evening?" The suited man extended his hand to my kidnapper.

"Just fine, sir," he answered, clearing his throat and not sounding just fine at all. "I thought you might want to know I caught this child stealing a Popsicle this morning."

"Is that so?" The older man shifted his attention to me.

The look on Mr. Marshall's face made it clear how I was supposed to answer.

"Yessir."

"What's your name, young lady?"

"Jasmine Fowler."

"Fowler." He repeated the name a second time, and I wished I had given him another name, like Sarah Sanders, the biggest tattletale in my class. "Any relation to Cooper Fowler?"

I wanted to kick myself for not saying I was Sarah Sanders or anybody other than Jasmine Fowler, daughter of Cooper Fowler.

"He's my daddy."

"And who's your mother? Does she work at the mill too?"

I should have said I was anyone other than the motherless child of a dirt-poor mill worker who couldn't afford to part with even the quarter I had offered Mr. Marshall. "No, sir. Her name was Liza, but she died when I was a baby. My daddy and I came here without her."

"I see." The boss turned to Mr. Marshall. Pulling a dollar bill from his pocket, he said, "Thank you for your help. I'll see to it that Miss Fowler gets home all right."

Mr. Marshall accepted the dollar and shook the older man's hand again. He walked through the door, holding it open long enough to turn to me and say, "Sorry to have caused you any trouble, miss. I hope you won't hold nothing against me."

The door slammed between us before Mr. Marshall could see that I did not intend to accept his apology.

"Do you know who I am, Miss Fowler?"

"The boss man," I answered with certainty.

He chuckled. "Do you know my name?"

"No, sir."

"My name's Jerry Duncan. I run this mill. Everyone here works for me."

I nodded my head to show him that I was familiar with the general definition of the word *boss*.

"Do you understand what you did wrong today?"

"I wasn't stealing that Popsicle, and I told Mr. Marshall that. I was gonna put it back. My daddy would tan my hide if I ever stole. I know better than that."

Mr. Duncan sighed and sat down beside me, loosening his tie. "Mr. Marshall, he's an ill man. Got sick a year ago and can't handle the dust inside the mill anymore. His wife still works for us, and he does odd jobs, whatever needs to be done, one of which is to keep the neighborhood children in line. I pay him a dollar every few weeks, usually for making me aware of some adolescent boy's antics. He might have jumped the gun with you because he hasn't come across any trouble this last month."

"So you believe me?"

"If you say you had no intention of stealing a Popsicle, I believe you."

"Thank you."

Mr. Duncan slapped his knees. "Well! I think we've spent enough time in this little room. Why don't I take you home?"

"I can manage," I assured him. "It ain't too far."

"I insist. My car's parked right out front."

Car? I hadn't been inside a moving car since Dupre brought me and Daddy to the mill village.

"I guess that'd be all right." I tried to hide my excitement as Mr. Duncan opened the door and freed me from Popsicle jail.

Parked outside was a topless car as bright red and as attention-grabbing as a fire engine. Mr. Duncan lifted me under my arms and set me onto the front seat. The warmth of smooth leather seeped through my overalls. I closed my eyes and pretended I was flying as the car charged forward through the neighborhood.

"This one yours?" Mr. Duncan asked as my flight stopped abruptly in front of my house.

He clearly already knew the answer, but I mumbled, "Yessir," as I fidgeted with the door, anxious to get inside and start explaining my day away.

"Let me help you." Mr. Duncan lifted me over the door and I thanked him for the ride.

"You're very welcome. I think I'll tell your daddy hello while I'm here."

I led Mr. Duncan through the yard, wishing I was delivering him to Sarah Sanders' daddy and not my own. If Mr. Sanders was half the snitch his daughter was, he and Mr. Duncan were probably great friends.

I cracked the front door and stuck my head inside. "Daddy?"

"Where ya been?" He turned from the stove, thankfully sounding more curious than concerned.

"Somebody's here to tell you hello," I said, still standing in the doorway.

"And who wants to do tha—" His voice trailed off as he opened the door and saw Mr. Duncan waiting in the yard.

Daddy stepped around me and jogged down the steps.

"Evening, Mr. Duncan," he said, shaking the man's hand. "Is my youngin causing trouble?"

"Not at all, Mr. Fowler. She's just a child being a child, and there's nothing wrong with that, is there?" Mr. Duncan forced a laugh my daddy did not return.

I stood on the porch, leaning against the house while the conversation continued.

"Your daughter tells me she lost her mother when she was very young."

"Yes, sir. During childbirth." Daddy shot me a glance that said I had divulged a secret to the last person who was supposed to know it.

"That's too bad she never knew her mama."

"She knows about her, sir, and we've got a picture or two around the house."

"So it's just you and the girl living here?"

"Yes, sir."

"And she's home alone while you work all day?"

"Well, most of the time she's at school, but she's home by herself during the summer." After a second of silence, Daddy added, "She don't cause no trouble though."

"Oh, I'm sure she doesn't. It's just that we need somebody who can deliver shopping lists to the company store and gather items for the customers. I thought you might be interested in a little extra money each week."

"We get by. I'd rather let my girl be a child while she can."

"She can still be a child, Mr. Fowler. We'll only use her one hour after school and four hours a day during the summer. And never on Saturdays or Sundays."

Daddy shook his head, his eyes fixed on a patch of dead grass. "I don't think so."

Mr. Duncan turned away from the house and led my daddy a few steps farther into the yard. He lowered his voice, but my young ears heard every word.

"Mr. Fowler, I don't want to make this difficult. You and your daughter live in this house on one income. We have families in the same type house who have five and six people working at the mill every day. And there are families who have that many able bodies, all of whom would be willing to work if we had a house such as yours to provide them."

"Whatchew saying, Mr. Duncan?"

"Son, you know what I'm saying. This is a business, and it requires hard work from everyone involved. When given the choice of having one man such as yourself, or having a man, his wife, and his passel of children contributing to the mill's productivity, we have to think about the economic implications."

After a long pause, Mr. Duncan looked my daddy right in the eyes. "That's not a choice I want to have to make, son."

"So you're telling me that if I don't turn Jazzy over to the mill, I ain't gonna have a job on Monday?"

"I'm telling you that allowing Jasmine to work a few hours each week is in everyone's best interest, including hers. She's lucky, Cooper. If this were ten years ago, she would have gone from the nursery to the mill floor, possibly bypassing school altogether. The way the law is now, she won't even be able to set foot on the mill floor until she's fourteen years old, and that will only be with your permission. Keeping busy never hurt nobody, son."

Daddy stared at nothing in particular and took a labored breath. "So if she works, it'll never be for more than four hours a day, she can still go to school, and her weekends will be free?"

"That's right."

"And she'll only be working in the company store?"

"Only in the company store. She's too young to be placed anywhere else, son."

"I don't want her on the mill floor. Ever."

"You know she's too young to be up there, and whether or not she goes up there in the future will be left up to you and your daughter. I assure you no one under fourteen does any work on the mill floor."

Daddy cut his eyes at Mr. Duncan. Even I knew that was a lie. It may have been the law, but people broke that rule all the time. My twelve-year-old neighbor worked on the mill floor every day. His mama and daddy just said he was fourteen, signed a piece of paper, and everybody overlooked the fact that he wasn't legal.

"Whatchew gonna pay her?"

"Fifty cents a week during the school year and two dollars a week during the summer."

I could see the whites on all four sides of Daddy's eyes. I was thinking of how many Popsicles I could buy for fifty cents a week, but since he made less than seven hundred dollars a year, he was probably thinking something else.

Daddy quickly glanced my direction before announcing his decision. "All right, Mr. Duncan, Jasmine can work. But I want it in writing exactly how much she'll work and what her duties will be."

Mr. Duncan pulled a pen from his breast pocket and conveniently found a blank sheet of paper folded in his pants pocket. He scribbled something on the paper and handed it to my daddy, who signed his name at the bottom before passing it back to Mr. Duncan to do the same. Daddy was given the piece of paper and the two men shook hands.

His mission complete, Mr. Duncan waved and said, "It was so nice to meet you, Miss Fowler. I look forward to seeing you again soon."

I weakly raised my hand in farewell. Daddy brushed past me, telling me to come inside for supper but not waiting for me to obey. The screen door slammed between us.

I wasn't sure I had room for supper, given the size of the knot that had formed while Mr. Duncan was talking to my daddy. I had been sold to the mill. My life had been decided. I stood on the porch and listened to the crunch of gravel as Mr. Duncan's car drove away—a fitting finale to the snatching of my childhood.

CHAPTER 6

JULIET

London

1930

EIGHT YEARS AFTER I LAST SAW or heard from my mother, I had come to the realization that I was abandoned not because she had stopped loving me, but because she had never loved me. Eventually, she stopped feeling guilty for her neglect and chose to pretend I never existed.

I wished to feel the same nothingness for her, and while I could no longer see her face, at times I ached for the mother I did not have. Sister Ava was my world, and I reveled in our time together, but she could not be my mother because according to a piece of paper, I already had one. I didn't know if it was worse to have a mother who did not want me or want a mother who could not have me, but had I known I was about to find out, I would have chosen no mother at all.

၈ ၆

SISTER AVA and I were eating breakfast on her patio as we did every Saturday morning. Graham Douglas, her husband of two years, was suspiciously absent. I attributed the uneasiness I felt to his unoccupied place at the table.

I searched Sister Ava's face while I chewed a bite of eggs more times than its consistency required. She appeared to be having an internal argument with herself, her head moving side to side and her eyes alternating between alarm and disbelief. She focused intensely on her breakfast, taking no time to chew and stabbing the food with such force that the fork clanged against the plate with each bite.

Having attacked every available morsel and still refusing to look at me, Sister Ava murmured, "Juliet, I have something to tell you. I should have told you sooner, but I put it off and now I fear I've waited too long."

My heart pounded in my throat. I had been waiting for news of Sister Ava becoming a mother—a real mother—since the day she was married.

"Is there going to be a baby?" I whispered.

Surprised eyes briefly met mine before falling again. "No."

My heart returned to my chest as I could think of no other news deserving of such a grief-laden delivery.

A lone tear splashed onto Sister Ava's plate, her poise crumbling under the weight of the news she was about to deliver. Blurting the sentence with such haste that it was strung together as one continuous word, she said, "Graham has taken a teaching position in Scotland."

I began to think Sister Ava's heartache had nothing to do with me. "Has he left you?"

Sister Ava closed her eyes. "No." She inhaled all the air her lungs could hold and breathed, "I'm going with him."

A sliver of a crack threatened my world. The crack spread when Sister Ava added, "We are to leave on the mid-afternoon train tomorrow."

One last glimmer of hope remained. "Am I going with you?"

Sister Ava forced her eyes to mine and her lips formed an unspoken no. The cracks shot like wildfire, my world imploding and leaving a heap of too many shattered pieces to ever hope to put back together.

"No?"

"I have no say in the matter, Juliet." Sister Ava reached for me, but I leapt to my feet and backed away from her.

Angry tears cascaded down my cheeks as I erupted. "You do have a say! You do!" I screamed. "You're choosing to leave! Just as my mother chose to leave! I expected as much from her, but not from you! I wish I had never met you! You're as horrible as her! Worse! I hate you!"

I hissed the word at her, recalling her opinion of it. *Hate is a strong word, Juliet, and I don't want to hear you use it again.*

Sister Ava begged forgiveness through her sobs, but her distress only enraged me more.

"I'll hate you until I die!" Heat rushed through my legs and demanded that I move. I stomped down the steps and onto the lawn.

"Juliet!" Sister Ava briefly composed herself. "Please don't leave in anger."

I turned around and matched her composure. "You have made your choice. Now you must live with it." I watched Sister Ava's gaze fall to the ground before I turned and walked away.

"Juliet!" Sister Ava's wails grew louder the farther I walked. "Juliet!"

The desperation in her voice caused me to stop. I prayed to find her tearing after me. Turning and seeing her slumped in her chair, resigned to our fate, I cried, "I thought you loved me! I loved you!"

I broke into a run. I pushed through the front door of the dormitory, bounded up two flights of stairs, and stormed into my room.

Veronica looked up from her desk, startled. Wild-eyed and full of rage, I began slinging books—all gifts from Sister Ava— from their shelves.

Veronica stood up and slinked toward the door. As she crossed behind me, she quietly sang, "Little baby Juli-ette, having quite a little baby fit."

I spun around and let my emotions explode across her face. A splotchy handprint formed on her cheek as she stared at me in shock. Shock turned to outrage, and she threw herself forward and tackled me. I heard the back of my head crack against the cement floor, but I felt nothing but the desire to fight. Veronica and I rolled back and forth with our arms clutching each other in what, under different circumstances, might have resembled a hug. Our legs alternated between providing traction for the girl on top and acting as a weapon for the girl underneath.

I wrestled my arms free, twisting and kicking until I was straddling Veronica at her waist with my hands around her neck. For a moment we were still, staring into each other's eyes, exchanging the looks of years of hurt.

Suddenly Veronica's eyes left mine. Her abdominal muscles tightened as her left arm reached for something. I was in the process of following the path of her outstretched hand when the corner of one of the books I had thrown to the floor clipped my cheek, narrowly missing my right eye.

The metal edge sliced my skin. Heavy drops of blood burst upon impact with Veronica's face and slithered down her chin. She raised her hands in disgust, and with no more fight left in me, I released her and dropped to the floor.

We lay side by side, staring at the ceiling, heaving. "I'm sorry," I whispered after I had caught my breath. "I'm sorry," I whimpered again as Veronica crawled to her bed.

I stayed on the floor and did nothing to stop the trickle of blood from seeping into my eye. My face burned with a fury I'd never before experienced, but I knew I deserved every second of the pain.

C3 80

THE GASH had not fully clotted by late afternoon. I had wiped most of the blood from my face and hair, but a trip to the infirmary was inevitable. Two stitches, a bag of ice to decrease the swelling, a pill for the pain, and a fabricated story about tripping into my desk later, I crawled into bed, hungry from having only eaten breakfast and ashamed for all that had taken place since.

When Veronica entered the room later in the evening, she left the lights off, gently closing the door behind her. My first thought was that she was sneaking in to kill me, and I was not altogether sure I didn't wish for her to succeed.

She made no effort to disguise her footsteps as she clomped across the room and stopped at the head of my bed. Her weight sank into the mattress. Fearful that feigning sleep would render me too easy a target, I popped my eyes open as her breath tickled my cheek.

If Veronica was startled, her face made no show of it. She lowered her lips to my ear and whispered, "Little baby Juli-ette, her actions today she will regret. If she ever touches me again, her time at this school will come to an end. She belongs on the street and my pleasure it will be, to see to it that she goes there if she ever crosses me."

My lips parted, but no words came forth. A sly smile crept across Veronica's face. Satisfied that she had the upper hand in our relationship again, she slipped into her bed. Before laying her head on the pillow, she sang, "Night-night, baby Juli-ette. Sweet dreams."

Cß Þ

I WOKE the next morning with a head full of dreams that had been dominated by Sister Ava. Determined to make the dreams a reality, I formed a plan to right my wrong. I would apologize to Sister Ava immediately after chapel and together we would find a way to visit during summer and winter holidays.

Despite my tender cheek and sore body, I had a renewed sense of hope as I hummed my way through the courtyard and entered the chapel. As if Veronica intuitively knew my spirits had risen, she sought me out and sat down beside me on the pew.

She possessed no visible remnants of our scuffle, and she was quick to tell anyone who would listen how clumsy I was for tripping and how foolish I was for keeping my grasp on a book as I fell, which made it impossible for me to catch myself and resulted in a collision between my cheek and the corner of the book. It was not a believable story, but neither was falling into the edge of a desk, so I kept silent as she told it time and again, growing more boisterous with each retelling.

With the entire room apprised of my foolishness, the organ began playing and two hundred girls stood to sing the morning's selected hymn. As the second verse began, Veronica leaned over and proclaimed loudly enough that I could hear over the singing girls, "Sister Ava came to see you this morning."

The words of the song kept flowing from my mouth and I maintained my focus on the nun leading the music, but Veronica saw my eyes dart her direction when she spoke. Seeing that she had my attention, she continued, "I told her you did not wish to see her." My rage from the day before began a slow ascent up my spine. "She didn't necessarily believe me, given our history, so she asked where you were. I might have sent her in the wrong direction."

Veronica stopped talking to sing the chorus. And to let me digest her revelation. The third verse started and she said, "But I gave her a farewell from both of us in the event she was unable to find you."

"A farewell?!"

Veronica rolled her eyes as though I were interrupting her worship experience. "Yes, a farewell." Pleasure oozed from her lips as she added, "She is boarding the train for Scotland as we speak."

I shook my head. Veronica was lying. Sister Ava would not leave without saying goodbye.

"Her train doesn't leave until this afternoon."

Veronica responded only by raising her eyebrows and lifting her shoulders to her ears. She had accomplished her mission and would say no more.

I spent the remainder of the service fighting the urge to rush to Sister Ava's cottage and prove Veronica wrong. When the last prayer was spoken, I pushed past her and ran to the house.

I knocked on the door. "Sister Ava! It's Juliet!" No response. I knocked again. I walked around to the back door and knocked. Still no answer. I cupped my hands to the window and looked inside. Everything was in its place, but Sister Ava was not home. Refusing to believe she would leave without saying goodbye, I sat down on the porch and waited for her to return.

Daylight turned to dusk. The mid-afternoon train was well on its way to Scotland, which meant Sister Ava was as well.

Hate is a hurtful emotion, and it hurts the one whom it consumes the most. Sister Ava had left without saying goodbye. My heart was not simply broken. It was ripped to shreds.

I trudged to my room. Veronica rose from her desk and mumbled, "I told you," as she hurried out the door, wishing to avoid a repeat performance of book throwing and floor rolling. But my rage had evaporated with my hope, leaving me with only despair.

È Ȋ

I TRAIPSED my mangled heart to the Petite Players Children's Theatre in London. The small brick theater sat nestled between a café and a clothing store, blocks from the grandiose theaters of the West End. The only acknowledgment that it served as a theater at all was a small plaque next to the entrance.

I trembled at the thought of entering alone, having never been to a theater without Sister Ava, but the theater was my only hope for survival. Only there could I be someone other than Juliet Jenson, twice-abandoned orphan.

I took a deep breath and stepped through the propped-open double doors. The small lobby showed its age. Two door frames with curtains in place of proper doors led into the auditorium. Through each opening an aisle ran along the wall, with a ragged red carpet leading to the stage.

One adult stood at the front of the room, facing a group of children. He remained oblivious to my presence as I walked toward him. Stopping behind him and tapping him on the shoulder, I timidly said, "Excuse me, sir."

The man turned with lanky arms folded across his chest. His slender frame made him appear taller than he actually was. Slick black hair sat firmly in place atop a long face. Thick eyeglasses magnified bulging eyes that searched for someone taller than myself before focusing on my forehead.

"Yes?"

I attempted to inconspicuously grow two inches taller. My forehead was unlikely to secure a position with his players.

"My name is Juliet Jenson, sir. I am a boarder at the girls' school in the countryside, and I've suddenly found myself with a bit of free time. The theater is my passion, and it would be my greatest pleasure to experience it from behind the scenes. I'll do anything you ask of me. Might there be a position available?"

In the midst my sudden growth spurt, the man's eyes fell to where mine were supposed to be. I quickly lowered my heels and met his gaze.

"How old are you, child?"

"Thirteen."

"And you've participated in the theater before?"

"I've attended the theater but never participated."

The man tapped the pointy tip of his nose with his index finger and looked me up and down. On the sixth tap he stopped, his eyes shifting upward and finding mine on the first attempt. "I might have something for you. Come back tomorrow afternoon at four o'clock sharp."

"Oh, yes sir! Thank you!"

I practically burst with relief as I skipped up the aisle. I had found my Neverland.

CHAPTER 7

JASMINE

South Carolina

1935

I ALMOST MADE IT to the eighth grade. By almost, I mean I was standing at the bus stop with seven of my classmates, waiting to be bussed into town to attend our first day at a non-village school. Eight out of nineteen graduated seventh graders were continuing their schooling, and I was one of them.

Miles's mama had taken me to the company store to pick out a piece of fabric for a new dress. I chose an eggplant purple with pinstripes and had never owned anything so beautiful, even when it was just a bundle of cloth.

The end result was the most exquisite dress I had ever seen. It was simple, with butterfly sleeves and a belt around the waist, but it was vibrant and clean and smelled fresh, unlike my other dresses which smelled like a mixture of washing powder and dirt. Most of all, it was mine. Mine first, mine forever.

I was examining the hint of a figure peeking through the dress when Miles poked me in the ribs. "Bus is coming, Jazzy."

I rose to my tiptoes to see over the cluster of older children waiting in front of us, my hand balancing on Miles's shoulder. The door swung open as the bus screeched to a stop, and the two twelfth graders climbed aboard. Two out of the twenty or more who had been in diapers with them.

The numbers grew by one or two as each successive grade boarded the bus. Miles and I got on last, but I was certain that one day we would be first. We would be the two to make it all the way to graduation.

Last on also seemed to mean last off as Miles and I passed the watchful eyes of the other four classes. Miles scooted across an empty row near the back, and I was still in the process of sitting down beside him when the bus groaned into motion, resulting in an embarrassing landing on his lap. I quickly slid off of his leg, and with the fire in my cheeks leaving little question as to what color fruit I resembled, I turned away from him and watched for the swimming-hole turnoff as the bus jostled down the badly paved road.

Unfortunately, I didn't make it that far. The bus stopped suddenly in the middle of the road, bouncing my flushed face off the back of the seat in front of me. A car door slammed, the bus door opened, and seconds later Mr. Duncan hoisted himself up the steps.

"You think he's come to wish us good luck?" I whispered to Miles.

"No." Miles cracked his knuckles nervously.

"What's he here for then?"

"Don't know. Don't bring attention to yourself, Jazzy."

I frowned at Miles's sudden paranoia but heeded his advice and folded my hands in my lap and stared at them.

Mr. Duncan's footsteps thundered across the steel floor until they stopped at my seat. "Miss Fowler."

I kept my eyes on my lap. "Yessir?"

"I need you to come with me."

"I'm on my way to school, Mr. Duncan."

"Not today, Miss Fowler."

"Yes, sir. Today's the first day."

"Jasmine, please come with me."

"Why?" I pulled away from the hand he tried to set on my shoulder, my calmness quickly deteriorating.

The older students were losing their patience. "Just get off the bus!" one boy yelled.

"We're gonna be late because of you!" another chimed in.

I looked to Miles for help, but he offered none. "Jazzy, just go with him. Straighten out whatever this is, and you can go to school tomorrow. It's just one day."

In disbelief that he would side with Mr. Duncan, even if he was still a little humiliated by the lap incident, I gathered my bag and stood up. "If I get off this bus, Miles, I'll never get back on."

Miles just shook his head and rolled his eyes at my dramatics.

I followed Mr. Duncan to his car. The bus passed us and disappeared toward town while Mr. Duncan and I sat unmoving on the side of the road.

"Why did you pull me off the bus?" I folded my arms and waited for an answer.

"Jasmine, there's been an accident at the mill."

My abrupt bus removal forgotten, I struggled to breathe. "Is my daddy okay?"

"He's all right, but he's broken at least one of his arms. The other one may be broken as well. He's at the hospital right now."

I was sorry to hear that my daddy's arm was broken, but *accident* seemed like an unnecessary designation, given that the word often meant loss of limb and occasionally meant loss of life. Learning that my daddy still had his life and his limbs, my focus shifted back to the matter of my not being on the way to school.

"So you're taking me to the hospital to visit him?"

"He needs to rest. The pain medicine will make him sleepy. He'll be home this afternoon, and you can see him then."

"Then why did you take me off the bus?" I demanded an answer, not caring if he was my boss.

"Jasmine, your father's not going to be able to work for at least two months."

"So you need me to work at the store until he's better? And then I can go to school?"

"Not exactly."

"Not exactly to which part?"

"Well, both. You're not going to be working at the store anymore. We have a spot for you in the sewing room."

"Inside the mill?"

"Yes."

"I'm not old enough to work inside the mill! And if you think my daddy's going to sign me away, he's not! He promised my mama I'd go to school all the way through, and that's what I'm going to do!"

Mr. Duncan reached into his jacket pocket and pulled out a folded piece of paper. Its contents swore I was old enough to work on the mill floor.

"My daddy didn't write this!"

"You're right, Jasmine. He didn't write it. He can't write anything at the moment, seeing as how he has casts on both arms. But he did sign as best he could." Mr. Duncan pointed to a scribble at the bottom of the paper. "Your daddy will lose his job and the house if no one in your family works while he's out of commission. Do you want that?"

"Of course not," I muttered.

"I don't like this any more than—"

"Do I start today?" I interrupted him mid-lie.

"The cloth is waiting on you as we speak."

I ran my hand along my beautiful new dress, rare tears welling in my eyes. "Can you take me home to change my dress first? Please?"

"If you'd like."

I nodded, the tears sure to be set free if I spoke.

Mr. Duncan drove me home and waited in the car while I carefully folded the dress and tucked it away in the back of a drawer, fully expecting to never have use for it again.

I reappeared in a faded pink dress I had received some-multiple-of-second-hand from the community clothes closet. Mr. Duncan told me I looked lovely, drove me to the mill, and insisted on giving me a tour himself.

I followed him inside the building and up two flights of stairs to a closed door. The constant hum that hovered over the neighborhood was nothing compared to the discord of rumbles and grumbles and squeals that threatened to invade my eardrums as soon as the door set them free.

"This is where the men work!" Mr. Duncan yelled over the commotion. "I'm gonna walk you through real quick so you have an idea of the process, and then we'll go downstairs!"

The door swung open and I stepped inside what could only be described as a disaster area. The floor vibrated under my feet as machines bounced and shook from one end of the room to the other. Some men ran from one machine to another, dodging other workers and machines as they went. Others stood in one spot, performing the same motion over and over.

Little boys in possession of advantageously small, nimble fingers manned machines ten times their size. Old men who should have been spending their remaining time in the comfort of their homes stood hunched over work stations, their arthritic fingers fumbling the task at hand.

Sweltering heat made breathing a chore, and every breath tickled my throat as dry cotton dust sank to its final resting place in my lungs. I stood with my back against the wall and tried to picture my daddy working in such an environment every day for the last thirteen years, but the thought was too staggering to entertain.

I was fighting tears for the second time that day when Mr. Duncan boomed, "Let me show you around!"

We started down a narrow aisle. I saw Mr. Duncan's mouth move and his finger point, but because I followed the pointing finger, I didn't hear what was said.

"Well, have you?!"

"Have I what?!"

"Ever seen a bale of cotton!"

I assumed he meant in addition to the one he'd just pointed to, so I shook my head.

"First place the cotton goes once the bale is opened is to the drum carder!" He pointed to a machine a boy about my age was feeding cotton into. "That's where your daddy usually works! Once the cotton gets fed in, the drum carder does the rest!"

Mr. Duncan went on about the machine separating the fibers and forming slivers, another machine turning slivers into roving, roving being spun into bobbins, bobbins being transferred to cheese cones, cheese cones going to the weaving room where the cloth is made, and the cloth ultimately ending up in a cloth room before being ready to go out the door.

I half listened to the meaningless jargon but mostly watched the boy rhythmically push cotton into his machine and thought about how my daddy must have shoved in a million handfuls during his lifetime.

"Make sense?!"

Mr. Duncan chuckled at my bewilderment. "Oh, it doesn't matter! You don't need to know how to do any of this!" He swept his hand around the room. "This room's for the men!"

He led me down a flight of stairs that emptied into a long hall. My ears rang as the pandemonium from upstairs lessened to a muffled roar when the door closed behind us.

"This is your floor," Mr. Duncan announced. "The women's floor. Y'all do whatever the men don't wanna do." Smiling, he added, "Whoever said women were just good for cooking supper and making babies didn't know what they were talking about because they make darn good mill workers too."

I stared at Mr. Duncan blankly, not sure whether he was complimenting my gender or letting his own chauvinism peek through.

"Anyway," he said, waving me down the hall and stopping at a closed door. "Everything you'll ever need to know is right here in the sewing room. The women in here get the greige good ready to send out the door."

"Gray good?"

"Greige. *G-R-E-I-G-E*. Means cloth with no dye or finish. But you only have to worry yourself with one thing. You'll be sewing strips of cloth together."

"I don't know how to sew," I told Mr. Duncan as he led me to an unoccupied sewing machine.

"Marie here'll teach you." The middle-aged woman grunted, not looking up from her machine. Satisfied with—or indifferent to—her response, Mr. Duncan said, "Well, I best be getting back to work. So glad to have you join us, Miss Fowler."

I was given no further instructions before Mr. Duncan left the room. I sat down on what appeared to be a cross between a footstool and an actual stool meant for sitting and looked to Marie for guidance. When she offered none, I took it upon myself to send a piece of cloth on a jerky ride through the machine, which resulted in a quick lesson being given grudgingly by a woman who was not Marie. I was left with a pile of cloth, and by the end of the ten hour shift I had perfected my life's work of sewing a straight line.

I shuffled home, exhausted. Daddy was sitting on the front steps, one arm in a cast up to his elbow and the other splinted against his chest. The shame in his eyes released my tears that had been threatening to fall all day.

"It's okay, Daddy," I whispered.

"I promised your mama."

"You'll keep your promise. You'll go back to your job and I'll go back to school," I assured him, knowing that anything less would destroy him, but also knowing that Daddy would probably never see the mill floor again, and I would probably never see anything else.

CHAPTER 8

JULIET

London

1935

A SEA OF UNFAMILIAR FACES filled the auditorium. I was not surprised to see no one I knew, yet I was devastated at the same time. I had not allowed myself to hope she would come, but hope does not wait for permission.

Sister Ava knew exactly where to find me. She had known since the moment we met. Yet she was nowhere to be found. A tear escaped down my cheek as the Reverend Mother grew ever closer to calling my name.

"Louisa Catherine Englebert."

Louisa's family stood while she walked across the stage. Whether the practice was originally established to allow loved ones an unobstructed view of their graduate or to allow everyone else to see those who had participated in her upbringing, the longstanding tradition was an inane part of the ceremony.

"Georgia Antoinette Elaine Ingram."

Not only was no one going to stand for me, I was also going to be the only girl with no second name. I had certainly been given one, most likely two or three. The more names one had, the higher one's social class, and my mother would have never let herself be outclassed.

Upon my birth, she'd surely seen fit to write as many names as the certificate allowed. Upon my abandonment, she'd been in such haste to rid herself of me that she wrote nothing in the space provided for additional names on the application. At five years of age, I was not yet privy to my entire name, so when my mother walked out the door of the convent, all but my Christian name and surname went with her.

"Julie Ette Jenson."

Veronica could not have orchestrated the moment more to her liking. *Little baby Juli-ette, how pitiful can her life possibly get?*

I forced the corners of my mouth into a lopsided smile and walked toward the Reverend Mother. I was determined to keep my eyes fixed on her, but that unsolicited hope compelled me to scan the audience one last time.

Not one face rose above the rest. A tidal wave of despair crashed over me as five years of hope was destroyed in a matter of seconds. I accepted my diploma with a fragment of a smile still on my face, but instead of circling back to my chair, I walked off the stage and exited the auditorium.

My poise crumbled when I stepped out into a picturesque spring afternoon. The world would not have felt more right had my world not felt so wrong.

I left a trail of angry tears through a courtyard filled with a brightly colored array of flowers. *How could I have been so foolish to think she would come? She clearly wants nothing to do with me. Not only did she know where to find me tonight, but she knew where to find me all along. I did not leave; she did. And she never even wrote, much less visited. She really is no different than my mother, acting as though I never existed. How could she do this to me? And how could I so desperately wish to see someone who so easily forgot me?*

I had talked myself into such a fit of outrage when I reached my room that I went on a rampage, tearing through carefully packed boxes until I found what I was searching for.

I ripped the photograph down its center, leaving Sister Ava in her flapper dress on one half and my five-year-old self looking genuinely elated on the other. Our outstretched arms, which had led to interlocking hands, would now forever be searching for something to grasp.

I flipped the two halves over and, momentarily rejoining them, read Sister Ava's inscription on the back.

My darling Juliet,
May this be the beginning of a lifetime of joy and happiness. I only hope to be so fortunate as to accompany you on the journey.

Love always,
Sister Ava

What a fool I was to have believed such nonsense. With new resolve, I tossed the remnants of a happier time back into the box. I would search no more.

CHAPTER 9

THE TIMES ARTICLE

London

1940

THE WORLD is at least in agreement about one thing: there is something special about Juliet Jenson.

Stunning is the word used most often to describe her. Midnight-blue eyes are framed by long, dark lashes. Ebony curls cascade to her shoulders. Fair skin is without blemish.

Miss Jenson is not simply a beautiful face, however. She has appeared in over thirty theatre productions since the start of her career and has completed five pictures for an American film studio. She has yet to receive a negative review.

For the few who are unfamiliar with Miss Jenson and her accomplishments, her story is quite extraordinary. She walked down the aisle of the Petite Players Children's Theatre nine years ago, wishing to fill a void in her life but unaware that she was to fill a void in the theatre.

Miss Jenson spent two days sweeping the auditorium floor before being given a bit part as a street child in *The Little Match Girl*. When the play opened in November of 1930, Miss Jenson *was* the little match girl.

After her first performance, the director noted, "The child is phenomenal. She absorbs the material, becomes the part, and delivers every scene to perfection. Her ability to effortlessly transform herself is a gift few possess."

For two years, Miss Jenson played every female lead at the children's theatre, single-handedly saving a theatre that was on the brink of bankruptcy. Show after show sold out as patrons were eager to see "the future of British stage and screen."

During her time with the Petite Players, increased ticket sales not only rejuvenated the struggling theatre, but the profit was used to remodel both the interior and exterior of the building, transforming it into what it is today.

Miss Jenson was plucked from the two-hundred-seat theatre in early 1932, and bypassing mid-grade theatres in the city, she landed at the twelve-hundred-seat Grand Majestic, the site of her first theatre experience. She spent the next three years playing the female lead in eleven productions to sold-out audiences.

At the age of eighteen, an American production studio sent Miss Jenson across the Atlantic, casting her in a supporting screen role. Overshadowing the lead and drawing more attention, she was cast as the lead in four subsequent pictures.

After a successful stint in the United States, Miss Jenson returned to the British stage. Currently, she can be seen as Juliet in Shakespeare's *Romeo and Juliet* at the Grand Majestic, where crowds wait outside after every performance, hoping for a glance at the beloved actress as she exits the theatre.

Word is spreading that by next year Miss Jenson will return to Hollywood, where her career is sure to flourish.

CHAPTER 10

JULIET

London

1940

THE ARTICLE DID NOT LIE, but it did put a front-page spin on the truth. Yes, crowds waited outside the theater, eager to flood me with waves of overwhelming attention. I did not care for the notoriety, but the article was not about the real Juliet Jenson. The real Juliet Jenson existed only in the confines of her own home.

The Juliet Jenson the article spoke of delighted in the adoration. Every photograph request spread her smile slightly wider. Every autograph made the pen move more eloquently across the paper. Every glance, nod, and outstretched hand was met with graciousness and humility, a part all successful actresses are required to play.

Yes, I appeared in over thirty stage productions in ten years and never received a negative review. Yes, I received nothing but praise and acclaim for five American pictures. I was willing to accept and perfect any role I was offered because the more time I spent being someone else, the less time I had to spend being Juliet Jenson—unwanted, unloved, and twice abandoned.

Yes, I returned to Britain despite a promising career in the United States. It appeared as though I returned to my adoring fans as a thank you for giving me my start, but the sole reason I left Los Angeles was because my agent gave me no choice, promising to find me the role of a lifetime.

No, the role of a lifetime was not a part that had been portrayed by countless numbers of girls and women for four hundred years and would continue to be portrayed by anybody and everybody for all of eternity, but even that Juliet's reality was more appealing than my own.

CHAPTER 11

JASMINE

South Carolina

1940

DADDY WENT BACK to his drum carder when his arms healed, but I never saw a classroom again, and by the time I was too old to see a classroom even if my circumstances allowed it, I was resigned to the fact that I would spend the rest of my life behind a sewing machine.

After ten hours of mind-numbing boredom, I shuffled home along the edges of yards, the worn soles of my shoes no longer an adequate shield against the gravel in the street. I opened the door and found Daddy standing in the middle of the living room, wearing a suit and tie. His slightly graying sandy-blond hair was freshly trimmed and parted, and his face was smooth from the rare luxury of a close shave by the barber.

A smile stretched across Daddy's face. His eyes were bright with genuine happiness, an image of him I had only seen in pictures from when he lived on the farm. The passing of time and his work at the mill had definitely aged him, but for the first time in my life, I thought I saw a glimpse of the man Cooper Fowler was before he moved to the mill.

"You look handsome, Daddy." I kissed his cheek, inhaling a rush of aftershave. "Why are you all dressed up?"

My best guess was that someone had died. He only wore suits to church and to funerals, and it wasn't Sunday. His smile seemed out of place for a funeral, though. Matching his grin, I said, "You going on a date?"

In his southern drawl that grew slower as the years passed, he said, "I sure am. With you. I'm taking you downtown for supper, Sugar."

A wave of self-consciousness rushed through me. "Tonight? Daddy, I smell like dirt. And look at me." I pulled an arm's length away. As he looked me up and down, I did the same to him. The suit, the tie, the polished shoes, the sparkle in his eyes. He had done all of that for me.

I quickly tried to cover my hesitation. "I'd love to, Daddy. I just need a few minutes to clean up."

Daddy told me to take however long I needed. I shut myself inside the bathroom, thinking that if I truly took however long I needed, the restaurant would be closed for the night before we arrived. I kicked off my shoes, shimmied out of my dress, and stood in front of the mirror, not knowing where to start.

I hadn't taken a good look at myself in so long that the person staring back at me wasn't the me I remembered. I had become a woman, but I couldn't attach a date or even a year to exactly when that transformation had taken place. The mill didn't care that I practically left one day with a flat chest and returned the next with a bosom, and I had only cared because my dresses were suddenly too tight. A visit to the some-multiple-of-second-hand clothes closet had solved that problem, and I had never thought about it again.

I leaned in close to the mirror. Daddy had done the best he could, but because I had no mama and because of the nature of my work, fashion and beauty weren't part of my vocabulary. Pale skin revealed the beginnings of gray semicircles above my cheekbones. Aqua eyes had lost their shine. I released my hair from the band holding it back and the strawberry-blond mess fell limply above bony shoulders. I pinched my cheeks to bring color to a drab face, but no amount of squeezing achieved the desired result.

I submerged myself in the bathtub, praying the effects of mill life would miraculously wash off of me. With no time to soak, I quickly washed myself and took a hopeful glance in the mirror, disheartened to see only a wet version of what I had seen minutes earlier.

I sifted through the limited options folded inside my chest of drawers and decided on a pale violet church dress, the fading less obvious than a darker color would be. As I pulled it over my head, I remembered my long-forgotten purple school dress. I slowly opened the bottom drawer and there it lay, untouched for five years and as vibrant and gorgeous as the day I first saw the fabric.

I doubted the dress would fit, but Miles's mama must have known it would need to get me through my growing years. She had left space where space was needed, and the buttons came together effortlessly.

I forced a comb through tangled hair, water droplets falling from the ends and soaking the neck of my dress. I had seen pictures of girls in magazines with loose curls bouncing off their shoulders, but I'd never so much as seen a crinkle in my straight-as-straw hair.

I gave my cheeks one last squeeze and walked into the living room, where I did a quick twirl for Daddy.

"You sure do look real purdy, Hon." Daddy would have paid me the compliment regardless, but maybe he did think I was pretty, like how no mother believes her baby to be ugly, even when it's obvious to everyone else.

Daddy led me to the old Roadster he had borrowed for the evening. We lurched into motion, his experience with cars as limited as my experience with bicycles. When we got to the covered bridge, which had been re-covered between my first and second fateful trips through it, Daddy jammed his foot into the brake pedal. We sat in silence for a few seconds before he sighed and said, "I know you was supposed to graduate today, Jazzy."

The principal at the school would have probably thought otherwise since I missed five grades, but I knew what he meant. As Daddy and I sat on the bridge, Miles was fulfilling one half of my one and only dream that we would be the two to graduate.

Not only was Miles graduating, he was leaving for college at the end of the summer. He had stopped by my house to show me an acceptance letter, and when he stepped off my porch that day, so did my hopes for a husband.

Not that I liked him in a husband sort of way. The closest we had ever come to a date was sharing an ice cream sundae at the dairy bar when we couldn't each afford a whole one, but he was my age and he was my neighbor, and that seemed to be how marriage worked on the mill hill.

My momentary pity party ended when I realized Daddy was having a much bigger one.

"I promised your mama I'd give you all the opportunities in the world, and I couldn't even afford to get you out of sight of this mill for eighteen years. Sometimes I think you'd have been better off if I'd left you with your grandparents."

"Don't say that, Daddy. That's not true." I searched his face for a glimmer of the man he used to be, but that man had disappeared.

Daddy shook the thought from his head and drove across the great threshold. We rode through the country for miles, passing nothing but cows and fields and an occasional truck.

The roads grew busier as we neared a small cluster of buildings. Daddy drove us straight into the heart of town, made a turn, passed more cars than I had seen in my lifetime, and parked in front of a restaurant situated on the bottom floor of a three story building.

I suddenly felt very out of place as well-dressed men led their well-dressed wives up and down the sidewalks, going in and out of the stores along the street. My dress was inadequate, my hair was still damp, and every time my wooden shoes clunked across the pavement they screamed poor white trash.

Daddy held his head high and ushered me inside the restaurant's lobby where people better dressed than those outside waited to be seated. He spoke to the host while I tried to fade into the wall.

We were quickly shown to a small table in the back corner of the restaurant, as close as we could be to the kitchen without

actually being in it. Daddy and I were clearly the last people the
restaurant wanted other customers to see as they arrived.

Daddy thanked the man kindly, not seeming to mind the
location of the table. We were both handed an oversized menu
and told the waiter would be with us shortly.

My eyes ran down the list of prices, and finding the smallest
number, I looked over to see what I would be having. Chicken.
My selection complete, my focus drifted to the white table cloth.
An oil lantern sat in the center of the small round table, adding
little light to the dimly lit room. Beige walls were decorated with
mirrors offering a view of the other diners. Seeing no one staring
or whispering or pointing, I began to feel like maybe I wasn't
such an eyesore after all.

I was almost at ease when I locked eyes with a man across
the room. He quickly looked away and jotted something into a
notebook. His suit was black—a color I thought was only worn
to funerals. Instead of a necktie, he wore a black bow tie. The
strip of hair wrapped around the sides of his shiny bald head was
so purely white it looked unnatural. The earpieces on his glasses
stretched to contain a round face. Holding up the face was a
thick neck and providing a perch for the neck was a rotund body.

Like an uncontrollable tic, my eyes darted between the man
and the menu. With every glance his direction, my anxiety
escalated. My mind raced, and all I could think about was why
the man across the room couldn't take his eyes off of me.

CHAPTER 12

GORDON GREEN

SHE WAS EXACTLY WHO I was looking for. She passed my table, head down and shoulders slumped, refusing to make eye contact with the host as he seated her in the farthest corner of the restaurant.

When she lifted her face, her eyes found a large mirror on the wall, through which she examined every inch of the room with the extreme concentration of a baby examining a new toy.

Concentration turned to consternation when her eyes met mine. She quickly looked back to the menu, but the moment we shared was enough. She was perfect.

By no means was she beautiful, but she had the potential to be pretty. Blue-green eyes, undoubtedly her most promising feature, leapt from a pale face. Exhaustion framed the whites of her eyes, their color appearing more lustrous against the shaded backdrop.

The girl carried on polite conversation with her dinner companion as she ate, managing to refrain from shifting her gaze my direction. I studied her every move, scribbling notes in my book.

Baffled by the selection of silverware in front of her. Napkin has not been touched. Speaks with mouth full. Thin, but not scrawny. Homely appearance, but not necessarily unattractive. Nice eyes. Pleasant smile. Has potential, but can she do it?

When their plates were cleared, I stood and made my way to the girl's table. She noticed my movement out of the corner of her eye and followed my approach without turning her head toward me.

Her dinner companion mistook me for an employee of the restaurant, holding his plate out when I offered a handshake. Drawing my hand away from the dirty dish, I said, "Good evening, sir. My name is Gordon Green. I'd like to have a word with the young lady if you don't mind."

Realizing his error, the man quickly returned his plate to the table and shook my hand. He was no older than forty, but life had obviously not been very kind to him. The circles beneath his eyes were many shades darker than those of the girl across from him. His suit disguised a thin frame, but prominent cheekbones proved he was little more than skin and bones.

"Evenin'." His deep-south drawl oozed from his lips with the sluggishness of the last drop of honey as it clings to a jar.

"This hur's my dawter. Whatchew wont wither?"

"I'm here on business, and I may have a proposition for your daughter, sir."

"A proposition?"

The man's tone made it unclear as to whether or not he was familiar with the word.

"That's right. I work for a production studio. We're getting ready to film a new picture, but we've had difficulty finding the right girl to play one of the parts. When I saw your daughter walk into the restaurant tonight, something told me we had found our girl."

The man chuckled, shaking his head. "My youngin ain't no actress, mister. I think you got the wrong girl."

The girl lifted her head and eyed me suspiciously. Up close, she did have a natural attractiveness about her. It would take a great deal of work, but if I could get her away from whatever had worn her so ragged, I might have something lovely in my midst.

I offered her my hand. She cautiously accepted, not taking her eyes off of mine. Having already introduced myself to her father, I simply nodded and said, "Gordon Green."

She stared at me for a long moment and then said, "Jasmine Fowler."

I couldn't be certain, having been given only two words, but she didn't seem to speak nearly as frustratingly slow as her father.

"It's a pleasure to meet you, Miss Fowler. May I buy you a cup of coffee?"

Her shoulders rose as she looked to her father. He drew back a corner of his mouth and contemplated my offer. Reaching a decision, he nodded and said, "It ain't gawna hurtcha none to have cawfee with him, Jazzy. I'll be right hur. You g'awn."

Miss Fowler and I shared a surprised glance. She hesitantly stood and followed a few steps behind me as I led her to my table. I sat down across from her and was about to pitch my case when she spoke first.

"What exactly is it that you do, Mr. Green?" Her accent was definitely that of a country girl, but she spoke with a sweetness I was certain the public would embrace.

"I'm in the motion picture business."

"Like the ones they show at the community center at the mill?"

"I suppose so." I made a note in my book. *Mill child.*

"Well, I ain't never seen a picture show before. We can't afford it."

"You've never seen a picture?" I was astonished by her admission. Even the poorest children snuck into the theater or convinced someone to pay their way now and then.

"No, sir. Not even a cartoon on Saturday morning."

Naive, but that's what we're looking for.

"Miss Fowler, tell me about yourself."

"First, you tell me what you're writing in that book. I saw you writing in it earlier too."

"I write down my observations so that I can remember them later." She looked less than satisfied with my answer so I slid the notebook across the table. "See for yourself."

Her eyes ran across the page. I wondered whether she could actually read or if she was only making a show of it. She answered the unspoken question when she said, "Homely's not a very nice thing to say about somebody you don't even know."

I made a mental note to add that she could read, at least at a basic level, later and said, "Homely just means not made up. You're more...natural. See right there next to it where I wrote not unattractive, nice eyes, pleasant smile?" I pointed to the more complimentary words on the page.

"You wrote not *necessarily* unattractive, which means it is yet to be determined." Sighing, she said, "But thank you for the nice eyes and pleasant smile comment. I know I ain't pretty. I never had a mama to show me how to be pretty."

"Everyone has a mother, Miss Fowler."

"Well, I only had mine for a few hours. She died the day I was born." Passing the notebook back to me, she said, "What are you wanting me to do, Mr. Green?"

"I want you to tell me about yourself." My request did not answer Miss Fowler's question, but she complied.

"I was born on a farm in Abbeville, and like I said, my mama died right after I was born. Me and my daddy moved here when I was a baby, and we've been at the mill ever since." She shrugged her shoulders and raised her eyebrows in a way that said she had given me all she could but thought I expected more.

"Do you work at the mill as well?"

"Yes, sir. I started working at the company store when I was a little girl, but I've been inside the mill for five years."

"Do you enjoy your work?"

"Would you enjoy pushing cloth through a sewing machine for ten hours every day?" Miss Fowler's eyes creased, and I realized the question wasn't rhetorical.

"I don't believe I would."

"I don't like it either, but it's what I've gotta do. There ain't...isn't no other option."

Her attempt to correct her grammar showed that she was adaptable and had the potential to learn. I refrained from adding that to the notebook.

"What if there was another option? Do you think you'd be interested?"

"I guess it'd depend on what that other option was."

I was confident she would find anything that didn't involve cotton an appealing alternative. "I'd like to test you for a role in a picture."

Miss Fowler exhaled a quick breath of laughter and shook her head. "Mr. Green, I retired from test taking when I was thirteen years old. And I told you already, I don't know nothing about the motion picture business. I don't care to subject myself to a test I know I'm gonna fail."

"It's not that kind of test, Miss Fowler. All this test will involve is you standing in front of a camera and being yourself. It will be over in a matter of minutes."

"How do you expect me to be myself in front of something that's watching my every move?"

That question *was* rhetorical and was laced with a hint of irritation. If I didn't alter my approach, Miss Fowler was going to put an abrupt end to the test she didn't realize she was already taking and passing with flying colors.

"Let me put it to you this way. The girl we're looking for is a lot like you. She grew up on a farm in South Carolina."

"But I didn't grow up on no farm," she quickly interjected.

"No, but you did grow up in South Carolina. All you'll have to do is be yourself, and we'll give you some pretty clothes and teach you a few lines, and in just a few months you'll be back home."

Shaking her head with less determination than before, she said, "I can't leave home for a few months. My daddy won't be able to pay the bills if I'm not working."

It was my turn to eye *her* suspiciously. "Miss Fowler, you will be working. We'll pay you five thousand dollars."

Stunned eyes locked with mine. "Five thousand dollars?" She struggled to vocalize the amount.

"Five thousand dollars."

"All at one time? You'll just hand me five thousand dollars?"

"We'll pay you a set amount weekly, and when production ends we'll write you a check for the rest."

Her voice quivered as she said, "I need to ask my daddy."

I waved Miss Fowler up out of her chair and in the direction of her father. He stood with a concerned look on his face as she made her way to him. I couldn't make out the exchange that took place between them, but the conversation ended with a firm nod from each of them.

Sitting back down across from me, Miss Fowler whispered, "I can't say no."

"So you'll take the job?" I asked exuberantly, passing an already-prepared contract and pen across the table.

She nodded and took the time to read every word of the contract. After reading and rereading, she signed along the dotted line with a shaking hand. So not only could she read, she could also write, or at least write her name, which was all that was needed if the opportunity to sign autographs were to present itself.

"Thank you, Miss Fowler. Production won't start for a few months, so you have time to get everything in order." I pulled a slip of paper from my pocket. "This is a receipt for a prepaid train ticket to California. You'll take it to the station right down the street from here, where it will be exchanged for a ticket to Los Angeles. You'll have to change trains a couple times along the way, but before you know it, you'll be in sunny California." I paused, noticing Jasmine staring blankly at the receipt. "Are you following me, Miss Fowler? Should I be writing this down?"

"Please," she exhaled, clearly overwhelmed.

As I wrote, I continued giving verbal instructions. "Like I said before, the ticket you have will be exchanged for a dated ticket at the station. I'll make all the arrangements beforehand to reserve a ticket for you. Is there a telephone number where I can reach you with the details?"

"No."

I looked up from where my hand was prepared to write the number. "No?"

"There's a telephone at the company store, but I've never used it. The owner will take down a message for me since I used to work for him, but his wife will probably charge me the nickel it costs to make a call. It don't matter, though, because I don't know the number."

"Then do you have an address?"

"Of course I've got an address!" She looked momentarily offended before jotting it down.

"When you arrive in California, there will be a payphone at the train station. Dial this number." I pointed to the bottom of her instructions. "I'll come pick you up, all right?"

Without hesitation, Miss Fowler leapt up from the table and wrapped her arms around my neck. "Thank you, Mr. Green. You don't know what this opportunity means to me."

I had never been so graciously thanked for offering a bit part to a player. Slightly taken aback by her public, unprofessional display, I reminded myself that her lack of professionalism was exactly what we were looking for.

"Just doing my job, Miss Fowler. I'll look forward to seeing you in California." I patted her back and gently separated myself from her embrace.

A smile exploded across her face, and her eyes burst into all their sea-green brilliance as she extended her hand to me. "See ya in California!"

I shook her hand and watched her return to her father and fall into his arms. I leaned back in my chair and clasped my hands behind my head, lost in thought.

The studio was looking for a defeated personality. As defeated as she was, Jasmine Fowler displayed an unwillingness to fully surrender to her circumstances. Whether that feistiness would prove to be beneficial or detrimental remained to be seen, but at any rate, I had found my girl.

Part III

ॐ

The Beginning of The End

CHAPTER 13

JULIET

London

1940

Day One

THE WAR FOUND LONDON halfway through the third act. The air raid siren flooded the theater. The orchestra improvised a crescendo and the actors amplified their voices, but the warning would not be defeated. I was instantly ripped from Verona. Romeo's eyes pleaded with mine to stay in the scene and continue on as we had so many times before. But this time was different.

CB BO

THE INCONVENIENCES of a looming war had infiltrated my daily life for a year. Wailing sirens accompanied me to the theater in the afternoon, and nothing but the stars in the sky guided my path home at night.

The blackout was strictly enforced from dusk until sunrise the following morning as the war threatened to shift west to England. But that's all it was—a threat. Each day was a dress rehearsal for the day no one ever thought would come.

It was more than a bit eerie walking home alone in the dark. There were no illuminated streetlamps, no visible store fronts, no uncovered windows, and no headlights on automobiles. I was more worried about being hit by a blinded bus than becoming a casualty of a war being fought far from my own soil.

Though the likelihood of being assaulted by an automobile decreased exponentially once I reached my house, the probability of a more tactical invasion—however slight it seemed—remained the same, thus making my lesser concern my greatest concern when within the walls of my home. Thick black drapes separated me from the rest of the world, and I felt sure the Germans were intelligent enough to know that the city did not magically disappear at sundown and reappear the next morning.

Cß ßO

THE TENTH NIGHT of the blackout was when I met the stranger in the alley. I collided with his shadowy figure as I exited the side door of the theater.

"Pardon me," I hurriedly apologized, eager to find a more populated street. The scent of his cologne accompanied me to the main road. Safely there, I turned to find his silhouette where I left it.

"Until we meet again!" His breathy farewell floated through the alley as he turned and faded into the night.

The following evening I smelled him before I saw him.

"We meet again." His velvety voice made me suddenly aware of my heart beating inside my chest.

"I'd hardly call it serendipity," I responded tartly, taking several slow steps toward the street and wondering if he would simply watch me walk away again.

"You don't believe in fate?"

I turned and squinted to make out the mysterious stranger's features. "You clearly know when and through which door I exit the theater. Fate has nothing to do with it."

"And you clearly know that I know when and through which door you exit the theater."

"So?"

"So, even with that knowledge you still chose to exit through this very door. Destiny, I'd say."

He could not see me roll my eyes. He also could not see my chest heaving from the butterflies dancing around my abdomen. At least I hoped he could not.

"So," he continued, "if a gentleman were to ask to walk you home, would you be inclined to say yes?"

"Gentlemen don't wait for ladies in dark alleys." Thankfully my training had taught me how to keep nerves from quivering forth while speaking.

"True, but ladies don't enter dark alleys alone in the first place. I believe we have neither a lady nor a gentleman in our midst." He removed his hat from his head and placed it over his heart. Mimicking the accent of a street urchin, he said, "Just a lad wishin' ta walk a lassie 'ome's all."

An ever-so-slight inkling of amusement escaped my lips before I could swallow it. Regaining my stoicism, I said, "If you choose to walk alongside me on a public street, there's not much I can do to stop you, is there?"

"I suppose not." He returned his hat to his head and pivoted toward the street. When I made no effort to move, he swept his arm out in front of him. "Ladies first."

I took one cautious step and then another. My eager companion fell into stride and we exited the alley side by side.

With a decreased sense of sight, my other senses went into overdrive. I inhaled his cologne as though it were oxygen. I heard every slow, steady breath as though the usual sounds of the city had been muted. I felt every aspect of the back of his hand when it inadvertently brushed against mine.

Reaching the first intersection, our stroll suddenly stopped.

"All right, then. I live around that corner. I'll say goodnight now. It has been a pleasure."

"Oh." I could think of nothing else to say as confusion overtook the other emotions I was feeling. I finally managed a bewildered, "Goodnight, then."

"Ha!" The stranger became increasingly stranger as he reached for my hand and began walking again. I reclaimed my hand as quickly as he had grasped it, but he didn't seem to notice as he went on reveling in his victory of a game I had not realized we were playing.

"You do want me to walk you home! You acted nonchalant, but that's what you are—an actress. Now we both know the truth."

"And what might that be?" I was caught in the act, but feigning apathy was all that kept my heart from bursting through my chest.

"You're smitten by me."

I was the one who abruptly stopped walking with that announcement. He had to be an actor as well. No human being naturally exuded such egomaniacal self-confidence. Unless he was, in fact, an egomaniac.

I desperately needed to escape the fog of spiced aftershave lotion. I was interested in the companionship of neither an actor nor an egomaniac.

"I don't even know you."

"You're getting to know me as we walk."

"And I don't believe I like what I see." I started walking again, unsure if I wanted him to walk away or follow after me.

The cologne-filled air dissipated, and my sense of security went with it. I had all but broken into a run when suddenly I was overtaken by the stranger from the alley and his strangely comforting scent. He took my hand again, but this time in a grasp of introduction rather than affection. I instinctively tried to pull away, but he would not release me.

"Please allow me to speak, and then I will leave you alone. Forever, if you wish." His tone took a sincerity I did not know it was capable of. "I know you're not smitten by me or even fond of me. I can be a bit of a cad when I'm nervous. I'm a stranger to you; I know that as well. But I have been captivated by you since I first saw you on the stage. It is I who am smitten. I assure you I did not orchestrate our encounter last night, but when you bumped into me I could not let the moment simply pass. Please allow me one more opportunity to be a man worthy of your presence." He brought his hands into prayer position, and all seriousness disappeared.

"If you get down on your knees, I'm walking away." My first hint of a smile since meeting him did not go unnoticed.

He raised his arms in surrender. "Fair enough. You have already given me more than I could have ever hoped for this evening."

We walked on in silence. After turning yet another street corner, a skeptical voice said, "You walk all this way alone every night?"

"I never walk all this way. Alone or otherwise."

"You don't?" His confidence suddenly sounded shaken, as though he was unsure where I was leading him.

"There's a tube station a block from the theater and another two blocks from my home. Why would I risk my life walking the in-between with nary a streetlamp to light the way?"

After a second of silence, I heard a high-pitched, "Uh-huh," with strong emphasis placed on the last syllable.

I immediately regretted divulging such a confession and tried to recover. "I was distracted and missed the entrance."

"And you've missed two or three more since then." He chuckled at his quick-witted remark, and I picked up my pace. Less time spent with the stranger from the alley meant less time to unintentionally give him further reason to believe I wished him to be anything more.

As we neared my house, I grew increasingly apprehensive. He had already told me he was no gentleman and did not believe me to be a lady. I wondered if I was leading the wolf right to his prey.

I ascended the steps to my front door as one might approach a waiting noose. Realizing I was alone on the stoop, I turned to find what looked to be a chivalrous man standing at the bottom of the steps.

"It has truly been a pleasure, Miss Jenson. Until we meet again." He tipped his hat and, as a gentleman would, watched me safely enter my home before the door closed between us.

The next day anticipation grew as afternoon turned to evening. When I opened the side door of the theater, his dark figure bounced off the brick wall across the alley. He escorted me home, and when we reached my steps, he lifted my hand to his lips. Again, the perfect gentleman said goodnight at the door.

The fourth evening his lips found my cheek.

The fifth evening his kiss found my lips.

The sixth evening I met him halfway, and as I stood inside the door and listened to his footsteps fade away, I found myself wishing he was not such a gentleman.

The seventh evening, as we approached the steps, I took his hand and led him onto the stoop. "Won't you come inside for a bit?"

"Are you sure?" His lips besieged mine, leaving little room for contemplation.

"Mmm," I sighed.

I unlocked the door and we entered the dark room as a unit. When the door closed behind us, his silhouette vanished.

"Lovely home," he quipped, the blackness swallowing us. I fumbled for a light switch, but his hand caught mine midair and wrapped it around his waist. "No need for the light," he exhaled between kisses. "Wouldn't want to allow the Germans to ruin the moment."

What we did next, we did in the dark, and he was gone before daylight.

He was a welcome distraction from waiting to be blown to bits in the middle of the night. He took the loneliness away. He passed the time. Nothing more.

For a year he remained an elusive stranger waiting in the alley to walk me home. We rarely walked with long stretches of silence, but the conversations were largely one sided. My contributions were usually brief and always vague. I learned little of his life, and he learned nothing of mine. Some evenings he left me with only a kiss at the door, but I always found myself relieved when he wanted more.

We never turned on the lights. The only glimpse I got of him was through the natural light of a full moon. When gray London nights refused to give way to true darkness, I avoided him altogether. The elusiveness made his presence acceptable.

Juliet Jenson—adored actress—was a strong, independent woman. She was rarely seen dangling on the arm of a man because her standards were high and she would never settle.

But the real Juliet Jenson—unwanted, unloved, and twice abandoned—had built a protective barrier that no one could penetrate. She dangled from no man's arm because that man would no longer be a stranger, and only strangers were allowed into her life.

Strangers could not hurt her. Acquaintances could, friends likely would, and love was absolutely forbidden.

CHAPTER 14

JULIET

Night One

I SCANNED THE AUDITORIUM for the open door allowing such a blaring interruption. The siren was usually nothing more than a slightly off-key orchestral accompaniment, but now it demanded a solo.

The lights came up and the orchestra screeched to a halt as the stage manager appeared from the wings.

"Ladies and gentlemen!" His powerful voice momentarily smothered the siren. "It is necessary at this time for everyone to exit the auditorium and proceed to the nearest shelter. Please do so calmly and in an orderly fashion."

Few people rose from their seats, so accustomed to false alarms they were unwilling to be inconvenienced in the middle of the play.

The manager repeated himself in a firmer tone. "Ladies and gentlemen, you must leave the theater and go to the nearest shelter at this time. Remaining in the auditorium is not an option. Your ticket will be exchanged for a later date. Everyone must exit now."

The grumbling audience meandered toward the exits. Having never been inside the theater during a drill, they did not know the mandatory evacuation was abnormal. I knew, though, and I was terrified.

The urgency in the stage manager's voice signified that he was not simply being unduly cautious. Fear gripped my insides and I lost the ability to make purposeful movements. It was not until Romeo was physically ushering me across the stage that I regained myself.

I hurried backstage, tearing off my costume and retrieving my clothes as I passed the dressing room. I finished zipping my skirt as I burst out the side door of the theater, desperately hoping to see my blackout companion waiting in the alley.

He was nowhere to be found, and there was no time to wait. I had to go to the shelter alone.

The street was congested, but few people seemed concerned. Most were cheerful and laughing as if they were simply out for a Sunday stroll.

I was swept down the steps of the nearest Underground and found swarms of Londoners already gathered inside the concrete shelter. I nudged my way through the crowd, searching for a vacant place to sit against a wall as far from the commotion as possible.

As I passed a group of boys kicking tin cans back and forth on the tracks below, I heard my name. One of the boys swiftly hoisted himself onto the platform. I considered ignoring his approach, but the snail's pace in which I was moving made a confrontation inevitable.

"The other lads didn't think it was you, but I knew it was," the boy boasted when he saw that he had my attention. I attempted a smile, but fright did not allow it. "I saw you on stage once, and I've seen all of your pictures," he added proudly.

I stared blankly at the boy as he continued chattering. "My brother has your posters on his walls. He gave me one, but I have to keep it under my bed because my mum won't allow me to hang it. She says I'm too young for such foolishness, but I'm practically thirteen."

The boy's friends gathered around us. "I told you it was her," he grunted at another boy, shoving him as he spoke.

"I never said it wasn't her!" the second boy shouted.

A halfhearted pushing match commenced, the tight quarters not allowing elbows or shoulders to be fully involved. Under less dire circumstances, I would never walk away from an admirer of any age or level of maturity, but maintaining my reputation was not of utmost importance at the moment. I left the school boys to their argument and turned to continue my trek.

Noticing my escape, the first boy gave his opponent one final shove and followed after me. "Wait, Miss Jenson! Wait!"

I feigned oblivion, but soon he was in front of me, blocking my path. I held my gaze above his head as he spoke.

"If I don't at least get an autograph," he explained, "no one will ever believe I met you."

I forced my eyes to his. "I haven't got a pen."

"I'll find one!" the boy proclaimed, my lack of enthusiasm not a deterrent. Before he set out to complete the task at hand, he took hold of my arm. "You promise you'll wait here?"

"I promise," I answered listlessly.

"I'll be right back, then."

The boy disappeared into the constantly changing crowd. I considered breaking my promise, but not knowing how long I was going to be inside the Underground with him, and given his determination, I waited.

He returned with a pen and a page torn from a magazine. I hastily scribbled the usual pleasantries and signed my name.

Not yet satisfied, the boy made one final request. "Will you kiss me on the cheek, please? And try to leave lipstick marks."

For the first time since the siren sounded, my face came out of its solemn blankness. "No, I will not."

"Just one small kiss, not even on the lips!"

"No," I said, slightly more firmly.

"Please!" he pleaded, clutching both of my arms. "What's the problem?"

I shook myself free of the boy's grasp. More loudly than I intended, I said, "The problem is that we're in an air raid shelter. I gave you your autograph. Now leave me be!" Tears glazed my eyes and the boy scurried away, tucking his autographed paper into his pocket.

I had no choice but to continue to parade past the watchful eyes of what felt like all of London. The gawkers were the least bothersome. The whisperers were slightly more irritating. The loudmouths were downright rude.

"I knew she wasn't as great as everyone made her out to be," one woman snidely announced to the lady beside her.

The lady quickly proved she wasn't one. "She's not as pretty either," she snorted. "It must take quite a lot of work to get her looking the way she looks in the pictures," she cackled before quieting to muffled whispers.

"What are you doing inside the Underground with all the commoners?" a middle-aged woman sneered as I walked past her. "Isn't there a special place for your kind?"

Outstretched hands swept across whatever body part they could reach. A baby lamb at a petting zoo would have been less of a spectacle.

With the end of the walkway rapidly approaching—and the idea of having to retrace my steps increasingly unappealing—I spotted a sliver of vacant wall space beside a young woman. All that prevented the sliver from being an area large enough for me to sit down was a toddler standing by her side. Seeing that I was eyeing the spot, the woman shifted an infant to one arm and pulled the child onto her legs, motioning for me to sit down.

I sank onto the cool, dirt-stained floor. Walking room was becoming nonexistent as Londoners crowded into the shelter. Men, women, and children of all ages and all walks of life sat nestled along the wall. Latecomers sat down where they stood, realizing there was nowhere else to go. Train tracks, unused by disabled trains, were slowly occupied by those who found no space on the platform. The number of passersby gradually trickled down to none.

The noise level rose and fell rhythmically throughout the Underground. With every lull, the siren howled overhead while everyone sat in silence and strained to hear what was taking place. Realizing it was nothing more than the same drill we all heard for months, conversations resumed and the siren faded.

I straightened my legs to preserve what little distance was left between myself and the person directly in front of me, crossed my ankles, and rested my head against the wall. When I closed my eyes, my mind drifted to the man who was not waiting for me in the alley.

Why wasn't he there? Am I really nothing more than a bit of fun to pass away otherwise lackluster blacked-out nights? Of course I am, but that's all I want to be. Strangers cannot hurt me.

The desperate ache I felt over him not being with me defied my own logic. He *was* nothing more than a stranger, wasn't he?

"Excuse me, miss?"

My panic-stricken revelation was interrupted by a voice so close that the words tickled my ear. I opened my eyes and warily turned my head to find the young woman with the babies staring at me like a startled cat. She was barely more than a girl, drifting somewhere between adolescent and adult. Adolescent by age, adult by circumstance, and unkempt from head to toe.

The little boy was a miniature of the girl. Same disheveled brown hair, same saucer-shaped black eyes. Dirty, bare feet stuck out of the bottom of a jaggedly stitched sackcloth romper.

Once she had my attention, the girl's eyes shrank to their normal size. A smile stretched across her face, and I began to regret my seat choice, certain she recognized me. But if she knew who I was, she did not let on.

"Will ya 'old me baby for a minute, miss? Me arm feels loike it's roight ready ta fall off." Her thick Cockney accent suggested she was a bit too far west to have been at home when the siren sounded.

I glanced at the sleeping infant in her arms. A clean, pink face peeked out of a thin hospital-issued blanket.

"I suppose so," I agreed hesitantly.

The baby was plopped onto my forearms before I could move them into a proper infant-cradling position. I jostled him toward my elbows until his head was safely in the crook of my arm.

The toddler quickly splayed himself across the girl's freed lap. She wrapped her arms around him, rested her chin on his shoulder, and began to tell him a story about a little boy who could fly.

Sister Ava's words broke free from the place where I kept them hidden deep within my mind. *Without imagination one must spend all of his time in the real world, and the real world is not always a grand place to be. Create your own Neverland behind your eyes, and go there whenever you wish.*

There had never been a better time to heed her advice. I shifted the baby to my torso, his warm cheek sinking into my chest, and tilted my head against the wall, closing my eyes and trying to think of something pleasant.

Time passed and fear dissipated. I was as skeptical of the need to remain below ground as the restless few who began to leave, but I preferred the company of strangers to the solitude of my home, so I stayed put. Dozens managed to escape before a police officer blocked the exit, leaving the rest of us inside the shelter indefinitely.

The baby stirred. His face burrowed into my blouse as his mouth searched for nourishment.

"I don't believe I have what he's looking for," I announced, holding him out to the girl.

"No, but he'd 'ave quite a story ta tell, would'n he?" She chuckled as she unbuttoned her dress and put the baby to her breast, covering the exposed area with the blanket a bit belatedly.

The little boy immediately whined to return to the girl's lap. When his request was denied, he slumped next to his mother and pouted. I watched his face redden as he grew ever closer to giving the one performance perfected by all toddlers—a roaring, attention-grabbing tantrum.

To save myself from the unsolicited publicity, I offered to hold the baby again the instant he squirmed beneath the blanket, indicating he was full. The girl readily returned him to my waiting arms and the boy reclaimed his place on her lap.

The baby seemed perfectly content to share my warmth rather than his mother's. His hands wriggled out of the blanket and tight fists settled against his cheeks. When I stroked his arm, he released his grip and wrapped four tiny fingers around my thumb. My breath caught, and I allowed myself a moment of genuine emotion before I quickly slid my finger from his grasp, tucked the awe-inspiring child's arms back into the blanket, and set him onto my lap.

"I'll take 'im back now an' get 'im outta your way." The girl moved the toddler to one leg, making room for the baby.

She only needed to be told once that he was not a bother. She returned her attention to the older boy, and I returned to the solace behind my eyelids.

Several minutes later, I opened my eyes to find the girl's bulbous eyes studying my face.

"You're very koind. Nuffin loike I would've expected." I felt my face flush as she added, "But that's why ya don't judge a book by its cover, eh?"

"You know who I am?" I could not hide the shock in my voice, and she didn't try to hide the shock in hers.

"O' course I do. Who does'n?"

"I assumed you didn't recognize me."

"Cause o' me appearance?"

I could not tell whether she was trying to pick a fight or if a confrontational tone was simply her natural way. I turned toward her and adamantly shook my head. "No, not at all."

"I ain't always been loike this ya know. I might not 'ave been as 'igh falutin' as you, but I 'ad a home and things o' me own once."

"I, I meant no disrespect," I stammered, anxious to squelch the altercation that appeared to be brewing inside the girl's head.

"We 'ave different lots in life, you an' me. I don't 'old it against ya. Me name's Genevieve." The girl held out a grimy hand. I reluctantly set my hand against hers and she shook it firmly. "And you're Juliet. Pleasure ta meet ya. See, now we're friends."

No, we're not.

"I grew up in the orphanage two blocks from the bells. It was'n such a bad loife, but I ran away when I was fifteen so I could get married. Me 'usband was sixteen. Thought we could make it on our own."

I suppose you thought wrong.

"Michael 'ere, he came ten months after the wedding. Gave me a terrible toime. I almost died." Genevieve paused, waiting for me to acknowledge her near death experience.

"I'm sorry." For good measure, I added, "You both look healthy now."

"Oh, we are. Gabriel, he came six weeks ago. Did'n give me no trouble at all. Only thing is, we lost our place at the shelter an' have'n been able ta get it back yet."

I did not ask her to elaborate, but she apparently needed no encouragement.

"Walt, that's me 'usband, left for the war before I knew I was expectin' Gabriel. I could'n work, so we lost our flat. I'll get it back before he comes 'ome though."

If he comes home. Another reason to never grow attached to anyone. Even if he does not intend to leave, the circumstances of life may do it for him.

Genevieve's eyes swelled again. "I'm borin' ya, ain't I? I'll stop talkin' now."

I shook my head. "It's just been a long day. I'm tired and a bit concerned about what's transpiring up there."

I pointed toward the ceiling. Genevieve looked skyward and slowly said, "Roight," as though only then did she remember we were in an air raid shelter and not sitting on a patio sharing tea.

We were both still darting our eyes around the ceiling when a sudden hush swept through the room. The hum of casual conversations had been swallowed by a much more sinister hum off in the distance. A sound London never believed she would hear quickly grew in intensity until a grinding roar directly overhead faded opposite the direction from which it came.

Startled children clung to their mothers. Women buried their faces into their husbands' sides. Men sat stoically, but their eyes told a different story.

Genevieve's eyes reached an unprecedented protrusion. She gripped my hand so tightly that her fingernails pierced my palm. Gabriel's wails of discomfort suggested I was clutching him with the same vigor. I lifted my hand and found five red indentations where my own nails had come dangerously close to breaking his pristine skin.

Fighting tears, I moved closer to Genevieve until our sides were fully touching. I wrapped an arm around her shoulders and allowed her to melt into my side. Michael clung to his mother, his mother clung to me, and I had no one to cling to but a completely helpless newborn baby.

For a time everyone sat in chilling silence. The Underground was heavily saturated with apprehension, but aside from the constant blaring of the siren, there was no noise overhead.

Then a second plane flew over. It was gone as quickly as it had approached, and the harrowing silence resumed.

The pattern continued into the night, with a passing plane bursting the paralyzing swell of anticipation every few minutes. Gabriel and Michael cried themselves to sleep. Genevieve kept one ear against my shoulder and the other covered by her free hand. When her trembling body grew still, I knew sleep had found her as well.

My uncovered ears remained exposed to every sound. Silent tears rolled unimpeded down my cheeks, as I had no free hand with which to stop their progress. Eventually, physical and emotional exhaustion overtook fear and I also fell asleep.

I awoke some time later to a silence no longer accompanied by the siren. A sleeping Michael was draped across my legs and Gabriel was with his mother. My right arm still rested across Genevieve's shoulders. My left arm ached from holding the baby. My neck was tight from the awkward position it had taken against the concrete wall. My eyes burned from relentless crying.

As I focused on my various aches and pains, I realized I had not visited the toilet since late afternoon. Unable to will my right arm to move without assistance, I lifted it off of Genevieve's shoulders with my left hand. I carefully tilted her head against the wall and slid my legs out from under Michael. I felt like I had doubled in weight as I pushed myself up the wall and into a standing position.

I maneuvered my way through the shelter, tiptoeing over sleeping families. Those who were awake sat quietly, most of them looking the same way I felt.

A fully clothed schoolgirl sat on the toilet, enjoying a lollipop and reading a magazine. Her eyes acknowledged my presence but she made no effort to move.

"May I?" I asked with all the politeness I could muster.

She stood up and walked out of the room, craning her neck to keep her eyes on me as she left. I closed the door behind her and hurriedly used the toilet, growing more unsettled with every moment I spent alone inside the enclosed box.

Before I could fully open the door, the girl brushed past me and reclaimed her seat. Popping the lollipop out of her mouth, she asked, "Are you related to Juliet Jenson? You look a bit like her."

"Not to my knowledge." My knowledge told me that I had answered honestly, that I could not be related to myself.

"Huh." She tilted her head back, studying my face. "If you'd do yourself up a bit, you'd likely pass for her." Opening the magazine and haphazardly flipping through its pages, she said, "There's an article in here about how to make yourself look like a star. Let me find it."

"Don't trouble yourself. I need to get back—"

"Here it is." The girl ripped a handful of pages from the magazine, interrupting a sentence I could not have finished if she had let me.

Accepting and quickly folding what appeared to be an editorial with a photograph of myself in the bottom corner, I asked, "Have you been awake all night?"

"Yep."

"When did all go quiet?"

She shrugged. "Three magazines ago?"

I thanked her, less for her breezy answer which was more worthy of a lesson on manners than an expression of gratitude, and more to put an end to the exchange. Not surprisingly, the girl twirled her lollipop stick between her fingers in response and returned her attention to the magazine.

I weaved my way back to Genevieve and her boys. Finding Michael taking up every inch of the space I had vacated, I swept him onto my lap as I sat down. Genevieve stirred briefly before settling against my shoulder.

I closed my eyes, but sleep did not come. I remained wide awake, anxious to know what had occurred above ground. I had heard no explosions or fire brigades or other unwelcome sounds from the street, but that did not mean all was well.

My mind drifted to the man I was determined to believe was still a stranger, nothing more. *Is he all right? Is he concerned about me? Why should he be concerned? I'm only a distraction in an unsettled world, and that's all I want to be.*

I swallowed the flutters that took flight from my abdomen every time I thought about him and forced my attention to the little boy in my lap. Lack of a proper shampoo left his hair coarse and tangled. His pudgy hands and feet needed a good scrubbing, with caked dirt inhabiting long nails and leaving the tips black. The rest of his skin looked clean, but it was flaky in certain spots, likely the result of being rubbed too often with the same cheap soap used to wash his hair.

The more attention I gave to Michael, the less I had to give to what might have happened outside. As I focused on the rise and fall of my chest against his back, my breathing synchronized with his and conscious thought slipped away.

CHAPTER 15

JULIET

Day Two

A COMMANDING VOICE shook me out of an uncomfortable sleep. As I regained my senses, I shivered uncontrollably, partly from the night air and partly from sheer exhaustion.

"Thank you all for your cooperation last night," the police officer continued, having gained most of the room's attention. "We've been told it's safe to release everyone to their homes."

Bones cracked throughout the Underground as those eager to leave stood faster than hours of immobility allowed. Most people however, myself included, remained seated as uncertainty overpowered the desire to rush home.

One man in the crowd spoke up. "And what are we to find when we reach the street?"

"You will find everything as you left it. There was a minor disturbance at the docks, but this area received no damage."

Sighs of relief floated across the platform as people began gathering their families and belongings. I looked down at Michael one last time, intending to turn him over to his mother, wish them well, and be on my way.

"I thank ya again for your koindness," Genevieve said as I rose to my feet. "Maybe I'll see ya 'ere tonight if the sirens go off?" Her dark orbs waited intently for a response.

"I won't be coming here tonight," I answered honestly. "I was at the theater yesterday when the siren sounded, and this was the closest Underground. I don't believe I'll be working today, so I'll stay closer to home."

"Roight." Genevieve's face fell, and my heart would not let me leave, even though my feet desperately wanted to.

"Why don't you and the boys stay at my house until you can reclaim your flat?" What came out of my mouth was a much greater commitment than the one night's stay I had intended to offer.

Genevieve's eyes looked like they might spring from their sockets. "I can't impose on ya loike that?"

"I can't leave you here with nowhere to go," I admitted.

"If you're sure?" Genevieve was already attempting to stand with both boys in her arms.

I was not at all sure, but I took the baby from Genevieve and waited for her to lift Michael. Together we ascended the steps and exited onto a street crowded with others trudging home.

Aside from the congested sidewalks, it was a typical London morning. The sun was nowhere to be found but was still serving its purpose and spreading daylight across the city. The air was crisp, and the ever-present threat of a morning shower hung over our heads.

The streets came to life as Londoners reached their homes and started their days. Cars rolled by, city buses began their rounds, and the tube periodically rumbled beneath our feet. Businessmen walked past us on their way to work. Children and their mothers left their homes with school bags and lunch sacks in tow.

When I saw my house still standing, untouched, I let out a breath I did not realize I was holding. I unlocked the periwinkle-blue door and led Genevieve into my home.

"Why's your door blue?" she asked as she stepped inside.

"I don't know. It was like that when I moved in. I thought I'd paint it a more neutral color, but I've yet to find the time. What color do you suggest?"

Genevieve was paying me no attention. She had made her way to the center of the room and was slowly spinning like a ballerina atop a music box.

The room was wallpapered with the hundreds of books I had collected over the years. A pair of French doors spanned the back wall, providing a view of a shared garden filled with a brightly colored collage of flowers I could take no credit for. A staircase along the right wall led to the second floor. A writing table and a chair took up one corner of the otherwise bare room.

"All of this is yours?" Genevieve asked, her eyes fixed on my bookshelves.

I nodded, knowing she could not see me, but also knowing she already knew the answer.

"These books, they'd probly buy foive years' rent where I used ta live. Maybe more." Sensing my sudden unease, she spun around to face me. "I'm just sayin' ya 'ave a lotta books is all."

Interesting way of saying it.

"I've been collecting them since I was five years old." I ushered her toward the stairs. "They're very important to me."

"If there's one thing I respect, it's other people's property," Genevieve assured me. "Never so much as picked a pocket, 'ave I."

At the top of the steps, walls the color of the front door welcomed us to the living room.

"I know why the door's blue!" Genevieve smiled proudly as she announced her revelation with one meticulously pronounced word. "Continuity."

Noticing another staircase along the wall, she exclaimed, "I bet there's somethin' blue up there too!" and took it upon herself to find out.

I followed closely, the walls closing in on me with three extra people in the house—one of whom really liked to talk. At the top of the steps Genevieve turned left. I slipped around her and quickly redirected her. "Your bedroom is this way."

"Is that your room?" She tried to turn back around, but I kept her aimed at the guest room. My bedroom was just that. Mine.

"Yes."

"Is it blue?"

"No."

"Is my room blue then?"

I opened the door. Genevieve threw herself, and Michael, onto the bed.

"It is blue!" she squealed, running her hand along the royal-blue comforter. "Is this silk?"

Genevieve went on about how luxurious the comforter was while I swept a thick layer of dust off the footboard. The only piece of furniture in the room was the bed, and the irony was not lost on me. All Genevieve needed was a place to sleep. She had no clothes for a bureau and no accessories for a dresser.

"The bathroom is through there." I gestured toward an open door at the back of the room.

"In the room?" She hopped off the bed and peered inside the door. "How do you get in?"

"That one's all yours. There's another one off my bedroom."

"I 'ave me own toilet?" Genevieve's mouth hung open in disbelief. "We did'n even 'ave our own toilet when we lived in our flat. We 'ad to share wif the 'ole hall. I can't believe we 'ave our own toilet!"

Don't get too comfortable with it.

"There are washcloths and towels in the cabinet, and the soap and shampoo are under the sink. If you need anything, I'll be in my bedroom for a bit."

I held Gabriel out to Genevieve. Instead of taking him, she said, "Can you lay 'im on the bed for me? I think I'll 'ave meself a baf."

I centered the baby on the bed and framed him with pillows in case he somehow managed to squirm to the edge. I closed the guest bedroom door and then my bedroom door before locking myself inside the bathroom and filling the bathtub to the rim. With three closed doors sufficiently reducing Genevieve's chatter to a murmur, I lowered myself into the warm water and prayed that the last twenty-four hours would wash off of me.

CB BO

THE RINGING of the telephone pierced an unsettlingly quiet afternoon. Gabriel loudly expressed our mutual disapproval of being startled in such a way while I made a dash for the phone, not wanting to wake Genevieve from the nap she and Michael were taking upstairs.

"Hello?"

"Juliet!"

"Yes?" I strained to hear over the baby's wails.

"Are you all right?" The voice at the other end of the line was American. My agent. The man supposedly finding me the role of a lifetime.

"I'm alive, if that's what you're asking." I was in no mood for pleasantries.

"Sounds like you've been busy."

"I'm sorry?"

"I hear a baby."

"That's not my baby." *If you had contacted me once in the last year, you would know I did not spend nine months carrying a child. I spent nine months waiting for the role I was promised.*

"Well, in that case, can you please return it to its rightful owner so we can have an uninterrupted conversation?"

"His owner is occupied at the moment. What do you want?"

I bounced Gabriel up and down and rocked him side to side, less to appease my agent and more out of fear his mother would appear at any moment, fully re-energized.

"I have a role for you in Hollywood."

"What is the part?" I tried to sound even more uninterested than I actually was.

"I'll tell you when you get here. You leave for New York in the morning."

"Tomorrow?"

"Yes. Be in Southampton no later than ten o'clock."

His authoritative tone did not sit well with me. "You are in no position to give me orders."

"And you are in no position to refuse." He took a frustrated breath. "Listen, Juliet. I can't force you to leave, but did you not

115

spend last night in a bomb shelter?" He paused, not to wait for an answer but to allow reality to sink in.

"Juliet, I woke up this morning and sat down at my kitchen table, ready to leisurely enjoy a cup of coffee and read the newspaper. Do you know what I saw plastered across the front page? '*War Finds London.*' Those three words took up the entire top half of the paper. The bottom half contained a photograph of Londoners packed into an Underground station and a caption that read, '*Terrifying night results in dock damage; feared to be a prelude for what's to come.*' I read no further, Juliet, and my coffee went untouched. My single focus became getting you out of London. After two hours of pleading, I was able to secure you a ticket on a flight leaving tomorrow at noon."

He had me until he said flight. "A flight? I believe I'd rather take my chances here than take to the sky to cross an ocean."

I had flown short distances over land, and while I was not fond of it, I felt there was always a safe place to touch down if the need arose. Commercial transatlantic flights had been taking place for less than a year, and Pan-American's so-called airplane was nothing more than a flying boat. As far as I was concerned, boats weren't meant to fly and airplanes weren't meant to float.

"Juliet, listen to me. The article is right. The war has found London, and it's going to get much worse before it gets better. Tens of thousands of people are clamoring to leave the city as we speak. On a normal day, your ticket would have cost me over four hundred dollars, and I assure you this isn't a normal day. All I'm asking of you is to make it worth my while."

"I'll reimburse you for my ticket. And I'll take the first ship out and pay my own fare."

"No ships are crossing the Atlantic at the moment. The only place a ship might get you is across the Channel, and that's not a direction I'd care to go if I were you. I don't know when the next ship will leave for New York. It might be tomorrow. It might not be for weeks. Do you really want to live like this indefinitely?"

No, I'd rather not.

He took my silence as a no. "I thought you might change your tune. If I could get you out sooner I would, but you do whatever it takes to get to Southampton in time for that noon flight."

"I'm somewhat at the mercy of the Germans at the moment. They might not be inclined to accommodate my schedule."

Ignoring my discourteous remark, my agent said, "I'll be waiting at the airport when you arrive. Take care of yourself."

With that, there was a click. I returned the telephone to its hook and dropped onto the chair beside it. Tomorrow could not come soon enough.

CHAPTER 16

JULIET

Night Two

THE SIREN HOWLED ITS FIRST WARNING late in the afternoon. Genevieve rose from the living room floor and casually walked to the window.

"Do ya think it's just a drill?"

"Once you have a performance, you never rehearse again," I muttered, setting my book on the end table and standing up, ready to put the day's plan into action. "It's two blocks to the Underground. You gather the blankets and I'll get the food. Can you manage the blankets and Michael? I'll carry Gabriel."

I hurriedly scooped the baby from the floor and collected the picnic basket I had packed earlier in the day. I bounded down the stairs and turned to find Genevieve standing on the second step from the top. She gripped Michael's hand as his wobbly legs searched for the next safe place to land.

I rushed back up the steps. Holding the baby and the picnic basket with one hand, I snatched the bag of blankets with the other.

"Please lift him! You may teach him to use the stairs another time!" I was already back at the door and waiting for Genevieve to walk through so I could lock it.

As she passed in front of me, Michael now in her arms, she looked at me like I had suddenly sprouted polka dots. I ignored her glare and, with my forearm against her back, ushered her across the street.

"Why're ya pushin' me?" Genevieve twisted her head my direction.

"Watch where you're going," I instructed.

"What're ya pushin' me for?" she asked again.

"Because you're not moving fast enough. There, straight ahead. That's where we're going. Do you see?"

"Yeah. But me plates o' meat won't let me scarper any faster."

Genevieve planted her feet and I collided with her back. She knew she was speaking a language I did not understand, and she correctly guessed that I would be annoyed by her nonsensical response. I put several inches between us, as the thought of having to listen to her jumbled rhymes all night was worse than not finding sufficient space to spread a blanket.

Despite Genevieve's dallying, we were amid the first wave into the Underground and claimed a far corner at the end of the platform. When Genevieve did not voluntarily take a load from my arms, I exasperatedly said, "Michael can stand on his own two feet now."

"Ya ain't the queen, ya know."

"I'm asking nothing unreasonable of you. You're the one…" I finished the sentence with a frustrated sigh.

"And I ain't in need o' bein' told what ta do. I've fared just foine wifout ya for seventeen years."

Genevieve continued to grumble under her breath as she set Michael on the ground and searched for the largest blanket. She took great care to perfectly align two of the blanket's edges with the meeting walls and smooth out any creases. With her arms spread wide, she curtseyed and bowed her head. "Your blanket awaits, Your Majesty."

"Get up," I hissed through clenched teeth, looking around to see if we had attracted an audience.

Genevieve plucked the baby from my arms and sat down beside Michael, turning her back to me. Irritated, I sat down on the other end of the blanket and watched the shelter quickly fill to capacity.

The mood was somber. The murmur of quiet conversations remained faint. Children stayed close to their parents' sides. Smiles were exchanged halfheartedly and disappeared so quickly they went largely unnoticed by those they were meant for.

After an hour, only the occasional straggler appeared from the street. Genevieve and I kept our distance at opposites ends of the blanket.

When Michael tired of playing with two small wooden cars, his mother slapped a spoonful of clotted cream and jam onto a scone and handed it to him. He stuffed the scone into his mouth and with one slurp managed to lick the outside clean and avoid the bread altogether.

"Mo! Mo!" he demanded excitedly, holding the slobbery mess out to his mother.

"Ya 'ave ta eat it all before ya get more."

Michael looked down at his hand and then at me. With thick white cream clinging to his lips, he toddled toward me.

"Bite? Bite?"

I swayed away from his advancing hand as he tried to force the soggy bread into my mouth.

"Uh-uh." I declined the offering behind tightly pursed lips and looked to Genevieve for help.

"Just pretend ta eat it. That'll make 'im 'appy." She shrugged as though I should have already been aware of such a simple remedy.

Turning my attention to Michael, I forcibly swallowed my disgust and clasped his little wrist to prevent him from shoving the scone into my mouth at the first opportunity. After taking a quick bite of air and pretending to chew, I said, "Mmm, thank you, Michael. It's delicious."

Satisfied, he turned and plopped down on my lap. Resting his cheek against my chest, he took small bites of his bread. All was right in his world, and for a fleeting moment something felt right in mine.

I shifted closer to Genevieve. She glowered at the decreasing space between us.

Focused on the same strip of blanket, I said, "I apologize for losing my patience with you earlier."

"You can talk to me 'owever ya loike. It's your 'ouse. It's your food. It's your blanket. I'm intrudin'. I don't deserve ta be treated loike your equal."

"That's not true. I was being overly critical, and I'm sorry."

"When we get outta 'ere, I think it's best if the lads and I be on our way. I don't loike bein' a bovver ta anyone."

"You're not a bother."

Genevieve shook her head to disagree, and I searched for the words that might convince us both.

The first distant hum interrupted our conversation. My chest tightened and my heart pounded against it as the buzzing grew stronger, still concentrated far off to one side, no closer but louder. I felt like I was being bound and strangled as I struggled to take a breath.

The hum grew into a roar and passed overhead, surely on the way to the docks. Following the pattern of the night before, silence quickly resumed.

For two minutes no one moved. For two minutes anxious chests heaved out and in. For two minutes terrified eyes darted around the room.

For two minutes I thought the bombers had passed us by. For two minutes I thought we had been spared. For two minutes I thought the worst was over.

For two minutes a second group of bombers glided covertly through the night sky until one plane hovered above us, high enough to be unheard where we sat below ground.

The platform shook as an explosion burst through the silence. A barrage of bombs slammed the city, some so far away they were barely heard, others so close they were felt.

Cries erupted throughout the Underground. I breathed so rapidly that the air could not reach my lungs before I shoved it back out. Genevieve's hand shot out in search of mine, but panic prevented me from releasing my death grip on Michael. Finding the crook of my elbow, her arm rattled violently against my ribs.

Something pounded into the ground directly above the shelter. A thunderous roar blasted outward in all directions. The lights sputtered, and then the platform went dark.

With my vision suddenly snatched away, hysteria prevailed. No one else mattered—not the hundreds of shrieking strangers inside the Underground, not Genevieve, not the baby, not the child I held in my arms.

My trembling hands thrust Michael to the ground. He was no longer a comfort. I dropped my chin to my chest, covered my ears with my forearms, clasped my hands behind my head, and squeezed tightly, but I could not muffle the showers of distant pops and nearby crashes as they pelted the city.

The need to blink was all that told my brain my eyes were open. I lowered my eyelids but stopped there as my eyes were useless either way.

When I looked up again, the soft orange glow of a nearby lantern offered a glimpse of the terrified faces surrounding me. Michael had found his way to his mother's lap. He sat wide-eyed and open-mouthed with muted anguish. Genevieve's head was bowed, her tears soaking the boy's freshly shampooed hair. Baby Gabriel wailed angrily from where he had been tucked between my thigh and his mother's.

I lowered my head and cradled my face in my hands as I let all of my emotions come forth and made no attempt to do so gracefully. I heard and felt every aspect of each passing minute as it stretched into distinct parts. The moment a fresh wave of bombers convened in the distance. Each individual bomber as it passed overhead. Every bomb as it blasted into its unlucky target. Every scream as it ripped through the station. The emotional exhaustion that slowly overtook the screams, resulting in quiet horror. Every tear that rolled down my cheek. The familiar hand that grasped mine in the midst of it all.

"How did you find me?" I sobbed, raising my tear-soaked face.

"Someone recognized you before the lights went out. Said you were in the corner."

"Why did it take you so long to reach me?" I wanted to be angry but could not muster the emotion.

"He didn't say which corner. It was rather difficult fumbling around in the dark looking for you. You'd be surprised how many girls I've unintentionally comforted tonight."

I found the anger I was searching for. "How can you kid at a time like this? We're under attack!"

"What's done is done, Juliet. If London is destroyed, she's destroyed. But we're safe down here, and now we're together."

I was soothed by his melodic voice. I was calmed by his cologne. I was comforted by his touch. I was pleased to know he had searched for me. I was terrified to realize I had desperately hoped he would find me.

Too drained to be concerned that I felt more for him than I intended, I leaned into his chest, reaching for the sleeping baby at my side and lifting the tiny bundle.

"Is there something you need to tell me?"

"This is Gabriel." I was in no mood to play along. "I met his mother in the shelter yesterday. She's staying with me until she can reclaim her flat." I motioned toward Genevieve, who had cried herself to sleep.

"You've taken a housemate?" The look of surprise on his face spoke for itself.

"Temporarily. War makes one act unnaturally."

"Apparently so! You haven't so much as let me share a meal in your home in the year I've known you, but you meet a street child in the Underground and next thing you know, she's your roommate."

"She has nowhere else to go. She won't be staying long."

"How do you know I have somewhere else to go?"

"Well, you were going somewhere before I met you. And at the very least we know you have a talent for finding your way into girls' homes. I don't believe you'll ever have to resort to sleeping under a bridge."

I felt him put a few inches between us. "Is that what you think I am? A playboy?"

I'd not thought him capable of the emotion, but he sounded hurt. I shrugged my shoulders.

"Is that what you want me to be?"

I shrugged again.

"When we first met, and I told you I had been captivated by you since I first saw you on stage, I wasn't referring to the big stage. I meant the small stage, when I was still a lad and you were just a girl. Before you became Juliet Jenson, shining star, and I became just one of your multitude of admirers."

He paused, inhaling deeply. "We met once before. I brought you a flower after a performance, probably eight years ago now. A small little thing I plucked from the side of the road. Still had dirt clinging to it when I presented it to you. You accepted it graciously, even though everyone else brought you a bouquet. I'm sure you don't remember, but it was that girl who first captivated me."

Fresh tears welled in my emotionally-ravaged eyes. "That girl on the stage, the one seen by the public, she doesn't exist. She never did. If you're waiting for her to appear, you'll be waiting forever."

He wrapped his arm around my shoulders and drew me to his side. "All walls crumble eventually, Juliet."

"Not mine."

He did not try to convince me otherwise, but as I relished in his embrace, I knew that while my walls remained intact, the stranger from the alley had surreptitiously scaled them and gained unopposed access to the other side.

CHAPTER 17

JULIET

Day Three

MY WHISPERED NAME woke me from a night of fitful sleep. I stirred, unable to bring myself to a full state of awareness.

"Hmm?"

"Marry me."

My stinging eyes sprang open, and I saw his devastatingly handsome face in full light. I swallowed a flurry of butterflies and, certain I had misheard him, stammered, "Pardon?"

"Marry me."

"Marry you! I've never heard anything so ridiculous!"

Emerald eyes sparkled with amusement. "Too soon?"

"Goodness yes!" I heaved, relieved to know that I would not have to decline a sincere marriage proposal.

He threw his head back, laughing. I shifted uncomfortably as glaring eyes expressed their disapproval all around us.

Shushing him, I muttered, "How are you always so jovial no matter the circumstances?"

"This is nothing more than a story we will tell our grandchildren one day. How Grandpapa proposed to Grandmamma during an air raid."

"More like how Grandpapa made a fool of himself during a serious, life-threatening event."

His grin widened. "As long as I'm Grandpapa and you're Grandmamma, it makes no difference to me what story you tell them."

"I don't care to be grandmother to your grandchildren." I was determined not to appear enamored of his charm.

"Not now, but you will," he replied resolutely. "It's already been decided."

"By whom?"

"Destiny."

I rolled my eyes. "You and your destiny."

"Juliet Jenson!" A booming voice jolted me from the reverie of distraction. "Juliet Jenson!" My name echoed off the platform walls a second time.

I untangled myself from a mess of limbs and blankets and hurriedly stood, not wanting my name to be announced a third time. Smoothing my hair and tucking my blouse into my skirt, I made my way to two police officers as they stomped through the crowd.

"Juliet Jenson?" The smaller of the two men addressed me while the burly one stood nearby with arms crossed and baton in hand, scanning the occupants of the makeshift shelter.

"Yes?"

"We have been instructed to escort you to Southampton." The uniformed man focused slightly beyond where I stood as he recited his orders.

"Now?"

"Yes, ma'am. Will the child be accompanying you?"

I glanced down at the baby I had momentarily forgotten I was holding. "No, he won't. But I can't leave right this minute."

"Of course. You have time to get the baby situated."

I shook my head at the officer's lack of understanding. "No, I need more time than that. I need to go home and gather my belongings. And I have house guests. I need to make sure they're taken care of."

"Miss Jenson, if we don't leave ahead of the crowd, you won't make it to the dock in time."

"Of course she'll go with you," a familiar voice interjected. I spun around and was immediately embroiled in a tug-of-war over Gabriel.

"Let go!" I demanded to no avail.

"Why would you consider staying here?" was his undaunted response.

I had no answer. At least not one I was willing to admit out loud. "You don't even know where they're trying to take me!"

"Well, it has to be better than where you are right now!"

The police officer with the baton stepped toward us. "Look, I'm sorry to get in the middle of a family dispute, but if you're not going to go with us, Miss Jenson, we have other duties."

"This is not my family!" My grip relaxed, and suddenly the baby was no longer in my arms.

The kidnapper's eyes looked to have lost a bit of their shine, but he remained as infuriating—and intriguing—as ever. Turning his attention to the officer, he said, "Not yet, sir. We're planning a spring wedding. I trust her legal matter will be resolved by early April? We just sent the last of the invitations yesterday."

I elbowed him in the ribs. "That's how rumors get started, you idiot!"

He winced but appeared to find pleasure in the pain.

"Gentlemen, if you will wait at the top of the stairs, I assure you Miss Jenson will join you in less than two minutes."

The men left us, and my self-appointed spokesman said, "I'll see to it that your friend and her children are settled into your home if that is your primary concern."

He knew that was not my primary concern. With my eyes focused on the ground, I mumbled, "And what about you?"

"Pardon?" A sly smile crept up the corners of his mouth.

"You heard me."

"Oh, you needn't worry about me. I'll be fine."

He reached out and took my hand, stroking it with his fingers. No part of me wanted to pull away, and I struggled to maintain the ruse of apathy as his fingers moved to my forearm, tickling the smooth skin underneath and working their way to my elbow. His palm slid across the small of my back and drew me closer to him until all that separated us was the baby secured against his chest. If he was trying to leave me longing for him, he was succeeding.

"And how do I know I'll be fine?" He raised his eyebrows, beckoning my reply.

I lifted my shoulders, afraid of what else might be revealed if I humored him with the desired answer.

"Say it," he urged, finding my gaze.

I shook my head.

"Tell me why we needn't worry," he whispered, his mouth enveloping mine.

After allowing all of my senses to take him in one last time, I exhaled, "Destiny."

"Exactly."

He threaded his fingers through mine and we ascended the steps to the street. At the top, I glanced around. With the first hint of disarray, I quickly found his eyes.

"We will meet again," he said decisively, tightly squeezing my hand.

I returned the gesture and quickly kissed each of his cheeks. He smiled at the impersonal formality but did not pursue a more affectionate farewell. I slowly backed away, maintaining eye contact for fear of what my eyes might find if they wandered. When the outstretched arms of our clasped hands could stretch no farther, he took a step forward, kissed the back of my hand, and released me to the officers waiting to whisk me away.

CHAPTER 18

JASMINE

South Carolina

1940

Day One

THE WHISTLE WARNED that the train would leave without me if I didn't board soon, but I stood in a trance, stupefied by the silver box about to shoot me out into the great unknown.

"Sugar, it's time to go." Daddy stepped in front of me, bringing me out of my blank stare.

I bobbed my head in agreement and tried to control my quivering lip while he helped me slide my arms into the brown jacket that completed the skirt suit Mr. Green had sent from California. I had never owned anything so grown up. Or so uncomfortable.

Daddy looked me up and down, from my new high-heeled shoes also sent by Mr. Green to the curls already starting to fall out of my usually stick-straight hair.

"I know you're scared, Jazzy." He rested his hands on my shoulders, a coach giving a struggling player a pep talk. "But this is the chance of a lifetime. I don't want you to be stuck at that mill your whole life. That's not what your mama woulda wanted neither. Do this for her, all right?"

"Five months is so long, Daddy. I can't be away from you for that long." I gave in to the quivering lip and focused on holding back tears that felt like they were clawing their way past my eyeballs.

"Oh Jazzy, don't you worry none about me. I'll be fine, you hear?"

I nodded, starting to whimper.

"I'm so proud of you, Jazzy." Daddy pulled me to his chest and squeezed tightly. I wrapped my arms around his neck and buried my face in his shoulder.

Gently prying me off of him, he whispered, "I love you, Jazzy."

"I love you too, Daddy." I wiped my eyes, sniffling and trying to compose myself. I lifted the small suitcase filled with a lifetime of belongings and took several slow steps toward the train before I realized Daddy wasn't beside me. When I looked back, he was standing right where I left him.

"Go on now." He motioned for me to keep walking.

I turned around and devoted all of my energy to raising one foot and dropping it a little closer to the outstretched hand of a man in a navy-blue uniform. Each step felt like I was trudging through tar. The train attendant's arm was suspended mid-air for so long his shoulder must have been screaming when I finally reached him. He grunted as his tired arm pulled my languid body up the steps.

I plodded down the aisle of the crowded train car, the rock sitting at the pit of my stomach weighing me down, and claimed an entire row for myself near the back. I scooted to the window and found Daddy on the platform. I set my hand against the glass and he lifted his arm in return.

The train chugged louder and the whistle blew again and again. Without warning—or maybe the excessive noise and violent vibration was the warning—the train lurched forward, and I watched my daddy slowly shrink until all that was left of him was a figment of my imagination.

CHAPTER 19

JASMINE

Washington, D.C.

Night One

I CRASHED INTO THE SEAT in front of me, not prepared for such an abrupt arrival. After apologizing repeatedly to the lady I dislodged from restful sleep, all the while thinking she should really be thanking me for letting her know we had reached our destination, I looked out the window, scanning the busy station for a clue as to where I could find the train to Chicago.

The same attendant who had hoisted me onto the train was waiting to see me off. He wished me well, and my last link to home disappeared as I was swallowed by a sea of people better dressed, better smelling, and better fed than myself.

I wandered aimlessly through the station. At the far end of a waiting room filled with what looked like more people than lived in my entire neighborhood, I sat down between two men dressed in fancy suits at a snack counter, thinking that eating something might calm my nerves.

"What can I get you?" The server swirled a rag across the counter, ran a towel over the streaks, and set a miniature napkin down in front of me.

I pulled a dollar bill from my pocket. "What can I get for fifty cents?"

"You can get two of anything on that board." He pointed to a chalkboard with a list of gibberish scribbled on it.

"I'll just have a sandwich please."

"Miss, you'll have to go to the counter across the room for a sandwich. This is beverages only." The man pointed at his board a second time. I didn't see the word *beverage* or *only* anywhere.

I turned around and spotted the counter across the room. Families filled those stools rather than men in their business best. Swiveling back around, I said, "So if I want a Coca-Cola with my sandwich, I have to come back over here to get it? Seems like you'd have it all in one place."

The man to my left chuckled and slid off of his stool. "Get this little lady an orange blossom, Johnny, and I'll go get her a sandwich."

He handed the man he called Johnny a quarter, and I tried to give the helpful man my dollar.

"It's on me, miss." He closed my hand around the bill. "You just sip on that drink till I get back."

Johnny sloshed together a concoction behind the counter, poured the mixture into a funnel-shaped glass, and presented me with what looked like orange juice but didn't smell like orange juice. I wrapped my hand around the tall stem and cautiously lifted the drink to my lips. The smell was so strong I set it back down.

"I don't think I wanna drink this." I pushed the glass toward Johnny. "I'll just have a Coca-Cola please."

"We don't serve just Coca-Cola here, miss. You'll have to get that across the way."

"I thought you said that was only sandwiches."

"No, I said this is only beverages."

"Isn't that what I just said?"

Johnny looked as irritated as I was confused. The man to my right quickly chimed in, bringing my attention back to the orange blossom.

"Only the first little bit tastes bad. The more you drink, the better it tastes. It'll taste so good by the end, you'll be asking for another."

I shook my head. Nothing that vile could ever become pleasant. "Only a miracle could make that happen, mister, and I don't expect God's much in the miraculous drink business."

"Actually, miss, that's a good word for it. That drink you've got is a miracle. All your troubles will slip further away with each sip."

I had my doubts, but the thought of my heart no longer aching for home made it worth a try. I held my breath and took a big gulp. A fireball slid down my throat, settling in my stomach and boiling my insides.

"Ugh!" I sputtered what was coated on my tongue into the tiny napkin as Johnny set a second glass down in front of me.

"What's that?!"

"Water."

I chugged the cool, tasteless liquid, desperate to put out the fire in my throat.

The man who had persuaded me to try the drink offered me his handkerchief. "You have to take small sips like the fella told you."

"I'm not taking any more sips of that!"

"But the worst is over, darlin'. The first swallow paves the way. The rest just glides down and works its magic."

"Magic ain't real," I argued.

"This magic is."

As the man went on trying to convince me of the drink's supernatural powers, the intense burn eased to a peculiarly comforting warmth. I slowly raised the glass and took one small sip as instructed. The taste still left little to be desired, but I didn't feel like shards of glass were shredding my throat either.

At first it was only a sip every thirty seconds or so, but the men were right. The more I drank, the better it tasted. Before I knew it, my second orange blossom was being purchased by the owner of the handkerchief.

"I sure hope the top of this one will taste as good as the bottom of that one did!" I announced to Johnny as he switched my empty glass for a full one.

Both men assured me it would taste even better. They were right again.

I didn't see who bought my third orange blossom, but I thoroughly enjoyed it. I was slurping down the last drop when I heard, "Last call for Chicago! Last call Chicago Express!"

"Oh no," I slurred to my original drink purchaser, my eyes unable to focus on him. "I'm gonna miss my train."

"No you're not. I saw your ticket when you sat down. We're both going to Chicago. I'll make sure you get there." His arms slid me off of the stool. I saw my feet hit the floor, but I felt like I was floating.

The man supported most of my weight as all of my mind power went toward putting one unsteady foot in front of the other. He lifted me onto the Chicago Express, and I swayed side to side at the top while he climbed aboard. I was led past what seemed like hundreds of closed doors until I was facing another counter and another man eager to serve me.

I turned away when I saw the bar, but I couldn't get my feet to follow. "I...I should probably...I just...I should just...go to bed."

"Nonsense." My self-proclaimed travel companion scooted a stool into the backs of my legs, leaving me no choice but to sit down.

"Bring me two whiskey sours," he instructed the man behind the counter.

"Are you sure she's up to that?"

"She just gets a little nervous when traveling. Best to calm her nerves."

"Her nerves already look pretty calm, if you ask me."

"I didn't ask you. I asked you to bring us two whiskey sours."

The server muttered his disapproval while he made two identical drinks. Setting both of them down in front of my travel companion, he said, "You'll have to give it to her, Jack."

The counter moved in slow motion toward my face. I blinked, and when I opened my eyes, my heavy head was staring down a more normal-looking glass. Short, but shaped like glasses I had seen before.

I batted my travel companion's hand away when he lifted the glass to my lips. "I can do it myself, thank you very much."

I made contact with the glass after two failed attempts, and with eight fingers and two thumbs clasped around it, I slurped to the last drop.

"I'll have another," I proclaimed, slamming the empty glass onto the counter.

The server wasted so much time making another whiskey sour that I had forgotten I was waiting for one when it suddenly appeared on my tiny napkin. I promptly lifted the unexpected surprise to my lips and gulped the liquid like it was my first taste of water after being lost in the desert for days.

While I drank my second drink on the train, and fifth overall, the server disappeared and returned with a man in a navy-blue uniform. I wondered if he was the attendant from home, but his face was a blur.

"Can I see your ticket, sir?"

Unfortunately, the man in the familiar uniform possessed an unfamiliar voice. My disappointment quickly disappeared when my eye caught sight of a glass in need of being consumed. I took it upon myself to empty it while my travel companion squabbled with the attendant.

"I showed you my ticket when I boarded the train."

"If you and this young lady aren't traveling together, it's time for her to be shown to her cabin."

"I'm not ready to go to my cabin, Mr. Ticket-taker-sir," I chimed in. "I'll be sure to let you show me the way when the time comes." I pushed his arm away with all the force I could muster, which wasn't much at all.

My travel companion spoke up. "I take this train every other week. I would never disrespect a lady in that way. She was scared and nervous, so I bought her a drink and it went from there. I didn't know she was such a lightweight, but at this point we might as well let her pass out and then take her to bed."

Appalled by his suggestion, I said, "I'm not going to bed with you. No, sir. I don't even know you." I saw three of him, but I tried to focus on the face in the middle.

"Name's Jack. Now you know me."

"Well, I still...I ain't...just cause I know your name now, I still ain't going to bed with you."

"When you are ready, Miss I-don't-know-your-name-either, I will be a gentleman and see you to your private cabin where you can sleep your evening off."

Tired of all the back and forth nonsense, I slurred, "Server! I'll have another one of those orange drinks like before I got on this train. Jack here can tell you all about it."

Instead of an orange blossom, I was given a clear liquid that barely covered the bottom of the glass.

"Somebody's done drank mine," I announced.

"A little goes a long way," my travel companion assured me as I drained the glass in one swallow.

Suddenly my eyes were so tired I couldn't hold them open. I gave in to the overwhelming urge to lay my head on the counter, and the room faded away.

CHAPTER 20

JASMINE

Chicago

Day Two

I WOKE UP LONG ENOUGH to vomit onto the floor beside the bed. I didn't care who the bed belonged to or what might have been done to me while I was in it. I just wanted to sleep, without interruption, forever.

Some time later I stumbled down the hall to the bathroom, which was apparently too far from my cabin for me to remember how I got there. I was quickly intercepted by a train attendant and led back to the bed. Noticing the vomit on the floor, he went off in search of a mop, but I was asleep before he came back.

When I woke up again, a man in a navy-blue uniform was standing over me. I knew he wasn't the attendant from home, but beyond that, I couldn't say if I had encountered him before.

"Miss? We're in Chicago. You've got less than an hour to get to Dearborn."

"Dearborn?" I mumbled, closing my eyes and feeling like I might never open them again.

"Yes, ma'am. That's where the train departs for Los Angeles. We're at Grand Central. Dearborn's a few blocks from here."

I wasn't exactly sure where a block fell on the measurement spectrum, but I knew I was unable to get myself a few anythings right then. I was lying flat on my back. Every inch of my body ached, especially my head. It throbbed, like all of the fluids had been sucked out, leaving a no-good, shriveled-up brain that was unable to think straight anymore.

"Can't I just lay here," I moaned, "and go wherever this train goes next?"

"This train goes back to Washington, D.C., miss. I don't imagine you care to relive that experience. Here, let me help you. We'll go slow."

I managed to stay upright as he sat me up, my eyes still closed and my head feeling like it was going to roll off of my neck.

"There you go, miss. Now, let's get your shoes on, and we'll get you to a cab."

The attendant and I walked painfully slow to the train's exit. Painful for him because of the pace in which we moved and painful for me because I was moving at all.

"Stand here," he instructed when we got to the steps. "I'll go down first."

I obeyed and, unable to fully open my eyes, blindly began an excruciating descent. Each step felt like I was leaping from a mountain. My foot floated in the air for what seemed like forever before its return to solid ground reverberated into my head.

"What happened to me?" I groaned as we limped our way through the crowded station.

"You had a little bout with alcohol."

"I did?" If I was experiencing the result of a little bout, I hated to think what a big bout would feel like.

"Most people do at one point or another. You'll feel better soon." Cocking his head my direction and raising an eyebrow, he said, "You have no memory of last night?"

I searched my shriveled brain. It was devoid of all but one thought. "I think I might die."

The attendant suppressed a smile. "If you were going to die, you'd already be dead. In a few hours you'll feel good as new. It's just going to be an uncomfortable start to Los Angeles."

We finally reached the street with a good chunk of my hour to get to Dearborn already gone. The attendant left me hugging a lamppost while he stood at the curb and waved to every passing car. I desperately needed to lie down, and the sidewalk looked as good a place as any. I was sliding down the post when a car stopped beside us.

"She needs to get to Dearborn," the attendant told the driver as he hoisted me back to a standing position. Holding me up with one arm and reaching into his pocket with the other, he produced a handful of coins. The driver pocketed my fare, and the attendant dropped two more silver coins into his hand. "She's not feeling well, and she's never traveled before. See to it that she makes it onto the train to Los Angeles."

The two men lowered me into the car, and I proceeded to stretch out across the back seat as the driver took his place behind the steering wheel.

"Miss, are you all right?"

I couldn't answer. Nausea swept through my stomach and swirled around my wilted brain.

"Well, if you're going to lose your lunch, can you at least give me some warning?"

"I'll try," I muttered through clenched teeth.

I managed to hold on to my lunch, probably because I had no lunch left to lose. The car stopped before I had time to find a comfortable position and I dreaded the thought of moving again.

"Did we even go anywhere?" I asked as the driver removed me from the car with a little less gentility than the train attendant had displayed. With one sweep of his arm, I was outside and on my feet.

"A few blocks. Most people walk, but I don't think your legs would've gotten you here today."

The driver more or less carried me through the station. My feet went through the motions of walking, but they barely touched the ground. He lifted me onto the train, avoiding the steps altogether, and aiming me toward the passenger car and giving my back a gentle shove to encourage forward movement, he told me he could take me no farther.

I slumped onto the first vacant seat I found. The sudden drop flipped my stomach, and my head throbbed so badly I felt my heart beating inside my brain. I needed to find a bathroom immediately or else I was going to throw up on or in the near vicinity of my seatmate, which would make for an unpleasant trip for both of us.

Faced with quite a conundrum, I started to panic. Finding a bathroom meant moving my body. Moving my body would likely render the bathroom trip no longer necessary. If I was going to be sick either way, the least I could do was make an attempt to avoid an audience.

I stood to my feet and was instantly forced back down by shaking legs that refused to support my weight. I landed hunched over, holding my head with trembling hands and trapped in my misery.

"Are you all right?" An accent I couldn't place floated from my seatmate's lips.

"No." I could barely utter the one syllable. I rocked back and forth with one hand on my forehead and the other tugging the neck of my blouse away from my throat in a frantic effort to allow more air into my lungs. "I have to get off this train," I managed to blurt without gagging.

"I believe it might be too late for that. May I ask what's wrong?"

"Then I need a bathroom. Now." I stood and successfully stayed on my feet, but I was too dizzy to move. Gripping the back of the seat in front of me, I whispered, "I'm going to be sick."

The man—a soldier by the looks of his attire—stood and wrapped one arm around my waist. Clasping my elbow with his other hand, he said, "Are you able to walk?"

"I don't know," I whimpered, my head hanging and my eyes closed.

I saw no better alternative to testing my ability to walk, so I let the military man guide me down the aisle to the back of the car. Wind whipped against my face as we passed an open door, and the crisp Chicago air brought slight relief.

I veered off course and stepped onto the unoccupied metal platform situated against the train. Reaching for the side railing, I mumbled, "I need to stay here for a minute."

The soldier let go of my waist and took a step back. I leaned over the railing and quickly found out that the wind only masked the nausea. The motion of tipping forward and the rail's pressure pushed out what was left in my stomach without warning.

I realized I felt better as I spit the taste of vomit from my mouth. With my swimmy head clear, the reality of the situation rushed to the front of my mind. I had just thrown up in front of a complete stranger, and a young male one at that.

I hovered over the railing, frozen by humiliation, thinking that if the last forty-eight hours was any indication of the next five months, I would be better off marching down the steps and taking my chances hitchhiking back to South Carolina rather than continuing on such a dastardly trip.

The hand underneath my elbow brought me back to my senses. I couldn't believe he was still by my side after such unladylike behavior, but it must have had something to do with the uniform. Never leave a man behind and so forth.

Detraining no longer seemed like a good idea. If the soldier's military training taught him to not let a woman throw up without assistance, it probably also taught him to not let her make a rash decision that would leave her all alone in an unfamiliar city. I didn't want to make him late for whatever awaited him in Los Angeles.

I backed away from the railing and turned to thank the man for his help. What I saw almost knocked me off of the train whether I wanted to go or not.

I was facing the most handsome man I had ever seen. His bronze skin was as tan as any mill man I knew, but his color didn't look like the result of the sun. It looked God-given, smooth and even, without one freckle. Closely cut waves of golden hair brought out matching flecks of gold in brilliant green eyes.

I became acutely aware of his fingers tenderly clasping my wrist. Fireworks exploded inside my chest and I couldn't think of the two words I had turned to say. I stared into his mesmerizing eyes, flabbergasted.

The sudden charge of emotions brought on another wave of nausea. I pulled my arm from his grasp and threw myself against the railing, but my stomach was empty.

"I need to go sit down," I exhaled, avoiding eye contact with the spellbinding man as I walked past him.

After an arduous walk down the aisle, I lifted my suitcase, and without looking directly at his face for fear its perfection might leave me speechless again, I thanked him for his help, prepared to search for another place to sit.

The soldier leaned to his left, a sly smile on his face. I kept my focus on his ear until my eyes were so far to one side they involuntarily bounced back to his.

"Where are you going? We're still in Chicago. I know you're slightly delirious, but you've been doing all the moving, not the train." His crimson smile grew wider, revealing perfectly straight, glowingly white teeth.

I forced a weak smile, afraid of what might escape if I parted my lips. I swallowed hard and said, "I didn't think you'd want to sit with me after you watched me throw up." Swallowing a second time, I added, "And I feel like I might do it again."

The man nodded pensively. "What if you're contagious and I've already been exposed? If you leave now, who's going to be there later to hold my hair back?" He shot his shiny green eyes up at me and ran his fingers through his hair, leaving the perfectly placed waves disheveled.

I looked away from his shimmering eyes, not only because they were captivating, but the pounding headache and flipping stomach had returned full force.

"I'm not contagious." I dropped my suitcase and collapsed onto the seat.

"How do you know?"

"Because I've already been diagnosed." I pressed my fingers into my forehead.

"With what?"

"A little bout with alcohol."

"I see." The man beamed at my misfortune.

"It's not funny." I lowered my clammy hands to cover my eyes.

"No, of course not. Shall we head back outside?"

"Not yet."

"The train's about to leave the station. It's now or never."

"Never." I didn't want to move. Or talk.

I got my wish seconds later when the military man climbed over me and stepped into the aisle.

"Then if you'll excuse me for a moment, I believe I know the perfect remedy. Move over to my seat and lean against the window."

I followed his instructions and slid over. The cool glass immediately dulled my torment.

"Thank you," I sighed, not sure if I was thanking the man or the window.

"You're all right until I return?"

"Mmm."

He took that as a yes and walked away. The pre-departure frenzy grew and one good lurch shot the train out of the city. I hoped the soldier was still on board, but I didn't have the strength to find out.

I raised my weak, heavy eyelids until my pupils had a fuzzy view out the window. The train was passing through tightly spaced backyards, whizzing by house after house so quickly that my sickly eyes couldn't track them.

I was staring off into oblivion with partially opened eyes when my seatmate returned. He dipped a spoon into a glass and held it to my lips.

"Take this."

I backed away from the spoon. "That smells like how I got into this mess in the first place."

"It is. Now open wide." He circled the spoon in front of my face.

I wasn't going to open at all. Through tightly pursed lips, I grunted, "Uh-uh."

"I suppose you wish to go on feeling miserable then." He raised the glass to his own lips and held it there, anticipating my protest.

Right on cue, I sighed. "What are you doing?"

"We can't let a perfectly good dose of...medicine go to waste. You have refused to partake, so I will make the sacrifice."

"I didn't refuse." I set a shaky hand on his and lowered the glass. Despite the nausea, my insides fluttered.

"I believe your exact response was *uh-uh*. Where I come from, that denotes a refusal."

I had spiraled into such a state of agony that I didn't care if he was offering me poison. Actually, I hoped it was poison. The kind that would kill me, not just make me more violently ill than I already was.

"Kay." I was once again reduced to one-syllable responses.

"Kay?"

"Oh." Swallow. "Kay."

"Okay, you'll take it, or okay, you agree you refused before?"

"Both," I murmured.

The soldier tipped the glass against my lips. I grimaced as the first sip hit my throat.

"It might be best if you take it all in one swallow. Open your mouth and hold your breath and I'll pour it in."

When I had choked down the worst medicine I had ever tasted, my seatmate pressed a cold towel against my forehead. I reached up to hold it in place, but he lowered my arm to my lap.

"I'll hold it. You rest."

Feeling suddenly relaxed, the so-called medicine working its magic, I closed my eyes and welcomed the sleep that made me unaware of how horrible I felt.

CHAPTER 21

JASMINE

The Midwest

Night Two

WHEN I REGAINED consciousness, I was nestled against a warm body rather than the cool window. I had never been nestled against a warm body before, except maybe as a little girl when it got so cold that I crawled into bed with my daddy to keep my toes from turning to icicles during the night. But this was a different kind of body, and it definitely stirred up a different kind of warmth.

I opened my eyes and found myself within inches of the military man's flawless face. Golden scruff poked through a chiseled jaw line. The soft whir of deep sleep escaped through parted lips.

I carefully lifted my head off of his shoulder. The torture that had accompanied holding my head upright earlier in the day was gone. I almost felt normal. My eyes were peaked and my stomach churned from its emptiness, but the pounding headache and nausea seemed to have run its course.

My reflection stared back in horror when I turned to the window. Feeling better clearly didn't translate to looking better. My face was paler than usual, a blank slate for the gray circles outlining exhausted eyes. Several stray curls bounced off the left side of my face, and a flat, matted mess of drool and sweat was plastered to the other cheek.

I pressed my face against the window to avoid having to look at myself. Trees were only feet away as the train charged through a forest. The whistle blew its warning, and the train shot into a clearing and passed through an intersection. The roads weren't busy, but we weren't in sparsely populated farm country either.

The clearings became more frequent and the woods grew less and less dense until we were traveling through small clusters of towns. A span of buildings took shape in the distance. Every time the train burst out of the trees, the buildings were closer and had grown in number.

Since I was incapacitated during my brief visit to Chicago, the developing city was unlike anything I had ever seen. I was marveling at the view when my seatmate's warm breath tickled the back of my neck.

"Feeling better?"

A rush of butterflies left me feeling weak again, but it was a welcome weakness, not the sickly weakness from before.

"Are you a doctor?" I kept my forehead firmly attached to the window. I couldn't risk letting him catch a glimpse of my reflection, much less seeing me face to face.

"I'm a Simon."

"What's a Simon?"

"That by which I am called."

"Huh?" His accent remained a mystery, and he strung words together in ways I had never heard before.

"My name."

"Your name's Simon?"

"Yes. What's yours?"

"Jasmine."

"Jasmine." He pronounced the word prettier than I knew it could sound.

"Nobody's ever said it like that before."

"Like what?"

"Jasssmine." I held on to the *S* like a snake.

"Is it spelled with a *Z* then?"

"No. Just an *S*."

"So Jazzzmine, with a silent *S* and an imaginary *Z*?"

"I guess so." I shrugged. "Everybody back home calls me Jazzy though. That's got two *Z*'s and no *S*'s."

"So what shall I call you?"

"I like Jasssmine."

"All right then, Jasmine, are you feeling better?"

I attempted to nod without detaching my forehead from the window. "That's why I asked if you were a doctor. You cured me."

"Time cured you. I simply sped it up a bit."

"Well, thank you, whatever you did."

Simon shifted in his seat. He came so close that his breath snuck down the back of my blouse.

"What out there has you so intrigued?" he asked, his chin hovering millimeters above my shoulder.

I raised a finger and, quivering with nervous energy, pointed to the city we were rapidly approaching. "Are we almost there?"

"We're almost *there*, but just where do you think there is?"

I lifted my shoulders to say that I didn't know and bumped Simon's chin. His whole body was like an electrical socket. No matter where or how briefly I made contact, sparks flew.

I quickly dropped my shoulders. "Los Angeles?"

Simon laughed at my guess. "How long do you think you slept?"

I raised the shoulder that could move freely, careful to keep the other one in place.

"I believe that's Kansas City, according to the map I studied. Missouri. Do you know it?"

I shook my head.

"I'd never heard of it, either. I only learned of the state called Kansas last year, thanks to Dorothy. She made no mention of there being a city as well."

"Is Dorothy your wife?"

Simon laughed. Realizing my question was genuine, he composed himself. "I haven't got a wife. Have you a husband?"

It was my turn to laugh. "No."

"Why do you find that so amusing?"

Now was as good a time as any to reveal my unsightly appearance. I gave my cheeks a quick squeeze and turned to face him. I half expected him to recoil in disgust, but he didn't flinch.

"Look at me. Would you want to marry me?"

"Are you proposing?" A heart-melting smile stretched across his face. "Might be best to get to know one another a bit first. But we do have another day to accomplish that."

My face felt like it was on fire. "I…I didn't mean—"

Simon set his hand on my knee. "I'm only joking. I know what you meant. I do think you're lovelier than you believe you are, though. And I would like to get better acquainted if that's all right with you."

I was too flustered to know what was all right and what wasn't. I said the first thing that came to mind. "I need a bath."

"Is that a polite way of saying you'd rather not?"

"I'm just saying I've been to death's door and back since I last bathed."

"So you'll freshen up, I'll secure us a table in the dining car, and you'll meet me there in one hour?"

"It won't take an hour," I assured him as he stepped into the aisle to let me pass. What I could accomplish in an hour, I could accomplish in thirty minutes, and what I couldn't accomplish in thirty minutes, I could never hope to accomplish in an hour.

CB ⨯ EO

I WASHED my face and hair, brushed my teeth, and changed into a second suit from Mr. Green. My face needed to be no paler than it already was, so I dabbed powder beneath my eyes and elected to go all natural everywhere else. Satisfied with my dark-circle concealment, I opened a mascara box and swept the brush once through each set of lashes. After running a lightly tinted lipstick across my lips and smacking them together, I looked at myself in the mirror.

I had never worn any type of makeup before. The modest amount I was wearing was barely noticeable, but I did see a hint of the pleasant-looking girl I envisioned in my head rather than the homely girl who always stared back at me in the mirror.

It was my hair that was completely hopeless. Nothing could be done for it. Hair rollers were too unpredictable, and I didn't know how to begin an attempt to sweep my hair into the complicated styles worn by other girls. So flat, damp, and limp it would remain until it dried, at which time it would just be flat and limp.

I rummaged through my suitcase for the finishing touch. Finding the small box, I opened the lid and ran my thumb along two small hair combs. They were my mama's, made by my daddy. They had no jewels or adornments. They were just simple wooden combs stained a dark cherry color to match Mama's hair. I slid one into my hair above each ear and experienced the moment of reverence that always came with touching something of hers.

My cheeks were already warm with the anticipation of seeing Simon, but I gave them one last squeeze, smacked my lips one more time, and made sure none of my eyelashes were stuck together before I headed down the hall.

Simon's beaming smile welcomed me to the dining car. He had clearly done some tidying up himself. His scruff was gone and his golden waves had been reined back in toward his scalp. When he stood up, the smell of spiced leather followed him around to my side of the table.

"You smell like a brand new pair of cowboy boots," I told him as he pulled a chair out for me. "The real kind," I added when he did nothing but humph at my first comment.

Sitting down across from me, Simon said, "I must say I don't know whether to say thank you or apologize. I've never been told I smell like footwear before."

Aside from one raised eyebrow, his face offered no help in determining if he really thought I was insulting him. "I wouldn't have said it if it wasn't a good thing."

Simon smiled. "So if I smelled like a pair of worn loafers, you would keep that to yourself?"

"Well, you kept it to yourself when I smelled like vomit earlier, and you somehow managed to not even turn up your nose, so no, I don't think I would tell you if you smelled like feet."

My own eyebrows shot up as I realized I was talking about vomit and dirty feet at the dinner table. Mortified, I quickly lifted the menu in front of my face to end the conversation. A finger hooked the top of the paper and lowered it until I was looking into Simon's eyes.

"I thank you for the compliment, and while I may not be as creative in my delivery, I am no less sincere in saying that you look lovely this evening."

Heat splashed outward from my cheeks until I felt like my whole face was the color of a blistering sunburn. I didn't believe Simon really thought I looked pretty, but the fact that he had the courtesy to say it made my heart patter.

I murmured my thanks and took great interest in scanning the menu, hoping my face would cool to a happy medium between beet red and ghostly white before I looked up again.

Simon and I got acquainted over a meal with more courses than I usually ate in an entire day. Over soup we talked about where we were from. Over salad we talked about how I lost my mama and he lost his daddy. Over steak and potatoes we talked about his education and my lack thereof. Over an assortment of desserts we talked like we were old friends.

I excused myself to the bathroom when Simon ordered two cups of coffee to finish off the night. I did need to use the facilities, but mostly I needed to count the money left in my pocketbook. I was having food ordered for me and spoons forced at me, and if I didn't put a stop to it, I was going to be rolling up my sleeves and washing dishes. Or given my luck so far, I would be taken straight to the Los Angeles police station upon arrival in California, which would surely be a very different experience than Popsicle jail.

I returned to the table resigned to the fact that I had eaten my last meal until I found a soup kitchen in Los Angeles. Simon was paying the waiter for his dinner. I emptied my pocketbook and prayed that what I had to offer would be enough.

Simon sat quietly as the waiter refused my money. Heat erupted on my cheeks again, my fears being realized right in front of him so he could see just how destitute I was.

"Your dinner has been paid for, miss," the waiter explained.

"It has?"

"Yes, ma'am."

"By Mr. Green?"

"By the young man." The waiter nodded toward Simon.

Simon raised his eyebrows when I glanced at him for confirmation. I dropped onto my chair, looking at him with a mixture of amazement and amusement.

"What is it?" Simon's eyebrows were still lifted, and he seemed to be sharing my amusement despite being unaware of what I found amusing.

He was as handsome as when I first saw him, but the longer I knew him, the more I was able to control my emotions. The spark was still there, but I had subconsciously stopped igniting it at some point, probably when the mirror or my pocketbook gave me a good dose of reality, and the attraction had fizzled to a more manageable level.

"I just went on my first date, and I didn't even know it!"

"Your first date?"

"And last!"

Simon playfully narrowed his eyes in disbelief.

My head bobbled around as I tried to nod and shake it side to side at the same time. "Where I come from people don't date. Not like this anyway."

"Then how on earth has the population not gone extinct where you come from?"

"You don't have to date to procreate," I sang, grinning.

Simon smiled. "You're right about that."

"If I get married—and that's a big if—my husband and I won't be going on any dates. Before or after the wedding. So you, sir, are my one and only date ever."

Simon shook his head. "I don't believe you, but let's say you are correct. In that case, I want a redo."

"A redo?"

"If I am truly your one and only date," Simon explained, "I want to make it memorable."

"You've already made it memorable," I assured him.

Simon rose from the table. "You've yet to meet memorable Simon. Meet me here tomorrow morning at ten o'clock. And be prepared for the most memorable day of your life."

The embers were momentarily rekindled as Simon's lips grazed my cheek. As I watched him walk away, I was thinking a more memorable day was not possible. But what I should have been thinking was that memorable does not necessarily mean pleasurable. And nothing is impossible.

CHAPTER 22

JASMINE

Los Angeles

Day Three

A MEMORABLE MORNING turned into a memorable afternoon, but nothing could have prepared me for such a memorable evening.

I knew the best day of my life was coming to an end when Simon pointed to the outline of a city much larger than the Kansas City I had been in awe of before.

"Los Angeleeze."

Twinkling lights against the setting sun welcomed us to our final destination. A lump formed in my throat and slowly grew as we rapidly approached the station. A blurred line of palm trees separated into distinct trunks and leaves as the train slowed to a stop.

With his fingers pressed into the small of my back, Simon guided me down the aisle and onto the platform.

"I need to find a telephone." I struggled to push the words past the lump.

"If you have the address, I'll see to it that you get there."

"I only have a telephone number."

Simon weaved us to a pay phone. I was searching for a dime when he dropped one into the slot.

"You didn't have to do that," I said, dialing the number Mr. Green had scribbled on a piece of paper.

"We're on a date."

One ring.

"Still?"

Another ring.

"Until a taxicab do us part."

A third ring.

"And the most memorable portion of the evening is still to come," Simon added. "I'm saving the best for last."

After ten rings with no answer, I returned the telephone to its hook. "I guess I'll try again in a few minutes."

Simon led me to a bench at the end of the platform. The sun was out of sight, but it had painted a lingering pink and orange sky in its descent.

Simon sat down, taking my hands and pulling me down with him. With his knees hugging mine, he said, "Was the day all you hoped it would be?"

"It was better than I ever imagined." I tried to swallow the lump that had settled in my throat. The thought of a permanent goodbye brought tears to my eyes.

"What's the matter?"

"You've just been so nice to me," I sniffled. "I don't want to say goodbye."

"I never say goodbye." Pressing his cheek against mine, he whispered, "It's until we meet again."

I blinked back tears and opened my eyes to find his face so close to mine that my lips felt every word he whispered.

"It has truly been a pleasure, Jasmine Fowler. You have a beautiful soul. Outward beauty fades, but what you possess is eternal. Remember that. You make me want to be a better man. I consider it an honor to have been your first, but certainly not last, date."

Simon gently kissed my cheek. His lips moved across the skin above my upper lip to the other cheek and eventually rested on my lips. I closed my eyes and tried to get control of my rapid breathing. My whole body felt warm, more out of sudden fear than anything else. With my eyes still closed, I pulled my face away from his.

"I don't know how to do this," I whispered.

"That's all right," he breathed, his lips finding mine again. "Relax and let your feelings lead you."

I took two drawn out breaths, making a failed attempt to slow my racing heart, and slowly moved my lips around his until I was an active participant—no longer simply recipient—of my first kiss.

Simon worked his hands up my arms, reeling me in like a baited fish. My lips found a rhythm and frightened nerves gave way to little sparks of exhilaration.

Feeling lightheaded from lack of oxygen, I separated my lips from Simon's and watched our chests heave in unison.

"I thought I was saving the best for last," Simon exhaled. "I had no idea you were as well. Where did you learn to kiss?"

"Nowhere," I whispered. "I just followed my feelings like you said."

When my oxygen supply was replenished, I said, "Thank you for a day I'll never forget."

"Next time I'll make it a night you'll never forget."

"Yes, next time you might fall pregnant."

Simon's eyes darted from our interlaced laps to my face and then came to a stunned stop somewhere above my right shoulder as the unfamiliar voice spoke again.

"Or is that a gift you saved exclusively for me?"

As his heart pounded through his uniform with such force I thought it might beat right out of his chest, I started to think that maybe the voice I didn't recognize wasn't so unfamiliar to Simon at all.

CHAPTER 23

JULIET

I WATCHED in stunned silence as his fingers clasped her hands. Leaning toward her, he whispered sweet nothings into her ear. His lips lightly brushed hers with further cajolery and dared her not to succumb. He slowly traveled from one cheek to the other, leaving plump persuasion in his wake. When his lips returned to their resting place, succumb she did.

The shock of seeing Simon under any circumstance left me struggling to accept that the man on the bench was really him, but as hands I knew better than anyone's made their way up her arms, there was no doubt. Simon was in California. With another girl.

As the shock wore off, anger prevailed. I was angry with Simon for confirming so blatantly what I had always suspected but allowed myself to be foolishly convinced otherwise. I was angry with the girl simply because she existed. Most of all, I was angry with myself for letting my guard down, only to be annihilated at the first opportunity.

I stealthily made my way to the bench and positioned myself behind the girl. When Simon's eyes opened, I wanted to be front and center.

My composure wavered when he spoke.

"I thought I was saving the best for last," he panted, lost in a moment of euphoria. "I had no idea you were as well. Where did you learn to kiss?"

"Nowhere." Her backwoods drawl oozed murkily through tainted lips. "I jus follered ma feelins lak you sed."

I suddenly felt compelled to slap her dirty mouth away from his and wrap my hands around his neck before either of them came down from the cloud on which they floated. But fearing his return to reality to find the woman who professed apathy for a year strangling him in a jealous rage would do little but boost his ego, I refrained.

With fists clenched firmly around my handbag and my upper lip secured between my teeth, I waited for the right moment to make my presence known.

"Thank ya for a day I'll ne'er forgit."

"Next time I'll make it a night you'll never forget."

The bitter taste of blood as my teeth cut through flesh indicated that the time had come. I took a deep breath, swept my tongue across the self-inflicted wound, and mustered an air of composure deserving of an Academy Award.

"Yes, next time you might fall pregnant." I spoke calmly, without inflection, as though the words carried no weight at all. The statement was directed at the girl, but I stared intently at Simon's bowed head.

I had not finished the sentence before his eyes shot to the girl's in a state of bewildered panic. He stared at her, wide-eyed, as if she had conjured my voice from her own larynx. After a moment, his focus shifted beyond her face and his eyes locked with mine.

"Or is that a gift you saved exclusively for me?"

For the first time since I met him, Simon was speechless. I suspiciously eyed the military uniform that pulsated with each anxious breath. There had been no mention of his joining the service when I left him in the Underground, or in the letters I had received since. He did not strike me as someone who would be first in line to serve his country, and I was doubtful as to whether the uniform he wore even represented his country.

"What did you do? Strip a man's shirt from his back?" I remained poised, but my words were laced with venom. "Got yourself free passage across the Atlantic in gratitude for your commitment and sacrifice? A bloody whore at every rail station, swooning to satisfy your needs free of charge?"

The bit of blood pooled on my gum sputtered out with the word *whore*. My feigned restraint was rattled, and the irony was all Simon needed to regain himself.

CHAPTER 24

JASMINE

SIMON LOOKED TERRIFIED, like an axe murderer was standing behind me ready to swing. The voice though, the melodic female version of his, didn't sound like it belonged to someone who'd be inclined to create a public bloodbath. But if looks could be deceiving, so could voices.

I fought the urge to turn around and see what, or who, had Simon in such a stupor. If she was an axe murderer, I did not seem to be her target, and I was more likely to stay that way if I could give no physical description of her in a witness statement.

I kept my back to her while she accused Simon of being a thief, among other things. His emerald eyes suddenly regained control of his pupils and a lopsided smile crept up one cheek, twitching like he was trying but failing to get rid of it.

He leapt up, shoving me off of him like I was his bed covers and leaving me in plain view of his accuser. I stole a glance her direction and saw everything I always hoped to be the moment before I looked in the mirror and saw what I actually was.

Silky black hair fell to her shoulders in loose curls spread evenly beneath a wide-brimmed hat. A tailored skirt suit revealed a perfectly proportioned figure. A hint of makeup intensified the natural beauty of a face that needed no manmade assistance. Fierce, midnight-blue eyes bore into Simon.

If looks could kill, he already had the rope around his neck and was just waiting for the floor to fall out from underneath him. And I had an uneasy feeling it was about to.

CHAPTER 25

JULIET

SIMON SPRANG TO HIS FEET, pursing his lips in an effort to suppress an infuriating smile. When all trace of amusement was contained, he spoke.

"Never have I seen a more literal rendering of the spoken word."

"What are you doing here?" To my relief my voice remained steady.

"I came to surprise you." He smiled timidly and said, "Can we at least agree that you were surprised?"

If Simon thought he was going to charm his way back in my good graces, he was mistaken. My eyes fluttered upward as I shook my head at his frivolity. As far as he was concerned, life was a farce, and I was but a player in his grand production. He had cast me as a fool, and I had readily accepted the role.

As I met his self-assured gaze, I recast myself. Simon had directed the first act, but I would be usurping Act II. His comedy was about to take a tragic turn.

"Shouldn't you be in Italy?"

Simon's brow creased, unsure where I was leading. "Italy?"

"Is that not where they're sending their most dispensable men? No wife, no children, no vital occupation? The world will go on just as well without them?"

His Adam's apple jutted from his throat as he swallowed my impudence. I raised my eyebrows and waited for a quick-witted response, but when one did not come, I continued my diatribe.

"You're as expendable as they come. You ought to be the poster boy. Brawny, unattached, able-bodied hothead. They're likely to march you straight to the front lines."

"Juliet, I know you're angry, and you have every right to be, but if you'll allow me to explain—"

"I'm not angry." I took a step back as Simon reached for my arm.

"I don't believe you'd be wishing death upon me if you weren't a bit miffed," he quipped, still believing himself to be in complete control of our fate.

Matching his flippancy, I said, "I'm not wishing anything on you. I'm simply observing that you're a likely candidate."

"For death?"

I shrugged as though I had not a care in the world. "That will be left up to the Germans, I suppose."

Simon and I glared at each other. When he did not break the silence, I said, "If you have nothing more to say, I have business to attend to. And you have a girl to get your money's worth from, so I'll leave you to her."

"If you leave like this, you will regret it," Simon warned.

"The only thing I regret—"

I was so close. So close to beating him at his own game. So close to removing myself from his life without revealing my crushed heart. I thought I could remain detached, but as I spoke, the last year raced through my mind. Meeting Simon. Allowing him to walk me home. Allowing him into my home. Realizing he was more than a stranger. Realizing I wanted him to be more than a stranger.

A fleeting thought knocked the breath out of me. Was it a ruse? All of it, from the moment I bumped into him in the alley? The war had already started and Britain was going to fight, be it on her own soil or someplace else. Men were being called up, and it was only a matter of time before all young men were expected to serve. Simon's best chance to avoid direct combat was a wife, and not just any wife. A prominent wife.

Tears burned their way toward freedom, but I refused to let them fall.

"The only thing I regret," I began again, "is not walking away the night we met and making sure our paths never crossed again." One stray tear made a slow descent down my cheek. I was as livid with its escape as I was with Simon.

"I know you're hurt, Juliet." Simon clasped his hands around my fingers. I did not have the strength to pull away. "If I saw another man's arms around you, I assure you I would not like it, but I would assume it all a misunderstanding unless proven otherwise."

Simon's eyes glistened. Anyone's eyes glistened if they were held open long enough. He was pulling out all the stops to achieve his desired result, but I was his fool no more.

"And if you saw his lips on mine? And if he left me breathless? And if he offered me a night I would never forget? Still, you would think it all an innocent blunder?"

Only then did Simon realize all I had observed. The ever-present gleam in his eye disappeared.

"I would be devastated. But I would still give you the benefit of the doubt. And even if my worst fears were realized, I would forgive you. Because I can't live without you."

I slowly nodded my head. Simon's grip tightened around my fingers in hopeful anticipation.

"You might not be able to live without me, but I can live without you." I attempted to free myself from his grasp, but he would not release my hands.

"Don't say that, Juliet." Simon dipped slightly, but thinking better of it, he straightened up and pleaded, "You told me once that if I got down on my knees, you would walk away. Juliet, I'm on my knees. I traveled all this way for one more day with you. Please, give me that day. I'm begging you."

I could gently remove my hands and leave with my dignity still mostly intact. Instead, I forced my eyes to his. "And you told me once that you felt your father resented you and your mother for giving him something to live for during the Great War. That he envied the men who died on the battlefield. That the final ten years of his life were not spent living. Well, I release you of that burden. If you find death a more appealing prospect than living with the scars of war, know that I do not stand in your way. I will not be awaiting your return."

The color drained from Simon's face one shade of vivacity at a time. Familiar hands turned foreign as they shivered with cold perspiration. "You don't mean that."

"Oh, but I do. And you shall see that I mean it if you survive long enough."

Simon's nostrils flared as though he might be sick. Or as though he might kill me with his bare hands. I began to think it was the latter when his color returned, bypassing neutral and turning a shade of ripe plum.

"How dare you," he fumed.

I cut my eyes to the girl on the bench, silently sharing his sentiment.

Simon turned me loose and lifted his hands to his face, looking skyward and slowly dragging his palms down his cheeks.

"This is not how it was supposed to be," he groaned to the heavens.

We stared at each other, winded and dazed. The last five minutes felt like five hours. One of us had to walk away, and I desperately wanted to take the first step, but I feared my legs would give way if I moved.

I was coaxing my feet into attempting a graceful exit when Simon said, "If you're quite finished, I have a young lady waiting. Maybe she will give me something to live for."

Stung, but determined not to show it, I stoically gestured for him to proceed. Simon turned and took a step toward the bench. Turning back, he squinted at me, searching for my soul.

"You're not really pregnant, are you?"

The corners of my mouth curled into the beginnings of a smile as I realized what a convenient inconvenience that would be for him.

"Of course not."

I coolly held Simon's gaze until his eyes surrendered to mine and fell away, and then I turned and left him with an unraveled destiny and a two-bit jezebel.

CHAPTER 26

JASMINE

SIMON DROPPED ONTO THE BENCH all in one piece, but I felt like I'd just witnessed a butchering. He slapped his palms against his forehead and leaned forward until his elbows hit his knees. His shoulders bounced up and down, and I thought he was crying until he turned a dry face toward me. Bemused laughter puffed through his nostrils with each breath.

"Not exactly the memory I wanted to leave you with."

"You didn't tell me you had a girl," I mumbled toward the ground.

"I don't."

"Not now you don't. But I think ten minutes ago you did."

Simon exhaled another snort. "It's complicated."

I shrugged my shoulders, at a loss for words. Where I came from, you either had a girl or you didn't. And if you did, you didn't go around kissing other girls.

"I wanted her to be mine," Simon admitted. "I pursued her relentlessly for a year, but she would have none of it."

"Then why did you think she could be pregnant?"

Simon sighed. "What was it you said before? You don't have to date to procreate?"

Simon's kiss was starting to leave a sour taste in my mouth. She wasn't his girl, but he wanted her to be. She supposedly wanted nothing to do with him, but she seemed very upset to find him doing something with someone else. Simon was right. It was complicated.

I rummaged through my purse, searching for a dime and praying Mr. Green would answer the telephone and rescue me from the downward spiral I had gotten myself into.

The more crucial half of my prayer was answered right away.

"Miss Jasmine Fowler to the information desk! Miss Jasmine Fowler!"

I jumped up from the bench. Simon reached for my bag, but I swept it out from under his approaching hand. "I've got it."

"Let me help you," he offered, reaching out again.

"I can manage." I tightened my grip around the suitcase, and sensing my resolve, Simon dropped his arm.

Though I wasn't sure what the benefit of the doubt would be in the present situation, I decided to give it to him. I held out my free hand and said, "Thank you for your kindness on the train. I wish you the very best."

Simon wrapped both of his hands around my one. They were trembling, but I knew they weren't trembling for me. Barely able to look me in the eye, he whispered, "I truly am sorry."

Simon released my hand and slumped onto the bench, looking like he had just received the worst news of his life. Already forgotten, I turned and walked away, the whirlwind since getting off the train blurring more with each step.

What I saw when I stepped inside the building caused me to stop so abruptly, the door knocked me the rest of the way into the room. Standing at the information counter was none other than the girl Simon didn't get pregnant but could have because you don't have to date to procreate.

CHAPTER 27

JULIET

THE DOOR SWEPT Simon's bit of fun into the room. I had been too preoccupied outside to take a good look at her, but had I not seen it with my own eyes, I would have refused to believe his lips would ever touch any part of what stood before me.

Jaggedly cut dirty-blond hair limply touched her shoulders in certain spots and did not quite reach in others—surely the work of an inexperienced hand holding a pair of blunt school scissors. Faded freckles dotted a washed-out face. Prominent cheekbones suggested she was not well padded beneath the oversized gray skirt suit that had clearly not been fitted to her. A run in her stocking started just above a scuffed shoe and disappeared into her skirt. Shadows beneath her eyes did not look to simply be the result of a sleepless night with Simon.

Seemingly as eager to ignore my presence as I was hers, she kept her eyes averted as she walked toward the counter. Stopping little more than an arm's length away from me, she turned to the clerk.

"I'm Jasmine Fowler."

I did not feel my heart stop beating. I did feel it start back, racing to make up for the beats it lost in the interim. A lightning bolt shot down my spine and sizzled in my extremities. Surely I was having some sort of post-traumatic delirium. An aftershock. A wakeful nightmare. Anything but truth to what I'd just heard.

"Miss Jenson?"

I hesitantly met the clerk's eyes, praying he was going to tell me I had briefly slipped into unconsciousness.

"Miss Fowler has arrived."

With no such luck, my eyes drifted to the girl. Apparently destiny wanted an encore.

CHAPTER 28

JASMINE

SIMON'S WHATEVER-SHE-WAS was already aware of my arrival and didn't need a reminder. All I needed was to be pointed in the direction of Mr. Green, and I could leave a horrendous five days behind me.

I stared at the attendant while he stared at her. I played dumb, like I didn't know I was caught as a point on some type of angle, and hopefully not a triangle. The last place I wanted her eyes to be was on me.

The attendant's eyes shot to mine. "May I introduce you to Miss Juliet Jenson?"

I kept my eyes fixed on him. "Umm, no thank you."

"No?" His face twisted into a puzzled smile.

"No, sir. I think my ride is waiting."

The attendant looked back to Simon's accuser—Miss Juliet Jenson as she seemed to be more commonly known—and lifted his eyebrows. I heard a huff, and out of the corner of my eye, I saw her turn and walk away.

Finally gaining the attendant's full attention, I said, "Is Mr. Green here?"

"I believe he sent someone in his place."

"Then can you point me in the right direction, please?"

The attendant raised a finger and aimed it behind my shoulder. I turned around and scanned an unoccupied wall of glass. Unoccupied except for a pair of piercing blue eyes hatefully watching my every move.

"Outside?" I asked, searching for an additional exit to the one blocked by Miss Juliet Jenson.

Suddenly, the door was free as she rushed toward me.

"Are you dense?" she half whispered, half hissed, half spit inches from my face. She looked at me so intently, her eyeballs quivered.

I became very aware of the need to swallow, but I had lost the ability to do so. The urge grew, and with great effort I finally forced a giant dose of fright and confusion down my throat.

Like a fit of sneezes, I was caught in a fit of anxious swallows, the exertion showing on my face. Miss Juliet Jenson took a step back and waited, not trying to hide her disgust. When my face relaxed, so did hers.

"Well, are you?" she asked, gently shrugging her shoulders.

I rattled my head side to side, more reminiscent of a shiver than an answer. Her eyes rolled back into her head until I could only see the whites.

"Please see her to the car," she groaned to the attendant before turning and leaving the building.

The attendant walked around the counter and lifted my bag. He looked like he wanted to ask me something, but deciding I probably didn't know the answer, he motioned toward the door and followed me outside.

I realized dumb had been playing me all along when the attendant opened the door of a car that already contained Miss Juliet Jenson. My feet stopped mid-stride as I looked to him for confirmation. He gave me a pitiable smile and nodded, answering the question he had chosen not to ask before.

I lowered myself onto the seat and took in a breath of air so thick with tobacco smoke that my lungs refused to accept it. I had no time to contain the cough, and Miss Juliet Jenson made her repulsion known by scoffing loudly enough to be heard over the hacking. I didn't think she could turn any farther away from me, but she managed to square her upper half to the window and stay that way no matter which direction the car swerved.

My lungs finally accepted the smoky air without protest, but the space Miss Juliet Jenson and I were forced to share grew more uncomfortable with each silent minute. I wasn't sure if I had been kidnapped from the train station, and I was just as undecided on my preference. Kidnapping seemed unlikely, but the alternative, the possibility that she and I were meant to somehow be involved in each other's foreseeable futures, seemed just as absurd. As unfortunate as the last few days had been, even the worst luck couldn't deal that many consecutive blows.

One particularly long, hard curve broke the silence. I didn't see the turn coming, and my shoulder slammed into her back. My momentum sent her forehead into a window she sat close enough to that the impact was unavoidable but far enough from that the thump sounded painful.

"I'm sorry," I apologized, still in the turn, pressing her farther into the door and flailing to right myself.

"Just get off of me," she demanded, shoving her elbows into my ribs.

I flung an arm toward the door handle and, making contact, pulled myself to the other side of the seat. Miss Juliet Jenson turned away from the window and faced forward with her fingers pressed into her forehead, her eyes squeezed shut, and her upper lip tucked behind the lower one.

I was thinking that she probably deserved a little headache if she didn't already have one after her behavior at the train station when my daddy's voice squelched the thought. *Treat others as you would like to be treated.* Having witnessed how brash her treatment could get, if there was any chance we would be seeing each other again, his advice seemed pertinent.

"Is your head okay?" If I had just slammed my face into a window, I would want someone to make sure I was all right.

She didn't acknowledge that she'd been spoken to. I sighed and turned to my own window, keeping a tight grip on the door handle.

"Yes."

The response was so soft it didn't want to be heard, but I did hear it, and I took what I thought was an olive branch and ran with it.

"I'm not a prostitute."

The car jolted as the driver suddenly remembered he had passengers in the back seat. Miss Juliet Jenson's eyes opened, but aside from an occasional blink, she sat perfectly still while I kept talking.

"If you had just let Simon explain, you would know that I'm not. I was sick when I got on the train, and he helped me. I fell asleep and woke up feeling better, so we went to supper and then we went to our own beds. Today we stayed in the dining car all day, and we had just gotten off the train when you showed up. I know you saw us kissing, but he was only showing me how. It didn't mean nothing."

She was so still, I thought the truth had put her in a trance.

CHAPTER 29

JULIET

BAD GRAMMAR rendered Jasmine Fowler unwittingly correct. She rambled on about all she and Simon had shared during their rendezvous, reiterating every other sentence that a bed was not one of those things.

She couldn't be so naive as to think she was helping matters by relaying every detail of her encounter with Simon. Each mention of his name was like a drop of iced water splashing onto already raw skin. And she would not simply dump the bucket of information onto me; she let the particulars drip out bit by bit with no relief in sight.

The longer she spoke, the clearer I saw Veronica Adams' face. The misery from which it all began. Bitterness, resentment, and regret woven through almost twenty years of life.

A pang of deep-seated agony came dangerously close to surfacing. I closed my eyes and tried to push Veronica from my mind. My heart could not take the added torment, but that one pang was sufficient. When my eyes closed, Sister Ava was behind them, looking exactly as she had the day I met her, with a warm smile inviting me to her supper table. There were no happy memories of Sister Ava because memories were all that was left of her. Reminders of what could have been. What would have been had I not ruined it.

A handful of obstinate tears crept down my cheeks while the present gradually sent the past back to the depths of my soul.

"And Simon really is going to war. Hopefully nothing will happen to him while he's fighting, so you won't have to feel bad for all the things you said. I wouldn't wish that kinda send-off on my worst enemy. He probably knows you were just upset and didn't really mean it, but still..."

Jasmine Fowler was sorely mistaken if she thought she had any right to act as my moral compass. I wiped the tears from my eyes and turned to face her. The driveling had to stop.

"I don't think you're a prostitute. I think you're adulterous trash."

Her mouth clamped shut mid-sentence. Her eyes briefly met mine and then lost focus as she went someplace else. I did not care to what recesses of her mind my words had taken her as long as she stayed there until we arrived at our destination.

CHAPTER 30

JASMINE

THERE IS NOTHING MORE SOBERING than hearing the worst opinion you have of yourself spoken out loud for the first time. Until that moment, the hope remains that it is only a distorted self-perception not shared by the rest of the world. Then it is spoken into truth and you realize it was always true.

I reeked of garbage, so much so that Miss Juliet Jenson, after knowing me for less than half an hour, accurately summed up my place in the world. Every ounce of homesickness I had shed along the way to California came raging back. Mr. Green had said all I had to do was be myself, but with it firmly established that myself was trash, I didn't care to be the rubbish of the motion picture business.

The first chance I got, I would call Mr. Green and tell him thank you but no thank you for the opportunity before finding a way home and spending the rest of my life paying him back for the wasted train fare. And in the meantime, I would treat Miss Juliet Jenson exactly as she was asking to be treated.

"Why would Simon need to pay somebody when he gets you to go to bed with him for free?"

I swallowed my aversion to making such a derogatory remark and made another one. "I don't know your definition of trash, but that's pretty much mine."

There was enough light left in the car to see her fingers curl into tight fists around her pocketbook strap. I immediately rethought my decision to confront her within the confines of a moving vehicle, but it was too late.

"You've no idea what you're talking about." She spoke in barely more than a whisper, not bothering to turn toward me.

"Yes I do," I insisted. "Simon told me."

"What exactly did he tell you?"

"That you didn't want anything to do with him except to go to bed with him at night."

Her suit jacket expanded until I thought a button might pop off. It slowly deflated as she sighed and said, "That's not true."

"You think I'm lying?"

"What you said is not true. Whether or not it was spoken to you is irrelevant."

"Well it *was* spoken to me. It was also spoken to me that Simon wanted to court you, but that you would have none of it."

There was a long silence. When she decided that whatever she had to say next was important enough to be facing me while she said it, she looked at me with eyes that were a brighter shade of blue than before.

"Did he also tell you that he proposed marriage?"

My heart stumbled around in my chest as she continued to talk.

"He asked me in the London Underground less than a month ago." Her voice rose slightly as she demanded, "Now you tell me why he would ask someone he doesn't love to marry him." Her eyes filled with tears, and she quickly swiped them away, seemingly aggravated at their formation.

She glared at me, waiting for an answer. *No, he didn't tell me* would answer the first question but not the second. *He said you don't love him, not the other way around* would answer the second question but not the first. *Now I think you're lying* would be better left unsaid.

I said the first thing that came to mind after I sorted through everything I shouldn't say. "You must've said no."

"What?" She clearly wasn't fond of my response.

"You're not wearing a ring." I nodded toward the naked finger still wrapped around the pocketbook strap. "So either he asked and you said no, he asked on a whim and didn't have a ring but you still said no or else you'd have one by now, or he didn't ask at all."

Her eyes blazed with the raw emotion she was fighting to suppress. "And which do you believe to be the case?"

"Well..." Again I thought it best not to call her a liar outright, and she seemed more passionate about this than anything else, so maybe there was some truth to it. "I imagine he did it on a whim. To get a rise out of you when y'all were on better terms. That's why he did it to me."

"Did what to you?" Her poise was unraveling like a tangled ball of yarn, holding steady while the knot was loosened and then coming undone until catching the next snag.

"Simon made a joke about me proposing to him while we were on the train." Sensing her extreme displeasure, I hurriedly added, "I didn't really, though. I just misspoke, and then he said something about getting to know each other first." I shrugged to let her know there was nothing more to it.

Changing the subject, or so I thought, she said, "Do you know who I am?"

I raised my shoulders. "You mean your name?"

"For starters, yes." She had reassembled the composure she lost along the way.

"Well, the man at the train station called you Miss Juliet Jenson."

"Not Juli-ette," she snapped. "I'm *Ju*liet Jenson."

If she wanted to be nitpicky about it, I could be a stickler too. "Well, I'm not Jasssmine Fowler. I'm Jazzzmine Fowler."

Clearly frustrated that I had missed whatever point she was trying to make, she said, "I don't care how you mispronounce your name."

"Then why should I care how you mispronounce yours? I've never heard of Romeo and *Ju*liet."

"Because mine matters!" She laid her hand across her chest and said, "I'm Juliet Jenson. An actress. The entire world knows who I am." Her voice rose a notch in pompousness as she added, "At least the civilized world."

Ignoring the insult, I leaned toward the driver. "I really need to use a telephone to try and find a way back home if you don't mind stopping."

"There are no public telephones in these hills. We'll be at the house shortly."

"Shortly?"

"Less than five minutes."

I leaned back against the seat. Having already survived what felt like hours, I could last another five minutes.

"Where are you from?" Juliet resumed her interrogation.

Less than five minutes.

"South Carolina."

"There are no theaters there?"

"There are, but I ain't never been to one."

"You ain't never been to one? So that's a roundabout way of saying you have been to one?"

Less than four and a half minutes.

Elongating each syllable, I said, "I have never been to a theater."

Juliet gave a moment's pause at not only my ability to correct my grammar but also the fact that I knew a double negative resulted in a positive.

"Where did you learn to form a proper sentence?"

Now she was just being difficult. "Same place as you."

"Did you graduate?"

"That's none of your business."

"I'll take that as a no."

I silently counted down from four minutes to three minutes. At two minutes forty-six seconds, Juliet spoke again.

"I can't believe you thought Simon would actually associate with someone like yourself. He saw you as nothing more than a cheap thrill."

Two minutes thirty-nine seconds. I wanted to say it. Two minutes thirty-eight seconds. I needed to say it. Two minutes thirty-seven seconds. I had to say it.

"Not as cheap as you."

Her finger was in my face before I saw it coming. Between her teeth, she warned, "If you compare yourself to me again…" She lowered her finger without finishing the threat.

"Thank goodness you're not really having a baby," I thought out loud. "I'd feel real sorry for any child who had to grow up with you for a mother. You'd ruin it, spewing your hate all over it all the time. It'd be better off with no mama at all than with you. My mama died before she could ever even hold me, but she would've been a great mother if she'd had the chance. Somebody like you doesn't deserve a baby. And a baby certainly shouldn't have to put up with you."

Maybe I was so blunt with Juliet because I only had two minutes and twelve seconds left with her and I was thinking of the greater good—the child she wasn't carrying but could have been because you don't have to date to procreate. Or maybe I was just extremely irritated by her holier-than-thou behavior. Either way, the last minute and forty-six seconds were filled with soft sniffles coming from both sides of the back seat.

The car stopped in front of a two-story brick house. Juliet threw her door open, hurried up the sidewalk, and was out of sight before the front door slammed shut. The driver took my suitcase from the trunk and opened my door. There was no need to ask. Of course Juliet and I were meant to stay at the same house.

"Do I owe you anything?" I dreaded where I would have to seek the money if I did.

"I work for the studio. I'll pick you and Miss Jenson up at seven o'clock tomorrow morning, all right?"

"All right." He might only be picking one of us up, but there was no reason to tell him that.

"Will you let Miss Jenson know? She seemed to be in a bit of a hurry to get inside."

I nodded.

"And Miss…Fowler?"

I nodded again.

"I'm not saying she doesn't deserve it, but you may want to go easy on Miss Jenson. She was spending her nights in a bomb shelter about a month ago. That'll rattle you a bit, I'd imagine."

I nodded a third time.

"See you in the morning." The driver pretended to tip the hat he wasn't wearing.

"See ya." I turned and slowly made my way up the sidewalk. Juliet had most likely locked the door. Rather than try the knob, I sank onto the porch steps. My thoughts were too jumbled to make sense of the last hour, let alone the last week, so I sat thinking of everything and nothing at the same time.

I hadn't been on the stoop long when the door opened a crack. Nobody appeared, and I was not about to mistake the gesture as another olive branch, but at the very least I wasn't going to have to spend the night outside.

I stopped inside the entryway and looked around for the trap I might be stepping into. The foyer opened into a living room on one side and a dining room on the other, neither of which looked like anything was out of place. The stairs directly in front of me led to a landing that continued along either side of the top of the steps. Each of the three upstairs walls contained a closed door. I hoped I could hear enough movement behind one of them to know which one to stay away from.

I slid my feet out of my shoes and took great care to avoid any creaking announcements of my presence as I touched each step with nothing more than the tips of my toes. Halfway up, I noticed a telephone sitting on the top step. I had never seen a telephone inside a house, but I was fairly certain that was not where one was usually kept. The wire ran along the floor and disappeared underneath the closed door to my left, presumably answering my question as to which door to avoid.

The urgent need to call Mr. Green had passed. I needed time to think, and as uncomfortable as it was going to be, I felt like I had a fence to mend.

I carefully set the telephone at Juliet's door without making a sound and didn't think about a wiggling cord giving me away until I heard the door unlatch as I tiptoed toward the other side of the stairs.

"I thought you needed to place a call."

I turned and saw half of Juliet's face peering through the crack. "I decided to wait till morning."

She didn't respond, but I felt her eyes watching me after I turned my back to her. My hand was on the doorknob when she spoke again.

Her voice shook as she quietly asked, "If it was as you say, nothing but two days of an innocent good deed to educate you in the ways of the world, why did Simon tell you that next time he would give you a night to remember?"

I wanted to tell her that I had the same question, but having already been warned not to liken myself to her, I acted as if I'd not been spoken to, letting myself inside the bedroom and gently closing the door. That was a question only Simon could answer.

CHAPTER 31

JULIET

THE QUESTION was not one she could answer. I fell across the bed. I wanted to cry. I wanted to vomit. I wanted to sleep. Any or all three would be better than thinking, but with the blinding fury abating in the solitude, the chaos of the evening began to sort itself out.

Jasmine Fowler was right. I had said no. And not only had I said no, I'd acted as though marriage was the most preposterous proposition I'd ever heard.

Simon had no obligation to me. When we parted in London, I had left him in a state of ambiguity with no promise of a future but no declaration that he was simply part of my past either. I kept him dangling along in an undefined relationship, answering his almost daily letters flippantly if I answered them at all. Simon was free to romp around with anyone he liked, but would he really choose to do so with her?

Not if he was in his right mind.

I sat upright with the revelation, heaving to catch my breath, waking from a nightmare. Only this nightmare was reality.

Of course Simon was not in his right mind. He was so out of his mind that he thought traveling five thousand miles to see me was logical. Five thousand miles to see the person who kept him at arm's length for an entire year. The person who scoffed at marriage in the Underground and would almost certainly do so again if the idea were presented a second time.

Simon had not traveled five thousand miles to receive a more favorable war assignment. He could have saved time and money pleading his case in a letter or by telephone, knowing the likely rejection would be the same either way.

There was only one reason Simon had traveled five thousand miles. To *see* me. He wanted to see me one more time. Possibly one last time.

I wouldn't wish that kinda send-off on my worst enemy.

The horror of what I had done ripped through me. I had maliciously stripped a man of his hope. A man who had refused to give up on me. A man who had fought for me no matter how hard I tried to push him away. A man who had tirelessly chipped away at my walls. A man who had loved me. A man who had waited patiently for me to love him.

I did love him, enough that I went mad when I saw him on the bench with her, and lost in my madness I had destroyed him with no chance to beg a forgiveness I did not deserve.

I could only hope Simon would refuse to give up on me one more time. But as the despicable words I said to him played relentlessly in my mind, I came to believe he had probably fought his last fight where I was concerned. The tears finally came, and I thought them likely to never end.

CHAPTER 32

JASMINE

CLOSED INSIDE the unfamiliar bedroom, I felt every mile that separated me from my daddy. The hills of Los Angeles offered a peace and quiet I wasn't used to. All of my life I had been lulled to sleep by the constant hum of the mill, and the last four nights I had listened to the commotion of the train. Now there wasn't so much as a cricket chirping outside the window.

I busied myself with unpacking my suitcase. It seemed silly to empty a suitcase that might need repacking in the morning, but I had to do something to fill the silence.

It took less than five minutes to organize two new cotton dresses—the least multiple of second-hand I could find at the company store—two nightgowns, a handful of stockings and undergarments, and two pairs of shoes into a closet bigger than my bathroom at home.

I dumped the contents of a second bag onto the floor. My brown skirt suit landed in a crumpled, foul-smelling heap. My memory of what had taken place while wearing it was spotty, but it stunk of bad decisions.

I had no choice but to wear the suit for my first day of work, but I couldn't wear it in its present state. I peeked into the hallway and saw Juliet's closed door with no light shining below it. Wanting to avoid another confrontation, I crept into the hall with my suit bundle in tow and slid along the wooden floor in stocking feet.

I correctly guessed that the bathroom was behind the third closed door. It was filled with what I assumed were Juliet's belongings. I also assumed she would not want me borrowing those belongings, but using her soap seemed like it would rank low on the list of faults she already had with me.

I lathered, rinsed, and repeated, wrung the suit out as best I could, and glided back to the bedroom. I hung the suit in the closet and hoped it would be dry by morning.

With nothing left to do, I climbed into bed. The sheets weren't cotton, or if they were, they felt unlike any cotton I had ever touched. They were cool and silky, and the heavy bedspread nestled me into a mattress that sank like a marshmallow.

Because there were no external sounds to drown it out, the blood flowing between my ears sounded like a rushing river. The loudness of something to which I was usually oblivious kept me wide awake.

I stared at the ceiling and imagined sheep jumping one by one over a fence. I counted them with my eyes open. I counted them with my eyes closed. I wondered why the trick was always tried with sheep. I tried horses. I tried goats. Sleep did not come.

I turned on a lamp and found a sheet of paper and a pen.

Dear Daddy,

I made it to Los Angeles. By the time you get this, I may be on the way back home. Things are very different out here, and I don't know if it's worth five thousand dollars to stay. I'm living at a boarding house with another girl. Unfortunately, I didn't make a very good first impression on her. We both said some things we shouldn't have. I didn't mean what I said, but I think she meant every word. Her name's Juliet Jenson. Have you heard of her? She seemed to think I should know who she is, but I don't. The driver said she was sleeping in a bomb shelter a few weeks ago. I don't know if that's true, but if it is, I guess I can understand why she's a little on edge. I don't imagine it's a pleasant feeling to have bombs dropping on top of you, even if you're supposedly safe from them.

I didn't act in a way I'm proud of today, Daddy. Or the last few days for that matter. It's nothing you need to worry about, and I'm fine, but it was a long trip. So long that I don't care to make it again any time soon. Never mind what I said about coming home early. I'll stay. This is our chance at a better life, and it would be selfish of me to quit. It will all be worth it in the end. I hope you're not having to work too hard without me there. I love you, Daddy, and I'll write again soon.

Love,
Jazzy

I turned out the light and hugged my pillow, wondering if what I wrote was true. Would it really all be worth it in the end?

CHAPTER 33

JULIET

I WOKE TO THE FAINTEST LIGHT of morning, the sun having not yet met the horizon. The room was still dark, and for a few brief seconds I lay in the ignorant bliss of the first moments of wakefulness.

Light tapping on the bedroom door sent me deeper into a cocoon of bed sheets. A hushed voice butchered my name, and I could not sink far enough to prevent the previous night's events from rushing into consciousness.

"Juli-ette?" Jasmine called a second time.

"Go away," I mumbled into the sheets.

Her footsteps actually faded away. And then they hastily returned.

"I promise I'll leave you alone as soon as I tell you what I was supposed to tell you yesterday. The driver's picking us up at seven. He asked me to let you know, but you didn't seem much like you wanted to talk last night."

A fresh wave of devastation washed over me at the thought of spending the day with Jasmine Fowler. Conniving adulterer she might not be, but obnoxious constant reminder she was. I was under the impression that she had decided to go home, but that no longer seemed to be the case.

I contemplated withdrawing from the picture myself. I was so emotionally wrecked that I did not know if I could pretend to be anything else. Breaking my contract would almost certainly mean returning to London, and the intolerable terror of that last night in the Underground outweighed any discomfort I might experience in Los Angeles. I could go to Canada, but what would I do there besides reprise my perfected role of Juliet Capulet?

No, I had to stay and fulfill my contractual obligation, which meant turning into Juliet Jenson, beloved film star, at seven o'clock sharp. I rolled over and freed my head from the sheets. The clock on the wall read six fifty-one.

I sprang from the bed and swung the door open. Jasmine, pressed against it, took a clumsy, unbalanced step into the room.

"I, I was trying to see if you heard me," she stammered as she quickly retreated back into the hall.

"I should have heard you an hour ago rather than with ten minutes to spare," I chided, pushing past her and closing myself inside the bathroom.

After a short pause, Jasmine murmured, "Sorry," before her footsteps clomped down the stairs.

In addition to the mental anguish, I felt as though I had been given the beating I deserved. I looked it as well. My cheeks were puffy and tender to the touch. Bloodshot eyes, normally well-rounded ovals, looked more like thinly sliced almonds. The skin above my upper lip was raw, and the lip itself was more plump than usual, courtesy of my self-inflicted bite.

A hurriedly applied layer of powder concealed the splotches, and the lip felt more swollen than it looked. A hat sufficiently contained slightly unkempt hair, and from the neck down, all of my wounds were far deeper than the surface of the skin.

My eyes were my only concern. They might not give away the truth, but they would certainly reveal that something was amiss. With no time left to deliberate, I slid on the largest pair of sunglasses I owned and prayed for a sunny day.

CHAPTER 34

JASMINE

"Miss Jenson always comes right out." The driver sounded a little concerned as he watched for Juliet to emerge from the house.

"She overslept." I couldn't be sure that was the reason for the delay, but I assumed she usually woke up with more than nine minutes to spare.

"Did you tell her I was coming at seven?"

"Yes, sir." I did. At nine minutes till.

At three minutes past seven, Juliet appeared in the doorway. She had managed to get herself completely presentable in twelve minutes.

"So sorry," she apologized to the driver as he opened the door for her. She didn't acknowledge my presence, but she didn't twist herself out of sight either.

She smelled of real perfume, not the homemade sickly sweet mixtures the ladies at the mill splashed on their necks. The scent quickly filled the car, and I silently prayed for some of it to stick to me.

"You smell nice." That seemed as good a way as any to start mending a fence.

Juliet sighed, not necessarily with exasperation, but not with relief either. I felt like the elusive sigh included an eye roll, but if it did, it was hidden behind sunglasses.

"You smell like my soap."

It wasn't the thank you I was hoping for, but it was better than nothing, and it sounded more like an observation than an accusation.

"Well, my suit—" I started to explain.

"You washed your suit with my bath soap?" I couldn't tell if she thought that was better or worse than washing my body with her bath soap.

"I didn't know where to find the laundry powder, and it needed to be washed. I'm sorry. I'll get you some new soap."

"I'll replace the soap myself." After another sigh, she added, "And you may keep the bar you used, but don't use it on your clothes. They'll be ruined."

Twelve hours ago she was calling me trash. Twenty minutes ago she was pushing past me because I was making her late. Now she was helping me preserve my clothes? I'd hoped for progress, but this much progress in such a short amount of time seemed too good to be true.

ᘓ ᘔ

JULIET'S transformation reached another level when we arrived on the set. She bounced out of the car, beaming from ear to ear and making her way to a group of workmen. They formed a circle around her, and she threw her arms around the neck of each man as she flitted around like a lightning bug caught in a jar. Only she seemed perfectly content to stay in the trap.

I stood back and watched the scene unfold in front of me with a snippet of wonder as to how Juliet's behavior was all that different from Simon's. After she had devoted her attention to each man a second and third time, Juliet turned her head my direction and, with the same beaming smile, rushed to my side.

"Come, darling Jasmine, and allow me to make the proper introductions," she practically sang as she took my hand and led me into the crowd.

She dragged me around to all of the men—the nice looking ones as well as the not-so-nice looking ones; we just spent less time with the latter. Linking her arm through mine, she squeezed me like we were old friends and talked so fast and in such a sing-song voice I could barely understand her.

The men were even worse. They couldn't take their eyes off of Juliet. Not a single one of them looked at me as I was being introduced. They simply stared at her with bugged-out eyes and gaping mouths, never expecting to be the recipient of Juliet Jenson's undivided attention.

Juliet and I passed through three more mobs of ogling men, each group a little closer to a middle-aged man we seemed to be heading toward in a roundabout way. The man stood alone next to a makeshift desk, so engrossed in the contents of his notepad that he didn't realize he had retrieved the cigarette resting on one ear instead of the pencil resting on the other until he tried to write with it. Rather than returning the cigarette, he stuck it in his mouth and lit it.

With all of the eager young men behind her, Juliet released me and ran ahead, pulling the cigarette from the man's mouth and kissing him smack on the lips. I stood nearby, more puzzled than ever as the pair hugged and pecked at each other.

Suddenly remembering my presence, or at least acting like it was sudden, Juliet led the man to where I stood. Still holding his hand, she said, "Roger, this is Jasmine Fowler, the girl Gordon found in South Carolina. She has no acting experience, so I have absolutely no idea what he was thinking, but here she is."

The man tore his eyes from Juliet and looked me up and down. The first person to look me in the eyes all morning, he said, "I think you'll fit the part nicely, Miss Fowler," as he held out his hand and gave me a firm handshake. "I'm Roger Pearson, the director. Yes, you'll do just fine."

Clearly not pleased with his assessment, Juliet took Mr. Pearson's arm and led him a few steps away. Speaking softly, she said, "Roger, I'm worried that she's going to slow production or make a mockery of the entire picture. She might fit the character description, but she's not an actress. She's never even seen a picture!"

Mr. Pearson glanced my way, and I reflexively shifted my gaze to the ground. "She'll have to do, Juliet. Our time was limited, and she's who we were able to find. She only has a supporting role—hardly any lines. You, my dear, are the star. Her sole purpose is to make you look better. You wouldn't want anyone to outshine you, would you?"

Juliet made one last appeal. "Roger, I can't work with her." She lowered her head and shook it side to side. It seemed we had both regressed since our soap sharing discussion in the car.

"Trust me. It won't be nearly as bad as you think." Mr. Pearson wrapped his arm around Juliet's lower back and kissed the top of her head. "Come now, let's go make a movie."

Juliet had only led Mr. Pearson about ten feet away, so while I was intentionally not included in the conversation, I was just as intentionally not excluded from hearing it. I tried to look busy with my suit buttons when Mr. Pearson motioned for me to take the five steps needed to join them.

Juliet and I followed Mr. Pearson to the folding table serving as his desk. We sat down next to each other, the closest we had been aside from our bizarre arm-in-arm parade through the gawking men. Mr. Pearson took a seat across from us and lit another cigarette.

"Well girls, first of all I want to thank you for taking the time to be a part of this picture. We believe it will lead to great success for all involved." He pulled two pieces of paper from a folder and handed one to each of us. "Here are your contracts. Go ahead and look them over. We ask that you commit to eight hours on the set each day, although some days it may be less or more. The entire filming process should take between three to four months, and of course you'll be expected to attend the premiere as well as any other publicity opportunities that may arise."

Mr. Pearson paused to let us read our contracts. I was still on the first paragraph when he started talking again.

"At the bottom of the page is your salary." He pointed to the number on my paper. "Yours is five thousand, Miss Fowler, I believe to be paid in weekly installments of one hundred dollars with the remainder paid in one lump sum on the last day of filming."

Turning his attention to Juliet, he asked, "What are you up to now? Twenty thousand a picture?"

"Twenty-five. Seven hundred a week." She rattled off the amounts like they had no significance, but twenty-five thousand dollars was more than my daddy had made in his lifetime and it was probably more than I could expect to make in mine, even taking into account the five thousand dollars.

Mr. Pearson handed a pen to Juliet. She quickly signed the line at the bottom of the page and held the pen out to me. I had one last chance to say thank you but no thank you. I sensed Juliet's hopefulness as she noticed my hesitation.

My eyes shifted to the amount just above the signature line. Money wasn't everything, but it sure was something when you had none.

Juliet didn't let the pen go easily, silently letting me know what she thought of my decision. She and Mr. Pearson watched intently as I wrote out each letter of my name with careful precision.

When that was done, Mr. Pearson dropped the contracts back into the folder. "I don't know what you've been told about the picture so far, but let me set the story up for you. The film is set in the late nineteenth century and is centered around a girl who moves with her family from England to a farm in South Carolina. Juliet, that's obviously you. The previous owner of the farm leaves his...let's just say slightly intellectually challenged daughter behind when the rest of the family moves away. That's you, Jasmine. To make a long story short, she more or less becomes a servant to the English girl. I won't give away the end, but the story is quite tragic."

Mr. Pearson slapped his hands to his knees. "Sound good?"

Juliet was quick to speak up. "So basically I abuse Jasmine's character for four months, and in the end she's involved in some sort of disaster?" Her tone was light, but I knew she reveled in the thought.

"You'll have to read the script to find out the details, but I don't think you'll be disappointed," Mr. Pearson teased. "And what do you think, Miss Fowler?"

I shrugged my shoulders. "It's all just pretend anyway."

Mr. Pearson chuckled. "That it is, my dear. That it is."

CHAPTER 35

JULIET

THE PICTURE DID NOT SOUND so dreadful after all. Being able to portray my actual feelings toward Jasmine in ways that would never be acceptable in real life seemed almost too good to be true. I cleared my throat to keep from laughing aloud when she commented that it was all pretend and made a mental note to enlighten her later.

Roger pulled two scripts from his briefcase and handed one to each of us. Jasmine immediately opened hers to the last page, and I in turn closed the open pages over her hands.

"You don't read the last page first. Surely you've read a book before."

Jasmine removed her hands from the script and placed them on her lap. "Sorry," she mumbled to Roger.

"There's no rule as to how to read a script, Miss Fowler. Although Juliet's right. It's better if you read it as it will be seen on the screen."

A commotion suddenly rippled through the production area. Roger rose from the table, scanning all that was taking place around us. Sets were being built, contraptions larger than automobiles were rolling by with lights and cameras and men hanging from them, opening scenes were being blocked, hundreds of people were working in organized chaos to make the first day a success, and a squealing pig was running amuck through it all with a young stagehand chasing haphazardly after it.

"I told that boy to stay away from those animals," Roger muttered through gritted teeth. His face softening, he said, "Well ladies, it looks like I have a pig to catch."

"Maybe Jasmine can corral him," I smirked.

Jasmine did not share my amusement. She did not respond at all until Roger asked her directly, "Do you have experience with farm animals, Miss Fowler?"

Jasmine shook her head. "I think you have a better chance of catching the boy and making sure it don't happen again. But no sir, the only pigs I've been around were tied to a house, and you can't even get ahold of them unless you throw yourself on them. That pig probably just found his freedom."

Roger smiled. "Unfortunately, I don't think his freedom will get him past the highway." Looking at me, he asked, "Is it bad luck to have a casualty before filming begins?"

"Not as bad as having two, which you will if you don't stop the stagehand. He's the one who walked right off the scaffolding last year and broke his leg. He'll be in oncoming traffic before he realizes it."

"Oh, you're right." Roger's tone turned serious. "You two have time to get acquainted with your scripts this morning. Your only appointment today is a costume fitting at one o'clock. We'll be working inside the studio tomorrow. I'll see you both bright and early."

Roger rushed off to prevent negative press, and I was left to walk Jasmine through the basics of reading a script. I turned to the first page, thinking she would do the same, but she sat with her hands clasped on her lap and stared straight ahead.

"You need to familiarize yourself with the script while you have the opportunity."

"I'll do it later. Mr. Pearson said I don't hardly have any lines anyway."

"You do hardly, and it's not only about the lines. But suit yourself." I returned my attention to the script, leaving Jasmine to stare into space.

The tension built as her breathing grew louder and more frequent.

"Is there something you wish to say?" I asked when I could no longer hear myself think.

"Yes."

"Then say it."

Jasmine firmly shook her head, still looking straight ahead.

"Whatever it is, say it."

She shook her head again. "No, because I don't want to say something I'll regret."

"I believe that ship has sailed."

She cut her eyes at me. "You're really one to talk."

I was not doing this again. Certainly not here. "I believe I'll go read my script elsewhere. Be at the costume trailer before one o'clock."

Jasmine let me stand before she burst. "Why were you so nice to me this morning?"

Of all the reasons I thought she might give for being upset, that was not one of them. I sat back down to draw as little attention as possible. "I wasn't."

"Yeah, you were. You even gave me your soap. But I think this whole day has been one big show."

"It has," I answered succinctly.

Jasmine looked astonished that we were in agreement. If she was honestly distressed over a bar of soap, I would gladly put her mind at ease if it meant ending the nonsense.

"My gifting the soap was not part of the show. The soap is yours."

"I don't care about the soap," she huffed.

"You just said—"

"Simon didn't do anything compared to what you've done today. Yesterday you actually had me thinking that he'd done something wrong. That I'd done something wrong too. I felt bad all night. I couldn't even sleep." She glared at me accusingly. "Then today you're flitting around kissing men on the mouth all morning, even your boss. I don't think you really cared about

Simon. You just cared that for a minute he wasn't thinking about you."

Jasmine folded her arms across her chest and leaned back in her chair. I thought she was finished, but she was only catching her breath.

"He was really nice to me, as nice as anybody's ever been, and I know he was just doing it to make me feel better about myself, but isn't that still a decent thing to do? I don't know why he said he'd give me a night to remember, but he didn't really wanna do that or else he'd have tried to do it while we were on the train."

Jasmine searched for my eyes behind the sunglasses I had not removed all morning. "Last night I thought I understood why you were upset, but after today, I think you just threw a tantrum because you weren't the center of his attention right then. You wanted to make sure Simon paid for that and didn't care that he might spend the rest of his life paying for it. A man shouldn't go to war without feeling the love of the person he cares about most in the world. Even if that person is you."

Tears welled in Jasmine's eyes as she finished her rant. "I don't like you. I don't like you one bit, and I don't think the bombs changed you all that much, so I probably wouldn't have liked you before then either. But apparently Simon did, and if I knew where to find him, I would tell you so you could make right what you made wrong yesterday. He was kind to me, and I wish I could return the kindness. If that meant giving you a chance to redeem yourself, I'd do it. But it's too late now, and I just feel so sorry for him!"

Jasmine said nothing I did not already know, but hearing the truth spoken aloud from her lips was torturous. Fortunately for her, I was still playing Juliet Jenson, adored actress, so I calmly stood up, quietly requested that she never speak of Simon again, and walked away.

☙ ❧

ONE O'CLOCK came and Jasmine was nowhere to be found. I waited until everyone inside the wardrobe trailer was annoyed with her tardiness before I offered to go find her.

She was sitting on the grass, leaning against a tree with her ankles crossed and her hands folded on her lap. When she saw me approaching, she stood up and brushed herself off.

"Why are you not looking for the wardrobe department? Everyone is waiting for you."

"I did look, but I couldn't find it. So I gave up and figured somebody'd come for me eventually." Eyeing me suspiciously, she added, "I didn't think it would be you though."

She was making this too easy. "The others are perturbed that you weren't on time, and they didn't care to look for you. They were ready to forget about you altogether."

Jasmine shrugged. "That sounds like what you'd want. Why didn't you just leave me out here?"

I looked her squarely in the eyes. "Because I'm not going to have you make my picture a farce. Your costumes are going to fit, your lines are going to be learned, and you are going to be the most believable intellectually challenged farm girl the motion picture industry has ever encountered. Now let's go before the seamstress refuses to see us both."

Jasmine followed a step behind me and entered the trailer apologizing. She continued to apologize until she was told she was forgiven by everyone there. She obviously thought she had wronged the entire wardrobe department. I tried to conceal the grin that refused to be suppressed.

Jasmine and I stood side by side and tried on dozens of period dresses. Mine were ornately designed with ruffles, lace, bows, and skirts on top of skirts. Jasmine's were simple, pale-colored frocks adorned with only an apron.

"Why are my dresses so different from hers?" she asked the seamstress.

"Different social status," was the shrugged response.

Jasmine did not speak again during the fitting. As we rode home, I took the opportunity to enlighten her on what was make-believe and what was real.

"Not such a deviation from real life after all, is it?"

"What're you talking about?" she mumbled, clearly not eager for conversation.

"What you said earlier about everything being pretend is only partly true."

Jasmine waited for me to volunteer more information. When I did not oblige, curiosity got the better of her. "What do you mean?"

"What the audience sees is not real, but it must appear real. So in order for the actors to make their performances believable, it needs to feel real for them."

"All right." Jasmine lifted her shoulders and her eyes grew round as though she had no idea what I meant.

I tried to put it simply for her. "If the characters are at odds, there is no reason for the actors to attempt to like each other or even make an effort to get along, really. You and I might as well act as though we are our characters when we're together. That way we can fully play our parts to the best of our abilities. Do you understand?"

"I guess so." She sounded uncertain.

"So from this moment forward, you'll be Maggie and I'll be Elaina."

"You want me to call you Elaina?"

"No. I want you to read through your script, and then I want you to treat me as you think Maggie would treat Elaina, and I'll treat you as Elaina would treat Maggie."

"I don't think I like that idea." Jasmine's face twisted with displeasure. "I imagine I'll be getting the short end of that stick."

"That is how one properly prepares for a role," I told her matter-of-factly. "I can't help it if your role is less than pleasant."

"Oh I'm sure you'll make it less than pleasant," Jasmine retorted. "And now you can blame it all on some imaginary girl named Elaina."

CHAPTER 36

JASMINE

IF JULIET INTENDED to make my life more unpleasant than it already was, she didn't act on it right away. She unlocked the door and walked straight through the house, stopping only to grab a bottle of wine and a glass before going out to the back porch with her script.

I took my script to the front steps, and while the seating wasn't as comfortable as out back, the fresh air was just as enjoyable. I read through the first twenty pages as I had been instructed to do. Then I read them again and again.

When the natural reading light disappeared, I went inside to look over the pages again. I was determined to show Juliet that I could run circles around her line learning.

Glancing at the back porch, it looked like I needed to study no further. Juliet's script lay unopened on the table next to her. The bottle of wine was half empty, and the glass in her hand was almost dry. She swallowed the last sip, reached for the bottle, and filled the glass to the rim.

She was facing the backyard, so I couldn't see what she was doing besides drinking. But with the majority of a bottle of wine gone, it was certainly nothing productive, so I gave myself the rest of the night off.

CB BO

THE FIRST CLUE came the next morning. I woke up to the all-too-familiar sounds of severe nausea coming from the bathroom. It sounded like Juliet was paying heftily for drinking that entire bottle of wine. I thought about checking on her, knowing what I felt like a week earlier—miserable from my own bad decisions—but decided the reception would probably not be a welcome one and talked myself out of it. On the verge of being sick myself, I covered my head with a pillow and drowned out the seemingly never-ending waves of coughing and gagging.

Juliet appeared to have made a miraculous recovery by the time the car picked us up. Her perfume smelled slightly stronger than usual, but no one would ever guess she had spent the first part of the morning hugging the toilet.

"Are you feeling better?" I asked as I wafted the pleasant-smelling air my direction.

"Am I what?" She responded with nothing short of absolute annoyance as she dodged my waving hand like it was a fly swatter and she was the fly.

"I heard you throwing up, and I know why you were sick."

The cheek I could see turned bright pink.

"You drank way too much last night," I proudly diagnosed.

"Oh." The rosiness faded. "I suppose I did."

And that was the first clue.

⋘ ⋙

THE SECOND CLUE came six weeks later. Juliet was determined to film the picture as quickly as possible. What were supposed to be eight hour days for four months became twelve hour days with the plan to have the entire picture filmed after only ten weeks.

She was banging on my door by six o'clock every morning, three hours before our scheduled arrival time. Juliet knew the crew reported to work at half past seven, and if we got there at the same time, we were filming by eight.

For four hours, Juliet became Elaina and was more or less encouraged to yell at me, hit me, slap me across the face, and do all kinds of other terrible things, all in an attempt to make a high-quality, believable picture.

I played Maggie, and I hated her the day I met her. She was nothing but a pushover and a coward. She let Elaina do awful things to her and not once did she stand up for herself.

Mr. Pearson said Maggie believed she would be able to save her family's land if she did as she was told, but that was a bunch of baloney. She was just a chicken who, even after she got her head chopped off by Elaina, still tried to follow all of her orders. Only then she was blind and brainless, which made it that much more difficult.

Lunchtime came around and Juliet asked to work a while longer, so work longer we did. A while longer became two hours longer until we were finally given a fifteen minute lunch break before the commissary closed down for the day.

After lunch I was further abused by Juliet for four or five hours until we were finally dismissed to start all over again before the sun came up the next morning.

Juliet and I were both so exhausted that we rarely spoke to each other off set. I had grown largely indifferent to her, mostly because she worked hard and I respected her for that, if nothing else. I did not necessarily think she felt the same way about me, but whatever her feelings were, she kept them to herself.

That was the routine for six weeks, but then something changed.

Juliet and I were standing beside each other in the costume trailer, being helped into our dresses for the next scene. I slipped into my dress and the costume assistant effortlessly buttoned it up the back. Juliet stepped into hers without trouble, but the buttons didn't want to come together.

"Did you take this waist in?" Juliet's seamstress asked mine accusingly.

"Of course not. You know I don't handle her wardrobe."

"It fit her just fine last week. Somebody altered something, and it wasn't me."

As the two ladies argued, my eyes shifted to Juliet. She stood between them with her dress half buttoned, her lips pursed, and her eyes glued to the ground.

The situation grew increasingly uncomfortable, with the two women unwilling to consider that the problem might be the person wearing the dress and not the dress itself. Juliet remained tight-lipped, so I spoke up.

"That's not the corset she wore last week. The other one had laces. Maybe you were able to make it tighter than the clasping one she's got on today."

"She's worn this corset with this dress before," the costume assistant grunted as she tugged at the uncooperative cloth. "I can't think of any reason why it suddenly wouldn't work."

Juliet looked like she wanted to melt into a puddle.

"Could be anything," I answered casually. "Maybe she ate too much salt for breakfast, something as simple as that. Did you eat something salty this morning?"

Without turning her head, Juliet cut her eyes my direction and muttered, "I suppose so," but she and I both knew that was not the problem.

For the first time in weeks, I broke the silence during the ride to the boarding house.

"Aren't you a little bit appreciative of my help today?"

"What exactly did you do today that was helpful?" Juliet's voice contained more animosity than usual.

"I got you out of a sticky situation when your dress didn't fit."

"You got me laced so tightly that I couldn't breathe the rest of the afternoon."

"Well, your dress buttoned, didn't it? It wasn't going to any other way."

"You embarrassed me."

"*I* embarrassed you? I saved you from more embarrassment from the costume ladies. They were going to leave you standing there half naked, arguing about who took in your dress the rest of the day, when we both know nobody altered your dress."

I waited for Juliet to respond. When she said nothing, I said, "I didn't embarrass you anywhere near as much as the truth would embarrass you."

Juliet tucked her upper lip between her teeth. That was her usual reaction to frustration, but it must have also been her reaction to fear because I could tell she was scared.

"That's right. I know the truth," I proclaimed.

Juliet took one deep breath before turning her entire body to face me.

"And what is the truth?" She was expressionless and mostly composed, but her bottom lip quivered faintly and her hands were clasped so tightly that the blood had left the tips of her fingers.

"The truth is..." My eyes wandered as I tried to find my words. "The truth is, you've been trying to drink away your troubles, and that's just gotten you into more trouble. You drink so much at night that you're sick the next morning. And now you're gaining weight because of it."

Juliet's expression did not change, but her lip popped out from its hiding place. "You may certainly believe that to be true if you wish."

She turned back to the window and rested her chin on her palm. A single tear slid out of the corner of her eye. I had seen her cry twice before, and both times she had angrily wiped the tears away before they could fall. This time she didn't reach for the escaped tear, allowing it to slowly roll down her cheek and drop onto her lap.

"I can let your dresses out a little bit," I quietly offered, suddenly wanting to keep Juliet's predicament between us and out of earshot of the driver as a second tear slid freely down her face. "And then I can take them back in if need be. We'll bring them home with us tomorrow, and I'll have them ready by the next morning. Nobody will ever know."

I expected her to question my abilities or snidely tell me that at least I was good for something, but Juliet just wiped a third tear away and whispered, "Thank you."

And that was the second clue.

C3 BO

THE FINAL CLUE wasn't a clue at all. Juliet and I were given the script for the last scene the night before we were to shoot it. Mr. Pearson said he wanted the ending to be a surprise for everyone. After reading it, I assumed he mostly wanted it to be a surprise to Juliet. Had she known from the beginning how the film was to end, she would have probably walked off the set the first day and never come back.

I was overflowing with excitement at what was to take place. Maggie was finally going to stand up for herself, and Elaina was going down in flames. Literally. Maggie's course of action was a bit drastic, but I was so glad she was doing something that I didn't care what that something was.

I rocked side to side on the way to the set, a little ditty playing in my head. Juliet ignored my behavior longer than I thought she would, but when I started humming, she made her annoyance known by letting out an exaggerated sigh. Her irritation had no effect on me, though. Maggie was about to take a stand and redeem herself for being such a sucker.

CR BO

MAGGIE STANDS over Elaina and watches her sleep. Elaina smiles softly, lost in a pleasant dream. Maggie smiles softly, knowing Elaina's soft smile is about to disappear. Maggie leans forward until her lips brush the tiny hairs on Elaina's ear. "Goodnight, Elaina," she whispers. "It didn't have to be this way, you know."

As quietly as she entered, Maggie leaves the room. Retrieving the brightly glowing lantern from the kitchen table, she tiptoes to the front door and carefully twists the knob until the door unlatches and opens to reveal a dark, moonless night.

Maggie waits until she is safely in the yard to complete the task at hand. With one swift motion she sends the lantern sailing toward the house, not caring if it lands on the porch or crashes through a window or goes straight through the open doorway. As long as the glass breaks and the flame is released, its path does not matter.

The fully intact lantern flies through the doorway and crashes into the kitchen table, which is immediately engulfed in flames. But Maggie does not see any of that. She is running away from the house as fast as she can. When she reaches the edge of the property, she turns to watch the event unfold.

The kitchen glows bright orange and flames leap from the windows of the other rooms. "They should be coming out now," Maggie mutters. "Surely they heard the lantern break, and they must feel the heat from the fire."

Fire blazes in every room, yet no one runs outside. Smoke seeps from the house, camouflaging itself in the starless sky. Wooden support beams crackle, popping so loudly that Maggie hears them from one hundred yards away.

Minutes after the fire starts, the roof makes a slow descent, taking down everything in its path. Maggie watches her house, the house her father built with his own hands, shrivel to the ground. And she watches its new residents go down with it.

Maggie sinks onto the grass with the realization of what she has done. "There's blood on my hands now," she states matter-of-factly.

There is only one thing left to do. When the night began, Maggie was unsure whether it would be necessary, but now she knows she must follow through. She reaches into her apron pocket and pulls out a small vial of liquid. She swallows every drop and waits patiently. Each breath becomes a struggle. She fights violently for air, and then suddenly she is still.

CHAPTER 37

JULIET

THE LAST SCENE was unexpected. I knew Elaina and her family were going to die, and I had been none too pleased to find out their demise was to be at Maggie's hand, but Roger saved the bit about Maggie ending her own life until the moment before it was filmed.

Jasmine sat atop a hill, gazing in the direction Roger had instructed her to look and giving her best performance of the entire production because she was not acting. She felt every bit of the satisfaction her face conveyed.

Roger ended the scene. He jogged to where Jasmine sat and dropped a small object into her apron pocket. Watching from a distance, I couldn't hear what was said, but Jasmine's satisfaction quickly turned to dismay.

Roger called action one last time. Jasmine retrieved a vial from her apron, lifted it to her lips, and swallowed its contents. Seconds later, she was heaving and flailing and rolling around on the ground.

Roger raised an arm, waiting for his moment.

"Die!" His arm chopped through the air, and Jasmine went limp.

CB 80

"I DON'T know why Maggie had to go and kill herself," Jasmine complained on the way home. "She finally stood up to Elaina, and she couldn't even enjoy it."

Jasmine did not ask for my opinion and most likely did not wish to hear it, but I gave it regardless. "You believe she felt joy watching the house she was raised in burn to the ground?"

"I think she did what she had to do. What she should have done sooner. Then maybe it wouldn't have gotten to that point."

"You believe the situation called for cold-blooded murder and that she would be able to live with herself knowing what she had done?"

"It wasn't cold-blooded and it wasn't murder. She meant for them to escape."

"Were it not for Maggie's actions, there would have been no need to escape. She might not have intended to kill them, but kill them she did. Killing is not necessarily synonymous with murder, but it results in a death all the same. And when that death is caused by another human being, however unintentional, the one who must go on living is the one who suffers."

"I think she would be able to move on with her life because she would know she didn't mean for them to die."

Jasmine's ignorance was astounding. I'd tolerated her for ten weeks and had even felt neutral toward her at times, but to think she could cause someone's death, be it physical or otherwise, and simply carry on with her life was ridiculous. I had certainly never recovered from the brutal death of my relationship with Sister Ava, and as a result I was damaged beyond repair.

"Did you get over your mother?" My own words stunned me. I was thinking of Sister Ava, the only mother figure I had known, when I spontaneously posed the question to Jasmine. She had only mentioned her mother once, during our first heated car ride together. I had thought no more of it, but apparently I had tucked the information away for future use in order to prove just how despicable I truly was.

I held on to the slightest hope that my inquiry had sounded genuine rather than caustic, but I could think of absolutely no scenario where asking such a question within the context of our conversation would come across as anything but malicious.

Jasmine's entire body began to tremble. She breathed in short gasps. Pools of tears filled her eyes. As they spilled down her cheeks, she erupted.

"You think I don't know that I killed my mama?! That it would've been better if I'd died instead of her?! That I took my grandma and grandpa's only child away?! My daddy's wife?! That he had to raise the child who killed the love of his life?! That he became a slave to the mill because of me?! That I remind him every day of what he could've had if I'd died instead of her?!"

I desperately wanted to bury the pain I had surfaced. I wanted to send Jasmine's perceived truth so deep that it would never rise again, but the only way to do that was to reveal my own truth. My insides knotted so tightly with the thought that I knew I could not do it. I could not sacrifice myself to agony in an attempt to alleviate hers.

"Jasmine, I didn't mean—" I extended my arm toward her, unsure what I reached for, but she slapped my hand away before I could commit to a resting place.

"Don't touch me!" she screamed, eyes blazing. "You've been waiting for this moment! Ever since I told you my mama was dead! Well, today was the perfect day! You even got a nice analogy to go along with it! Yeah, I know that word! Analogy! Maggie is to Elaina as Jasmine is to her mother!"

"Jasmine, please calm down."

"No! I will not calm down! I killed my mama, and my whole life's been a punishment! And the biggest punishment has been you because all you've done is confirm every terrible thing I already thought about myself! I'm trash! I'm a murderer! And I won't ever be nothing else! There, I said it! Are you happy now?"

Malicious I was, and malicious I would forever be to Jasmine Fowler.

CHAPTER 38

JASMINE

I WANTED TO SPIT in Juliet's pretty face. I had slapped her hand to no consequence, but I was thinking rationally enough to know saliva wouldn't be taken as well.

The car was still rolling to a stop when I flung the door open and ran up the sidewalk. The front door was locked. I angrily jostled the knob before turning to wait on Juliet. She sauntered up the sidewalk, making the short walk as long as possible and leisurely sifting through the contents of her pocketbook.

"Hurry up!" I stomped a foot with each word to fully convey my impatience.

"I'm looking for the key," Juliet replied in the calmest tone she had ever taken with me.

"It's never taken you this long to open the door before," I grumbled as she casually walked up the steps.

Juliet found the key and nudged it into the hole. She was still turning the knob when I swung the door open and pushed past her, despite there being ample room to step inside without touching her.

I rushed up the stairs and slammed the bedroom door with all my might. I threw myself onto the bed and continued to fume.

I couldn't lie still, so I got up and walked briskly around the room. Before my brain realized where my feet were going, I had opened the door and bounded down the steps and was headed straight for Juliet.

"Did you get over Simon?"

She didn't turn from the kitchen sink.

"Did you?" I demanded.

"I asked you not to speak of him again." Juliet's voice wasn't raised, but her hands clutched the edge of the counter.

"And I won't ever again, because I don't plan to ever speak to you again, but if one of us is a cold-blooded murderer, it's you. You stripped Simon of his weapons and sent him off to fight a war defenseless. All because you're cruel and don't care who you hurt. Now you have to live with the consequences of your nastiness, and for that I pity you."

Juliet spun around. "You pity me?" She spit the word out with the disgust I expected.

"I do. You want to be loved, but you're never going to be because you make it impossible. At least my family loves me, and the family I lost didn't have a choice. Your family chose to walk away from you—even your own mother—and so has everyone else who's ever been in your life. I guess Simon finally saw you for who you really are because I haven't seen so much as a letter show up for you since I got here. You're incapable of love because you're scared everybody's going to leave you, and they are, because you're unlovable. So yes, I pity you."

Juliet's blank expression didn't change, but her upper lip was invisible behind the lower one, indicating I had made my point. I turned around and marched out the front door, slamming it as I left.

Cg ⁂

I WALKED back to the house under the light of a full moon and a sky sprinkled with stars. I sat on the front steps and searched for familiar star formations until the night grew too cool to stay outside without adding more clothes.

I slipped through the door, on the lookout for Juliet. Her usual spot on the back porch was unoccupied, and if she was downstairs, she was in the dark. The thought that she could be watching me, invisible in the darkness, sent me racing up the stairs. Her bedroom door was closed with no light shining underneath, but I could hear the faint rustle of bedsheets on the other side.

I darted across the hall and readied myself for bed. I wasn't the least bit tired, but the sooner I fell asleep, the closer I would be to going home.

I tossed and turned for hours, my brain unwilling to switch off for the night. I tried every sleeping position known to man, including the awkward ones used only during the elasticity of babyhood. I flipped from my back to my stomach to one side and then the other. I draped one leg off the bed. I tucked my legs underneath me. I curled into a ball. I stretched my limbs to the four corners of the bed. I got hot and kicked the covers off. I got cold and brought them to my neck. Finally, pencil-straight like I had been positioned inside a coffin and with the covers down around my knees, I drifted off.

CB &CO

I WOKE UP shivering in a state of groggy confusion. My hand was reaching blindly for the blanket when I heard something scratching the other side of the door.

My heart pounded, my barely awake brain certain some creature of the night had hunted me down and was about to attack. Blood rushed between my ears, blocking out all external noise.

I fell back, throwing the covers over my head. Fully awake, I frantically tried to convince myself that my imagination was running rampant and there was no sound at all.

My heartbeat slowed, and I was relieved of my temporary deafness. I strained to hear the scratching, but I heard nothing except silence.

The intense pull toward sleep returned as quickly as it had left. My eyelids grew too heavy to hold open. I started counting how many times I could blink before drifting off but gave up at four, the nothingness behind my eyelids too inviting.

Conscious thought had slipped away when a crash bolted me upright before the room had time to settle. My mind raced and my entire body smoldered with sudden terror. *We're having an earthquake* was the only thought that separated itself from a jumble of incoherent panic.

I lunged for the door, remembering only one piece of advice regarding earthquakes. Stand in a doorway as close to the center of the house as possible. I had to get to the bathroom, and if Juliet was already there, she would have to move over or get out of my way.

I threw the door open and immediately toppled over a large mass in the dark hallway. With a hard thud, I landed on all fours and then all sixes as my hands slid across a wet floor and lowered me to my elbows. I scrambled to stand up, desperate to get away from whatever was blocking the doorway. My feet slipped out from under me and the creature broke my fall.

I could tell right away that the creature was human. An intruder had tried to break into my room, and he had been struck down before he could succeed. The mess on the floor was his blood.

As I pushed myself off of his shoulder, he moaned. Only he wasn't a he. He was a she. And she was Juliet.

I found my footing and felt my way to the light switch. When my pupils adjusted to the harsh influx of light, I saw a barely conscious Juliet crumpled on the floor. The fingers of her outstretched right hand were curled loosely around the neck of a broken liquor bottle. Her fisted left hand clutched her stomach. She wasn't lying in blood. She was lying in spilled alcohol.

Seeing that an intruder wasn't lying before me—and that the person who was lying before me wasn't bleeding to death or even bleeding at all—calling for help lost its urgency.

There was no dry route to Juliet. I sloshed through the freshly spilled puddle of alcohol and splattered her face as I dropped to my knees. How sorry she would be to learn she had wasted what looked like an entire bottle of liquor.

"Juliet," I whispered to no response. I took hold of her right hand and shook it loose from what was left of the bottle. Thin red lines along her forearm, brushed by the jagged edges of glass, looked to be the only injuries she had sustained. I grabbed her wrist and swung her hand back and forth across her face.

"Juliet, Juliet, Juliet." I sang her name repeatedly, being sure to emphasize the *et*. I was still flopping her hand against her cheek when her eyelids fluttered. "Wake up, little drunkling."

Juliet's eyes opened. She stared past me, unaware I was there. I leaned over her and found her gaze.

"What would all of your adoring fans think of you now?"

Her lips parted. The word *hospital* weakly passed through them.

"You don't need a hospital. You just need to sleep it off right here. You'll be fine in the morning." I had suffered through my little bout with alcohol just fine without medical assistance, and I was a novice. Juliet was a professional.

"Phone for an ambulance," she urged, the words coming out slow and scratchy.

I shook my head. "If you don't need a hospital, you don't need an ambulance. Tomorrow morning you're going to be so embarrassed that I saw you like this, you're going to thank me for not getting anyone else involved."

Juliet's eyes rolled upward and her eyelids closed over them. I gathered the broken glass into a small pile next to the wall and rose to my feet, ready to step over her and go back to bed.

I was straddling her when she whispered, "Please."

I took a step backwards. "I'll tell you what. I'll help you to your bed. That way there will be a telephone right beside you. If you want to go to the hospital that badly, you can call them yourself."

"No!" Juliet suddenly found her voice, her eyes wide open. "Use the telephone downstairs."

I stepped over her and into the bedroom. "I'm not using any telephone. And if you want to lay on the floor all night, that's fine by me. Goodnight."

I closed the door between us. As I crawled into bed, I heard, "You. Are. The. Murderer," with Juliet taking a labored breath between each word.

I rolled my eyes at her dramatics. "You're not going to die. Just go to sleep. You'll be fine in the morning."

Juliet weakly pounded the bottom of the door, and then all was silent.

☙ ❧

MY EYES burned for more sleep the next time they opened. I felt like I hadn't slept one bit. I shuffled to the door, expecting to find Juliet asleep on the other side.

I stepped into the sticky remnants of her having been there, but she was gone. Assuming she had crawled across the hall at some point and made it to the bed, I tiptoed through the muck to get to the bathroom.

After nodding off on the toilet, I weighed my options. Turn right, wake Juliet up, and be the recipient of splitting headache hate all day. Plod down the steps and head straight outside to clear my foggy head. Turn left and go back to bed.

I was raised to think it was a sin to sleep past sunrise. The sun flooded the house, making sure I knew it had started its day. Fresh air was the right choice, but it wasn't the most appealing choice. The inviting warmth of the bed was an offer I couldn't pass up as I shivered in my thin nightgown. I slipped back under the covers and was out before I hit the pillow.

☙ ❧

THE KNOCK on the door interrupted my day of uninterrupted sleep. I pulled the covers over my head as if I could be seen from the front stoop if I wasn't fully cloaked in bed sheets.

The knocking grew more persistent. Someone really wanted one of us, and I was sure that I wasn't the one who was wanted, but the other one of us was probably not up to entertaining guests. Or answering the door for that matter.

I trudged down the steps and opened the door, ready to disappoint the person on the other side. Our elderly neighbor had her hand raised and ready to knock again. While it wasn't unusual for her to stop by, I was surprised to see her empty-handed. I had never known her to come over without a cake or casserole or other edible excuse to visit.

"Hey, Mrs. Fields."

"Hello, dear. I didn't wake you, did I?" Her eyes scanned my nightgown.

"Oh. Uhh…" I squinted toward the sky. The sun told me that noon would strike within the hour.

Mrs. Fields waved the question away without waiting for me to stumble over an answer. "I'm sure you didn't get much sleep last night. I'm sorry to bother you, but I came for some of Juliet's things."

"Why? Is she at your house?"

"No, dear. She's at the hospital."

"The hospital!" I shook my head. "I told her she didn't need a doctor, but she wouldn't listen. Now the whole world's going to know what happened."

"I'm sure she would've preferred to keep the matter private," Mrs. Fields agreed, "but I don't think she had much choice."

"She had the choice not to get into this predicament in the first place."

Mrs. Fields visibly swallowed her reluctance to discuss such a sensitive subject. "I suppose you're right."

"Did she wake you up and ask you to take her?" Judging by the state Juliet was in when last I saw her, I found it hard to believe she had managed to walk across the street and knock on Mrs. Fields' door under her own power.

"The young man who drives you to work took her. I was up before dawn, brewing the coffee so it would be ready when Earl woke up. He has four cups every morning before he goes in to work. He still works, you know, at the train depot. Been with the railroad his whole life."

Mrs. Fields' husband was at least eighty years old, but maybe all that coffee kept him in the working world rather than enjoying the leisure of retirement.

"Anyway." She steered herself back toward the question asked. "I was looking out the kitchen window. It faces your house, you know."

"Yes, ma'am. I've seen you washing the dishes at night." I didn't add that I had seen her looking through her kitchen window and into our upstairs picture window just as often.

"Seems like I've spent my entire adult life standing at that window." Mrs. Fields smiled sadly, lost in the memory of years gone by.

I was more than willing to listen to her life story another time, but at the moment I was only concerned with the present.

"You saw Juliet go with our driver this morning?"

"I did."

"How do you know they were going to the hospital?"

"Well, I didn't notice Juliet sitting on the front steps until the headlights shone on her when the car pulled into the drive. There was barely any light outside, and her clothes were dark, and you know how dark her hair is, and she was half sitting, half slumped on the bottom step when I finally saw her. The driver...I didn't catch his name, dear?"

I shook my head. "I never caught it either."

Mrs. Fields was zoned in on her story and didn't seem to mind that I couldn't attach a name to the face. "The driver got out of the car and helped Juliet to her feet. They took about three steps before her knees buckled. Thank goodness the young man was supporting her. She didn't fall to the ground, but she didn't right herself either. The driver swept her into his arms and carried her to the car. That's when I hurried outside to see if everything was all right. I told the young man to call me when Juliet was settled."

What Mrs. Fields described was very similar to what I had experienced during the aftermath of my little bout with alcohol. Only I didn't make an unnecessary trip to the hospital. Gently reminding her of her purpose for stopping by, I said, "So the driver called and asked for some of Juliet's things?"

Mrs. Fields' brow furrowed, adding more wrinkles to her aged face. "Nobody called. For hours. I was worried sick. So I rang the hospital myself, and that's when the nurse told me she got there too late." Mrs. Fields bowed her head, and my heart stopped.

You. Are. The. Murderer.

My own knees were about to buckle. I staggered backwards and dropped onto the stairs.

"Too late?" The question came out as barely a whisper.

"She was too far gone. The nurse said nothing could be done to save her."

"Juliet's..." The word choked me as it crept up my throat. "Dead?"

Mrs. Fields lifted her sorrowful face. "Not Juliet, dear. The baby."

"What baby?!" I spit the question at Mrs. Fields like she had lost her mind.

Her face showed a lesser degree of the confusion I felt.

"Apparently Juliet was expecting, almost five months along. You didn't know?"

My eyes darted frantically around the entryway, my mind seeking to make sense of the last five minutes. Suddenly the world fell away and I was back at the train station, nose-to-nose with Simon.

Yes, next time you might fall pregnant. Or is that a gift you saved exclusively for me?

Juliet knew then, the moment she met me. The moment she saw me kissing the father of her unborn child. She knew when I told her she would be a terrible mother, that she was undeserving of a child, that a child would be better off with no mother than with her. She knew when she was sick almost every morning. She knew when her dresses would no longer button. She knew when I threw Simon's probable death in her face and told her she was incapable of love or being loved. She knew when she was lying outside my door, begging me for help.

You. Are. The. Murderer.

Devastating shame sank me so deeply into its depths that I couldn't look Mrs. Fields in the eye. "No, I didn't know. But I should have." I dropped my head into my hands. "The baby was fine until a few hours before Juliet got to the hospital? It was just those hours that made the difference between life and death?"

Mrs. Fields' knees creaked in protest as she sat down beside me. "I don't know, dear. Possibly. We can forever ask ourselves *what if*, but *what is* is the reality we must live with." She draped her arm across my back and gave my shoulders a tight squeeze. "Unfortunately, this sort of thing happens all too often. I don't imagine a couple of hours would have made a difference, aside from making it a little easier on Juliet. She lost a good bit of blood. The doctors want to monitor her for a few days, but she'll heal quickly. And she'll heal emotionally as well, although it may take longer. It's never easy losing a child." Mrs. Fields spoke like she knew her words to be true.

"So Juliet won't be home today?" I couldn't face her before I left, even if that meant spending the night at the train station.

"The nurse said they'll keep her at the hospital for forty-eight hours in case she loses more blood. Why don't you ride over there with me so you can say goodbye before you leave? It might boost both of your spirits."

That it most definitely would not do. What it would do was another one of those *what ifs* we would never know the answer to. A further loss of blood seemed most likely.

I couldn't think of a good excuse, so I gave a bad one. "I have to pack my things today. I'll have the driver stop by the hospital on the way to the station tomorrow."

"Well, I'll be sure to tell her you're thinking about her." Mrs. Fields grunted herself to a standing position. "Do you mind gathering Juliet's belongings for me? My knees don't handle stairs well, and you know what she'd like to have better than I do."

I mustered the strength to stand and wearily climbed the stairs, my legs shaking under the weight of the news Mrs. Fields had delivered. Juliet's closed door staunchly stood as the barrier it was meant to be, sneering at me for even thinking of opening it. I'd never been inside her room, aside from toppling into it the day after I got to California, and I was in such a hurry to get back into the hall then that I had been oblivious to the room itself.

With bated breath, I turned the knob. I peered inside and gasped so loudly that Mrs. Fields trotted halfway up the steps to see if I was all right.

Juliet's bedspread lay in a heap on the floor. A crumpled, blood-soaked nightgown partially covered a circular bloodstain that spread outward from the center of the bed. Large drops of blood—some squashed into the shape of footprints—mapped Juliet's path from the bed to the door to the closet and back to the door. Thankfully I had never witnessed a massacre to be able to make an objective comparison, but I couldn't imagine one producing a more chilling scene.

The bloody footprints mysteriously ended at the door, but when I looked closely, an ever-so-faint trail led to my bedroom. I suddenly understood why Juliet was so adamant about not being helped to her bed. She had gone to great lengths to keep me from knowing just how dire the situation was, changing into a clean nightgown and apparently using the already bloodied one to mop up the excess so there would be no visible trace of blood on her.

I didn't realize both of my hands were covering my mouth until I turned to discourage Mrs. Fields from hobbling her way up any more steps. Seeing her silver curls nowhere in sight, I pushed the door around and threw the bedspread over the mattress stain, which still looked wet with bright red blood at its center. As I crossed the room to Juliet's chest of drawers—the splotches on my feet clinging to the wood with every step—I wondered if I was being hindered by something much more sinister than what I had thought was red wine in the hallway.

I felt such guilt rummaging through Juliet's belongings, knowing I was the last person on earth she would want searching her room. I blindly grabbed a handful of undergarments, two nightgowns, and a pair of slippers and tossed them into a bag. I had one foot out the door when I remembered she would need something to wear home. The least I could do was help her have a dignified exit from the hospital.

I turned around and walked straight to the closet. I thumbed through the skirt suits, looking for the one she wore the first day of filming. I had never seen her more bubbly, and even if it had all been a show, she had chosen that particular outfit for her performance.

I found the suit and a pair of dress shoes and quickly left the room, closing the door behind me. I added Juliet's toiletries to the bag and hurried down the stairs, eager to pass it on to Mrs. Fields. We said our goodbyes and she turned to leave.

"Mrs. Fields?" I had one last troubling question to ask. "Did they know the baby was a girl?"

Mrs. Fields froze. Her knuckles turned white as she squeezed the doorknob. "I'm not sure. I didn't ask."

She might not have asked and she might not have been sure, but the distress showing on her face when she turned around told me she was at least fairly certain. Rather than taking that as my answer, I pressed further.

"You said *she* and *her* earlier. I guess that's why I thought you were talking about Juliet."

Mrs. Fields sighed. "Now that you mention it, the nurse did refer to the baby as a girl. I suppose by five months a baby is almost fully formed. Just a smaller version of what it looks like when it arrives."

My heart sank deeper, if that was possible. A baby was a baby, but the image of a fully formed baby girl with a perfect little face and ten tiny fingers and ten tiny toes made me feel sick to my stomach.

I quickly said goodbye to Mrs. Fields and ran upstairs to Juliet's room. I stripped the bloodied sheets from the bed. The heaviest pooling had soaked the mattress, and no amount of scrubbing removed the stain. I stripped my own bed and lumbered across the hall twice with a mattress by my side, trading hers for my own. I put fresh sheets on her bed, washed the bedspread, and hung it out to dry. I scoured the floor until it sparkled and then moved on to the upstairs landing.

The whole house was spotless by the time someone else's driver picked me up to start my trip home. My driver must have not wanted to be in my company, and I only wished I had the option of not being in my company either.

CR ED

THE TRAIN RIDE home was five days of absolute misery. There was no handsome man to help pass the time, but if there had been, I would have declined any and all of his advances. There was an abundant supply of strong drink, but if I ever saw one more drop of alcohol it would be too much.

I was left with only my thoughts. I thought about how I kissed the father of Juliet's child and then tried to convince her she was the one at fault. I thought about how I decided she was an alcoholic and then used the diagnosis against her. I thought about how I let her lie in a puddle of alcohol—after lying in a puddle of blood—and then taunted her before I left her to suffer alone. The more I thought about all the reasons Juliet should hate me, the more I hated myself.

CHAPTER 39

JULIET

MRS. FIELDS BUSTLED OUT of her house, mixing spoon in hand, waving it frantically as the car turned into the drive. I managed a weak smile and a cordial hello when she promptly opened the door upon reaching the stopped car.

"Hello, dear, I'm so glad you're home!" She ducked inside the car and gave me a delicate hug with her fingertips, as though the part of me left unbroken might shatter with her embrace. I returned the gesture by weakly raising a hand to her back.

When the driver suggested she step back to make room for my exit, Mrs. Fields looked ready to wallop him with the spoon. Their outstretched hands competed for my acceptance, so I placed one hand in each and awkwardly stepped out of the car.

My halfhearted smile evolved into a wholehearted grimace with the discomfort of standing upright and climbing the steps to the front door. After an arduous ascent, Mrs. Fields assured the driver that she could manage without his assistance. They both looked to me, and I nodded to confirm that one caregiver was sufficient.

Left alone in the foyer with Mrs. Fields, I gave pause to the daunting mountain of stairs rising before me.

"I believe I'll sit on the patio for a bit."

"You don't want to go to bed, dear?"

"My desire to avoid steps is greater than my desire for the bed at the moment."

Mrs. Fields kept a hand under my elbow as I slowly walked through the house and out the back door. When I was settled onto a lounge chair and covered with a blanket, sipping a cup of tea I did not wish to be sipping, she offered to sit with me.

"It won't hurt my feelings if you want to be alone," she added.

"I believe I would for now, thank you. The medicine leaves me a bit tired."

"I'm sure you're exhausted. You rest, and I'll come by and check on you later. I'll bring you a plate when I finish dinner. We're having chicken and dumpling stew. Does that sound all right?"

Nothing sounded all right. In two days, I had eaten no more than the minimum amount required to satisfy the nurse. She had assured me that if I forced myself to eat, my appetite would be stimulated. This was important, she had said, because the more nutrients my body received, the more energy I would have, and increased energy meant a faster, more complete recovery. My appetite had yet to respond to the coaxing, but I graciously accepted Mrs. Fields' offer.

Supplied with a reason to go home, she patted my shoulder and gave me a whirlwind of grandmotherly instructions before turning to leave.

"Mrs. Fields?"

"Yes, dear?" She eagerly turned from the door, grateful to be needed again.

"Did Jasmine already leave for South Carolina?"

Mrs. Fields looked surprised by the question. "Her train left yesterday. Did she not stop by the hospital on her way out?"

"Not that I'm aware."

"That's odd. Something must have come up."

I wanted to ask Mrs. Fields why she found it odd, but I feared the answer. I thanked her for her help, rested my head against the chair cushion, and closed my eyes. She took the cue and left me be.

I did not keep my eyes closed for long. Behind them lingered the reddish-pink face of a child born much too soon. A child no larger than the palm of my hand but with all the distinctive features of a developing human being from head to toe.

A child I had initially refused to believe existed despite a plethora of signs telling me otherwise. A child I had wished did not exist once her existence was impossible to deny. A child I had gone to great lengths to make sure no one else knew existed. A child whose existence I was finally accepting just as her existence faded away.

A child who, according to the nurse, would not have benefited from an earlier hospital arrival. A child who was already lost at the first sign of trouble. A child who had likely been gone for days before the deluge of blood loss sent me into shock.

A child who, contrary to the nurse's belief, was at least alive, if not well, long after the first twinge of discomfort. A child whom I felt fluttering inside of me as I lay in the bed praying for the pain to subside. A child who may or may not have met the same fate had I been less concerned with my well-being and more concerned with hers.

A child who would not have to grow up with me for a mother. A child who would have been better off with any other mother. A child whom I did not deserve and who certainly did not deserve to have to put up with me. A child whom I had completely and utterly failed before she was even born.

ℭℨ ℬↄ

MRS. FIELDS proved to be more adamant than the nurse in making sure my appetite received its proper stimulation. I convinced her to strain the broth from the rest of the stew, voicing the concern that such a hearty meal might be a bit too nourishing after being on a bland hospital diet for two days.

When every last drop of the liquid was swallowed and the chicken, dumplings and vegetables were stored in the refrigerator to be eaten the instant I felt up to it, Mrs. Fields saw me to the sofa. I had longed for the bed since late afternoon and I had no intention of sleeping on the sofa, but I also had no intention of allowing Mrs. Fields to accompany me to the bedroom. After I promised to ring her with even the slightest need, she bid me goodnight.

It seemed the least tormenting course of action would be to ascend the stairs as quickly as possible. As quickly as possible turned out to be excruciatingly slow. When I reached the top, shrouded by darkness because I knew Mrs. Fields was watching the house, I was faced with a decision. Go to my own room and face what I left behind or go to Jasmine's and face her ghost.

I could not bring myself to go to my bedroom. I opened Jasmine's door, thinking only of a place to sleep. All that remained of her bed was the frame. A mattress sat propped against the wall, and without crossing the room, I knew my blood stained the unseen side.

I collapsed onto the freshly made bed in my room, grateful for the kind gesture and too exhausted to wonder how my frail neighbor had managed such a feat on her own.

CR &0

MRS. FIELDS telephoned to tell me she was going to let herself in with a plate of breakfast. Two minutes later, I heard the key turn in the door and her feet shuffle to the living room. When she did not find me where she thought I would be, she anxiously called my name.

"I'm upstairs," I quickly answered, not wishing to send the elderly woman into a panic.

"Upstairs! You climbed those steps by yourself?" she asked as she padded back to the foyer.

"I did."

I expected to hear the stairs creaking beneath Mrs. Fields' feet, but when she spoke again, she sounded no closer.

"I'll go get Earl to bring your breakfast up to you."

"You don't have it with you?"

"I have it, but I don't want to make you come down. Earl will be happy to run it up to you."

I gingerly swung my legs over the side of the bed and stood up. I had yet to receive the energy the nurse had promised me, but the fiery pain had subsided to a much more bearable nagging soreness.

I stepped into the hall and leaned over the banister. "I can come down, but is there a reason you can't come up here?"

"My knees. I ran up about five of your steps the other day before I realized what I was doing, and I'm still stiff in one knee and can't put much weight on the other."

"So you didn't come up here and clean?"

I had known someone had seen the state of my bedroom when a bag of my belongings appeared at the hospital, but at the time, I had been too medicated to come up with the most likely candidate. The driver had no way of entering the house without being let inside, and even if the door had been opened for him, he would have sent the opener of the door to my bedroom while he waited no more than a step inside the foyer. Mrs. Fields had the ability to let herself into the house and wouldn't have shared the driver's disinclination to enter my bedroom, but if she could not climb stairs...

"Oh, that was Jasmine. She was busy for hours. Every time I walked past my kitchen window, she was on her hands and knees at the top of the stairs. She must have scrubbed her little fingers to the bone polishing the floor up there."

"Did you happen to see why she was cleaning?" I wondered just how nosy my neighbor's eighty-year-old eyes allowed her to be.

"I suppose she just wanted to do something nice for you. Tidy up a bit before you came home." After a short pause, she answered the underlying question. "I don't see everything that goes on here, dear. I just like to check in on you every now and then, you girls living all alone."

I did not care that Mrs. Fields was a busybody, and I cared even less that Jasmine Fowler knew the gruesomeness in which she had left me to suffer.

ଓ ଞ

THREE DAYS later I received a letter.

Juliet,

    I still believe in destiny, and I still believe you are mine. I forgive you for wishing me dead. I hope you forgive me for giving you reason to. I will be on leave for three days in March. I would love nothing more than to spend every moment with you, but I can only travel so far in three days, so it will require a sacrifice on your part.

    If you wish to bring a bit of joy to a weary soldier, please send all such correspondence to the return address on the envelope. If in fact you meant every word of our last encounter and your opinion has not changed, please act as though you never saw the return address on the envelope. Regardless of your feelings toward me, I will devote the rest of my life to showing you how much I love you.

    Yours,
    Simon

With that, I got out of bed and resumed my life.

CHAPTER 40

JASMINE

South Carolina

December

1940

My HEART POUNDED as a platform scattered with people came into view. I started searching for my daddy before the faces were recognizable. The small depot lacked the hustle and bustle of the larger train stations, making it easy to see that he wasn't among those waiting alongside the tracks.

As the train slowed to a stop, little Andrew Carter appeared outside my window, hopping up and down and waving both of his arms to get my attention. He wasn't so little anymore, but he would always be Miles's baby brother to me.

"What are you doing here?" I asked distractedly as I stepped off the train, still scanning the crowd.

"I came to take you home."

Andrew reached out and took my suitcase. With both feet on the ground, I realized I had to look up to see his eyes. When I left South Carolina we were eye to eye. Three months later, we were eye to nose.

"Where's my daddy? Is he working?"

"He's at your house, I reckon."

"Why didn't he come to get me?"

"Cause I told him I'd do it on my way home from school."

"He's not excited to see me?"

"I don't know, Jazzy." Andrew shrugged. "I'm sure he is."

I followed him to the parking lot. "How are we going to get home? Did you get the school bus to stop here?"

Beaming, Andrew proudly exclaimed, "I got a truck!"

"A truck! How'd you manage that?"

"I've been working when I'm not in school. Saving up."

Andrew jogged a few steps ahead of me and turned around beside a blue pickup truck. "Here she is! Ain't she beautiful?"

"Mm-hmm." I hoisted myself onto the passenger seat, little Andrew Carter starting to look little again as he climbed onto the driver's seat.

"I don't know how I feel about a scrawny little towhead driving me around," I teased as we crunched through the gravel parking lot.

"Well, how do you feel about standing in the cold, hitching your way home?"

I cut my eyes at him. "I suppose I'll take my chances with you."

"You suppose?" Andrew laughed. "I haven't ever heard you suppose anything."

I supposed he was right. "The girl I lived with in California said *suppose* a lot. I guess I picked it up from her." My heart felt like it was being pinched every time I thought about Juliet.

"How was California?"

"It was..." I hesitated. I had relived the last three months a hundred times on the train, and even though the picture was devastatingly vivid, the last thing I wanted to do was paint it for Andrew. "Different."

"Of course it was different. What was it like?"

"Just nothing like it is here. Some things were better. Some things were worse."

"You're talking like I'm interrogating you, Jazzy. You got something to hide?" He looked at me with his brother's grin spread across his face and gently elbowed my ribs.

The short answer was yes.

I shrugged his elbow away. "There's just not much to tell. I was either working or I was at the boarding house. I didn't have time to see the sights," I answered a little too sharply.

"Geez, Jazzy. I'll save my questions about the sights for someone else then. Sounds like you need to go back to California and let the sunshine thaw you out."

Andrew was quiet for all of five seconds. "So this boarding house. You said you had a roommate? Was she in the picture too?"

The pinch became a squeeze.

"Yes." My face showed the discomfort of very real pain, but it went unnoticed by Andrew who had suddenly decided to keep his eyes on the road.

"Is she somebody I would know?"

I shrugged my shoulders. It seemed he was selectively seeing out of the corner of his eye because that he saw.

"Well, put me outta my misery, Jazzy. What's her name?"

I felt like Andrew was wringing my heart out, twisting with all his might.

"Juliet Jenson." I hoped getting it over with and saying her name might put us both out of our misery.

"Juliet Jenson?!" Andrew's misery was forgotten, but mine was not. "Of course I know who she is! She's only about the prettiest girl I've ever seen!" He slammed his hands against the steering wheel and shook his head in amazed disbelief. "I can't believe you know Juliet Jenson!"

We rode the rest of the way home in silence, both of us thinking about Juliet, but for very different reasons.

ᘓ ᘔ

I OPENED the passenger door and was immediately bombarded by crisp winter air and the smell of dirt. Juliet was momentarily pushed to the back of both of our minds as Andrew lifted my suitcase from the bed of the truck.

"You want me to walk in with you?"

"Why would I want you to do that?"

"I don't guess you would." He quickly shrugged a shoulder and held my suitcase out to me. We were mid-exchange when he said, "Have you talked to your daddy since you left?" He kept his hand around the handle, waiting for my answer.

"He answered a couple of my letters, but I haven't actually talked to him. Why?"

"No real reason." Andrew let go of the suitcase. "See ya, Jazzy. If you need anything, I'll be at home."

Since Andrew had already dodged similar questions twice, I didn't take the time to ask him why I might need him. I ran up the stairs and burst through the front door just in time to see my daddy struggling to stand up from the couch.

I stopped in the doorway, dumbfounded. Daddy coughed violently into a handkerchief, the effort of standing up more than his lungs could take. His clothes, the same ones that fit him before I left, swallowed him. A pair of suspenders held up pants that otherwise would have been around his ankles.

The coughing fit subsided and Daddy repeatedly cleared his throat, tucking the handkerchief into the ample space between the waist of his pants and his shirt. He secured a second hand around a wobbling cane, steadied himself, and looked up at me, barely able to lift the corners of his mouth into a weak smile.

"You look good, Jazzy." Daddy's welcome gurgled up his throat and came out sopping wet like it had just been saved from drowning.

I forced myself out of my stupor and walked toward the frail man standing before me. His face was ashen and he looked like he hadn't slept in days. The closer I got, the louder each labored breath rattled inside his lungs. I gave him a timid hug, scared I might break him with the slightest touch.

"I don't guess this is whatchew was expecting, huh?" Daddy lowered himself back onto the couch.

"You've lost weight." I sat down beside him, my limited acting ability unable to hide the immense concern on my face.

He snorted. "I been losing weight for eighteen years, Jazzy. That's the least of my worries."

"What are your other worries?" I asked quietly, afraid of the answer.

"Well, for one, my lungs gave out about a month ago. I guess—" He coughed, trying to speak too many words at once. "I guess I finally breathed in all the dust they could hold. And for two..." Daddy's eyes glistened as he inhaled a raspy breath. "I don't got a job no more, and the reason we still got the house is cause they's expecting you at work tomorrow morning."

I had been too stunned to cry when I first saw him, but with that announcement my eyes filled with tears. I reached into my pocket and gently crumpled the check that was supposed to give us the life we dreamed of. The life Daddy dreamed of couldn't be bought, and the life I dreamed of I didn't deserve.

CHAPTER 41

JULIET

London

March

1941

I FIDGETED as the car approached London, anxious to get my first view of the city. The outskirts looked relatively the same as when I left, but the daily *Los Angeles Times* articles had described the city proper as having been hit the hardest.

"How long have you been away from London?" the driver asked when my eyes briefly met his in the rearview mirror as they darted from one window to another.

"Since September of last year," I answered, realizing I had chewed the center of my upper lip into a tender, misshapen swell. I took to gnawing on my fingernails to prevent further infliction to my lip.

"So you managed to avoid the worst of it," he surmised.

That was debatable. "I suppose so."

"If you left in September, especially early in the month, you definitely avoided the worst of it. You should consider yourself lucky."

Lucky I most certainly was not.

The car entered the city. Life appeared to go on as usual amid intact buildings showing no scars of war.

"Will you drive past the Grand Majestic, please?" I mumbled into my fingers.

The driver took a sharp left turn. At the far end of another unscathed street, the theater stood in all its glory. I let out a relieved sigh only to forcefully suck it back in one block over. A multi-story building had been reduced to a two-story pile of rubble. The adjoining wall had been ripped from an adjacent building. Several abandoned flats were exposed and offered a stomach-turning snapshot of the moment normal life abruptly ended for the building's tenants. The jagged facade of a third building stood on the other side of the rubble, its interior gutted.

I brought a trembling hand to my forehead to prevent further view of the destruction. Noticing my distress, the driver said, "I can take you straight to the country house if you'd like. I'm afraid it gets worse."

"No, please go on," I exhaled, although every part of my being wished to flee the ruins. My sole reason for venturing into the city was to assess the state of my home, specifically the belongings I had been hastily forced to leave inside.

The car weaved through a maze of devastation. Intermittent piles of debris lined the sidewalks in front of partially standing structures. I watched in disbelief as Londoners simply stepped around the heaps of wreckage as though they were nothing more than puddles of rainwater.

"How do you see this every day and not go completely mad with fear?" I felt like my heart might burst through my chest, the rubble becoming more frequent as the car approached my street.

"The bombers never strike in the daylight anymore, so as long as you're someplace safe at night, you can carry on as usual during the day."

"But this is not usual."

"It is if you've lived with it for the last six months."

"Aren't you afraid that one morning you won't have a home to return to?" I could not fathom how any human being could grow accustomed to living in a war zone.

"I can't say that I am," he answered after contemplating the question. "Possibly at first, when it seemed the whole of London would be destroyed, but that hasn't proven to be the case. London has persevered, and I must say I'm right proud to still call the city home. I don't believe I would leave even if I had someplace else to go."

"I admire your sentiment, but I can't say that I share it," I confessed, thinking of a host of other places I could go—would go in less than a week—and guiltily thinking how I did not feel the least bit guilty about leaving London behind to fend for herself.

Reading my mind, the driver said, "I don't blame you, Miss Jenson. There was a rush to leave London initially, especially among women and children, but after a time, many of them returned. You're experiencing the shock they dealt with months ago. If you stay long enough, you'll acclimate as well."

"I'll only be here five days," I reassured myself aloud.

"Then I suppose you'll leave feeling as traumatized as you do now. Five days is not long enough to get used to bombs raining down on you."

"Two days certainly wasn't," I remarked as the car turned onto my street.

"So you were in the city when the air raids began?"

"Mm-hmm." My fingers were jammed against my mouth, making intelligible speech impossible.

The driver said something else, but all of my attention was on the pristine row of houses lining the street. The entire block appeared to have been spared, surely coincidentally rather than intentionally, but my home was unharmed.

The driver agreed to return in one hour. I had no desire to stay in the city a moment longer than was necessary. I thanked him and slowly walked to the periwinkle door, deliberating the proper way to enter my house after being away for so long. I had not spoken with Genevieve since I left her in the Underground, so I could not be certain the house was occupied, but the fact that it still stood made the probability likely.

Acting on the assumption that I had house guests who were not expecting a visitor, I knocked on the door and waited to be invited into my own home.

"It's open!" Genevieve's voice called from upstairs. I shook my head and turned the knob, thinking of every reason the door should be locked—the primary one being that the house was filled with my belongings, not hers.

I meandered past the bookshelves, not taking the time to account for every title but finding no gaping holes where books once sat. My relief was short-lived as I realized Genevieve had yet to see who dawdled downstairs. She was uncharacteristically silent and I thought it best to make my presence known before I fell victim to some sort of homemade booby trap.

I walked to the staircase and found a little boy shyly peering through the railings at the top. I saw his eyes briefly flash with recognition as I climbed the steps. He knew that we had crossed paths sometime during his short two years of life, but unable to specifically remember the encounter, he ran to his mother's side and wrapped his arms around her legs, never taking his eyes off of me.

Genevieve turned from the stove when Michael plowed into her knees. A steaming pot turned with her.

"Hello, Genevieve." I quickly greeted her, picturing the pot and its contents sailing toward me.

Genevieve's eyes swelled. For a moment she stared at me as though I were an apparition. Perhaps I was, as far as she was concerned. The ghost from the Underground.

Her eyes remained frozen in a state of surprise as she returned the pan to the stovetop, freed herself from Michael's grasp, and walked toward me with a chubby baby attached to her hip.

"I'm so 'appy you're back!" she squealed, throwing her free arm around my neck. She held on tightly, as though we had known each other for a lifetime rather than for thirty-six hours inside a bomb shelter.

"It's only a holiday," I croaked, Genevieve's grip constricting my windpipe.

When my lungs decided oxygen was no longer optional, I pried Genevieve's arm from my neck and put several inches between us. Baby Gabriel took a handful of my hair with him, making further separation difficult.

"Seems the lad remembers ya. 'Ere ya go." Genevieve tossed Gabriel toward me, my hair still tightly clutched in his pudgy hand. If I did not take hold of him, he was going to be dangling by my hair, and by the looks of his size, he would not dangle long.

I drew the baby to my side, the newborn I cuddled with in the Underground unrecognizable in his round face and alert eyes.

"Look, I 'ave a fat baby!" Genevieve proudly announced the obvious, pointing to the rolls cascading down Gabriel's arms and legs. "Never thought I'd be able to say that. I 'ave two 'ealthy little boys. All because o' you."

Genevieve wrapped her arms around my neck again. I accepted the embrace and even halfheartedly returned it, but I personally thought her reverence was unfounded, given that I had abruptly left her alone in the Underground at the first opportunity without so much as saying goodbye.

I toted Gabriel from room to room as I inspected my home. I thought that if I held him long enough, I might actually believe a selfless act on my part had given him a chance for a better life. But the longer I held him, the more I thought about the child I would never hold because a selfish act on my part had given her no chance for life at all.

೦೩ ೪೦

I WAITED all day for Simon to meet me at the country house. When the telephone rang, my heart swelled at the thought of hearing his voice, even if he was phoning to say he was delayed.

"Hello?" I answered breathlessly.

"Juliet?" The voice belonged to Genevieve, not Simon. My elation burst.

"Yes?" She had been told the telephone number was to only be used during an absolute emergency. I found it hard to believe a catastrophic event had occurred in less than twenty-four hours.

"It's Genevieve."

"I know. Are you all right?"

"Yes."

Silence.

I did not care to have to pry the purpose of the call from her, but I sighed and said, "Are the boys all right?"

"They're foine."

More silence.

"What is it then?" I asked impatiently.

"Someone is 'ere ta see ya."

"Simon?" Maybe I'd misunderstood where we were to meet. That would explain his absence, but it would not explain why Genevieve was the one placing the telephone call.

"One of 'is mates," she eventually answered. After several more silent seconds passed, she said, "A soldier. He'd loike ta speak wif ya. I'll put 'im on now, all roight?"

I dropped onto a chair, my mind bombarded with thoughts racing too quickly to discern, not sure I would be able to comprehend the news about to be delivered.

"Juliet?" Genevieve was still on the line, awaiting permission to pass the telephone to the stranger beside her.

"I'm here," I murmured.

I heard Genevieve say, "I think she knows already," as she handed the telephone to Simon's fellow soldier who proceeded to tell me what I did already know.

Simon had been dead for three weeks. He and his bunkmate, Private Brooks Lawson, had an agreement that if anything should happen to one of them, the other was to personally deliver a letter to the fallen soldier's loved ones on his next leave.

"Shall I leave the letter?" Private Lawson asked, mercifully going into no specifics regarding the incident that necessitated his visit.

"Was it quick?" I asked, forcibly wiping tearless eyes.

Private Lawson did not answer right away, breathing steadily on the other end of the line, surely reliving a memory that would haunt him for the rest of his life. After clearing his throat, he said, "It was immediate, ma'am. He didn't suffer at all."

"Thank you," I whispered.

"The letter, Miss Jenson. Will you be able to come for it?"

"Yes. Leave it, please."

The silence was deafening, neither of us knowing how to end the conversation. When I could stand it no longer, I said, "Thank you for upholding your end of the agreement, Private. I wish you all the best."

I placed the telephone onto its cradle and continued rubbing eyes that should have been crying. But aside from the dull ache that was always present when I thought of all I had lost, I felt nothing else, as though I had always expected this moment to come.

CB ED

I RETURNED to London long enough to retrieve my letter and waited until I was back in California to read it.

Juliet,

If you're reading this, please know that destiny did not fail me. You were always mine, until the moment I died. You did not fail me either. I carried you with me every moment of every day. Every time I closed my eyes, you were by my side.

I died with absolutely no regrets, and I want you to live with none. I am forever grateful for our encounter at the railway station because were it not for that, I would not know your true feelings toward me. I died knowing you loved me, and I could ask for nothing more.

I also died knowing you can live without me. You were always my destiny, but I was never yours. I was but a moment in a destiny that includes me but does not end with me.

I tried so hard to destroy your walls, but now I see why I was only able to chip away at them. You were always meant to go on without me. I started a process someone else will finish when the time is right. I wish for you to find true happiness and love. You deserve nothing less.

I loved you until my last breath.

Yours,
Simon

I folded the letter and set it on the patio table, the first of a deluge of tears sliding down my cheeks. I wondered if Simon met his daughter after he passed. I wondered if he learned the reason behind her short time on this earth. I wondered if he would be safely working at a munitions factory, awaiting her birth, rather than lying dead in a coffin somewhere, if only I had told him of her impending arrival at the railway station. I wondered if he still had no regrets. I wondered if he still wished for me to have none. I wondered if he still thought I had not failed him. I wondered if he wished he could have his dying breath back to devote to someone worthy of it. I wondered if it was possible to hate someone from heaven.

CHAPTER 42

JASMINE

Los Angeles

June

1941

SIX MONTHS after I was devoured by mill life again, I was forced against my will onto a window seat on an airplane bound for Los Angeles. My will had already been defeated by the time I boarded, so there was no kicking or screaming involved, but in the weeks leading up to the trip I begged Mr. Green not to make me go and told him I would lose my job, my house, my life even, if I went to California.

He took it upon himself to disprove my first two concerns by placing a telephone call to Mr. Duncan, who assured him I would still have a job and a house when I returned. Laughing at my third concern, he told me it was safer to travel by air than by land and reminded me that attending the film's premiere was part of my contract. Five thousand dollars was also part of my contract, and the majority of it still sat as a crumpled ball of paper under my pillow, but apparently letting the studio keep its money did not render the contract negotiable.

So I found myself frozen with terror, shooting through the sky and praying desperately not to plummet back to earth, on the way to a reunion that might make free-falling thirty thousand feet seem preferable in hindsight.

The window seat ended up being an unfortunate assignment, especially for the man next to me. I crawled over him twice in a frenzied rush to get to the bathroom to throw up. I hoped I was only nauseated because it defied logic to look down and see a cloud, but when I got sick a third and fourth time in the hotel room—all clouds high above me where they belonged—I knew my fear was not of flying.

After a dreadful night that involved little sleep, I stared at the dress Mr. Green had sent over, the eighteen buttons along the front taunting me and daring my trembling hands to disassemble and reassemble them before I had to be downstairs.

I made a failed attempt to pull the dress over my head and then attacked the buttons one by one, more or less ripping the material loose. Fortunately, the dress was well made and not one button popped off. I had packed a needle and thread, but if I couldn't get a button through a hole, I certainly couldn't get a piece of thread through the eye of a needle.

I slid my arms into the dress and started fumbling my way through the buttons top to bottom, thinking that if I at least got the upper half secured, the rest could be finished in the car. I clasped the last button in time to clumsily dab powder around my eyes, pinch my cheeks, and throw a hat on top of lifeless hair before I hurried down the stairs and out the door.

I was shifting anxiously from one high-heeled foot to the other when a car pulled into the circular drive, a familiar face behind the steering wheel. I frantically looked up and down the sidewalk for his familiar passenger, not ready for a confrontation I thought was at least an hour away.

I turned my back to the oncoming car and prayed for it to pass on by, even as it squealed to a stop directly behind me and my name was called through the open window. When the driver called for me a second time, I turned around and trudged to the passenger door, keeping an eye out for Juliet.

"How are you, Miss Fowler?" He raised a hand in greeting while I peered inside the car to make sure the back seat wasn't occupied.

His question seemed like an unnecessary one to ask the person who left his passenger to die, knowing we were about to be face to face. Maybe he was unaware of the part I had played in his emergency trip to the hospital. But even if Juliet's state was too dire to mention it at the time, she had surely not kept my cold-hearted ways to herself for six months.

"Well as can be expected, I guess. You?"

"Doing all right. You ready to go?"

"You're here for me?" The paralysis of panic was all that kept my feet from dashing back inside the hotel.

Ignoring the actual question but graciously answering the question I really wanted to ask, he said, "Miss Jenson has already been dropped off," proving that he at least had reason to think we wouldn't want to share a car.

"Oh," I exhaled, momentarily euphoric with relief. I opened the car door and thoughtlessly said, "You got a new car?" as I slid across the seat. My mind screamed the likely reason before I finished the sentence.

"Mm-hmm."

The brief respite squashed, I covered my face with my hands and groaned, "I'm sorry," as I pictured Mrs. Fields' account of Juliet's trip to the hospital. She hadn't mentioned blood, but her version had taken place in the dark. Without being told, I knew there was blood—a lot of it—and I'd never thought about what the daylight had revealed.

"Was it that bad?" I murmured through my palms. I knew Juliet had gone to great lengths to confine her lost blood to the bedroom, but by the time the driver got to her, she had been lying in a puddle of alcohol, and any additional blood loss must have looked like a terrifying amount given that it was mixed with the contents of at least one spilled bottle of liquor.

The driver confirmed my thought. "She was soaking wet. She mostly smelled of alcohol, but there was a hint of blood too. I didn't know for sure that she wasn't covered in blood until I saw her under the lights at the hospital. There wasn't much blood on her, but as pale as she was, it didn't look like there was a whole lot of blood left in her either." Arching his back, he shook the memory from his head. "I'm sorry. I don't mean to give you the gory details."

"I have my own gory details," I assured him. "Yours don't make mine any worse aside from the fact that if it weren't for me, your car wouldn't have been ruined."

I waited until his eyes met mine in the rearview mirror before I whispered, "I left her to die."

The driver's eyes darted back to the road, and I slumped against the door, feeling like the weight I had hoped might be lifted with the confession had doubled in size instead.

⚃ ⁊

THE CAR came to a jolting stop in front of the theater. The passenger door immediately began to open, and it was only when I saw my arm going with it that I realized my death grip on the door handle was causing the unwanted exit path.

Thinking I was voluntarily trying to get out of the car, the driver quickly twisted around and looked me square in the eyes.

"Wait a minute, Miss Fowler. I know you and Miss Jenson have had your differences, and I don't know what took place inside the house that night."

My eyes wandered with the haunting memories of what I did know had taken place inside the house that night.

"Look at me, Jasmine."

I forced my gaze back to his.

"I do know that you didn't intentionally leave anyone to die. I'm as sure of that as I am that the sun will rise tomorrow, all right?"

Tears glazed my eyes as the other passenger door swung outward and Mr. Green's round body filled the open space.

"It's so nice to see you again, Miss Fowler!" He yelled the greeting like I was a mile away. "Come with me!"

His hand fished for mine and, finding its target, pulled me across the seat. I heard the door I had unintentionally opened slam shut and knew my arms could stretch no farther. My fingers slid off the handle and I was dragged out of the car and onto a red carpet lined with smiling, waving fans eager to see someone other than myself.

"I want you to go stand with Juliet and let the photographers take some photos," Mr. Green instructed.

I had known the moment was coming, but the desire to turn around and run was so powerful, I felt like I had lost control of my body. The weight of the expanding knot in my stomach was all that kept my feet planted.

"Can I not just go inside?" I quivered. "These people aren't here to see me."

"They are here to see you. At least long enough to get a photograph. Just follow Juliet's lead. Where she goes, you go. It will be the slowest walk you'll ever take, but you'll be fine."

"Where is she?" I whispered, my voice stuck behind the giant lump at the back of my throat.

"Right over there." Mr. Green spun me around and there she stood, less than fifty feet away.

She faced a crowd of people and smiled radiantly as one hand autographed outstretched pages while the other waved to those not close enough to reach her. She was wearing a form-fitting dress the exact shade of her eyes and was slimmer than I remembered, which should have been expected given that I had never known her as the sole occupant of her body. I wasn't sure if the real Juliet Jenson was standing before me or if she was putting on a show, but either way she looked stunning, like a movie star, and I looked like a mill worker lost on a red carpet.

I took one step forward and realized Mr. Green was wrong. The path to Juliet would actually be the slowest walk I would ever take.

CHAPTER 43

JULIET

I CAUGHT SIGHT OF JASMINE out of the corner of my eye. My hand scribbled something illegible, certainly not my name, across the paper in front of me. I handed the botched autograph to its elated owner, my smile fading faster than I could force it back into position.

I had been told she was coming but had convinced myself she would not and had managed to expel her from my daily thoughts. As she walked toward me, six months spent forgetting erased itself like it had never happened. I might as well have been standing over Jasmine and Simon at the railway station, only this time with the knowledge of what the next year would bring.

Apparently displeased with her languid approach, Gordon ushered Jasmine the rest of the way to my side. Addressing the crowd, he said, "Miss Jenson will have more time for autographs this evening."

He turned me away from the distraction and positioned me in front of Jasmine. Noticing our eyes focused on our respective left shoes and our chests heaving with such force that they came dangerously close to touching, Gordon tightened his grip on my arm.

"I want you two to make your way to the photographers. I want to see smiles on your faces, and I want you to stand there until every one of them has their shot. I don't know what's going on, Juliet, but if you can't walk yourself past the photographers and take Jasmine with you, I will take you by the hand and lead you straight into the theater, and the story tomorrow can be why you were suspiciously absent from the red carpet."

I raised my eyes to Gordon's and silently called his bluff before shifting my gaze to Jasmine. She looked positively dreadful. Six months had aged her ten years, and if she had attempted to conceal the rapid decline, she had failed miserably.

Jasmine's thin frame trembled as her anxiety played out in a succession of labored swallows. Confident a photograph would accurately portray her ragged state, I pushed my memories to the back of my mind, said, "Let's go," and walked away.

I forced a smile and strolled down the line of photographers. Jasmine walked a step behind and no one cared to ask her to move closer. No one, that is, except Gordon. We were almost at the end of what felt like a funeral procession when he came from behind, clasped our elbows, and marched us backwards to begin again.

"Now you're going to do it as though you like each other," Gordon warned.

"That was as though we like each other," I muttered.

"Then you're going to do it as though you love each other."

"No." I shook myself free of Gordon's grasp. The word *love* had been used so rarely and so fleetingly in my life that I could not associate its meaning with Jasmine.

"You may give the photographers whatever caption you like. I'll be inside."

⋈ ⋊

THE film's premiere provided two hours of uninterrupted agony. I did not see the story that took place on the screen, but I relived every moment of its production. I watched my body subtly change as the film progressed, like a ticking time bomb ever closer to destruction, unnoticeable to the casual observer.

I cringed at the first sign of a visibly snug dress, but my angst was short-lived. Moments later, the same dress appeared a bit loose in the waist. Tears burned to be released as I remembered Jasmine's simple act of kindness. She had spent an entire evening letting my dresses out one by one, leaving extra space for reasons that were severely misguided but compassionate all the same.

Jasmine, along with the fortuitously required use of properly laced corsets, had allowed the timer to tick silently for four more weeks until production ended. She had bought me enough time to return home and face reality out of the spotlight, and for that I would have been forever grateful. But then she had detonated the bomb herself.

As I watched Jasmine on the screen, her eyes dancing with genuine satisfaction as Elaina and her family were burned alive, I remembered why I despised her.

CB ED

JASMINE and I were seated next to each other at a celebratory dinner for the well-received film. Neither of us acknowledged the other until the waiter was walking around the table pouring wine into glasses.

I glanced at Jasmine, wondering if she still believed alcohol was responsible for my affliction. I knew what she had seen inside the house, but given her naiveté, I did not know what she had made of it. It was entirely possible that she thought excessive drinking could lead to major bloodshed.

The waiter filled my glass, and Jasmine's eyes followed my hand as I raised the goblet to my lips. She watched me take a sip, and then her eyes met mine.

"Is it all right with you if I have just one glass of wine?" I asked contemptuously. "I promise I won't overindulge."

Jasmine's eyelids grew heavy, her eyes fell, and she did not look at me again.

CB ED

JASMINE MADE a dash for the car when the driver arrived. After a brief conversation between them, I was summoned to the open window. I stood outside as the driver explained that he was to take both of us home. He added that it was our decision whether he completed the task in one trip or two, all the while looking apologetically at Jasmine in the rearview mirror.

If the driver was going to prematurely apologize to her, I might as well give him something to apologize for. I opened the door and waited for Jasmine to slide across the seat. A part of me hoped she would slide right on out the other door. Exposing Jasmine's horrific behavior meant reliving my own, but the thought of her having no remorse, thinking she'd done nothing wrong, was worse than dredging up a nightmare that surfaced regularly anyway.

Jasmine clung to the door with her entire body pressed against it, but she made no attempt to exit the car. The tension built until it was so thick it was suffocating, and the discomfort was not confined to the back seat. Jasmine and the driver swapped occasional glances, and I began to wonder what exactly they had discussed during their time together earlier in the day. To my knowledge neither of them knew the truth, yet they seemed to have exchanged their own versions of the truth and formed an infuriating confidence from which I was blatantly excluded.

Relief swept across Jasmine's face when the driver turned into the hotel's entrance. I waited for the car to come to all but a complete stop before I made my request.

"I'd like to speak to Jasmine alone. Will you please go have a cigarette or two?"

Jasmine's terrified eyes shot to the driver, but his eyes were on me, asking me to reconsider, knowing that my request could become a demand, leaving him no choice but to oblige. I owed him my life, but Jasmine owed me her guilt, and at the moment the latter was more important.

"Stop looking at him like you're some innocent victim in need of saving!" I demanded.

Jasmine's eyes fell to her lap and I turned my attention to the driver. "I have something to say to Jasmine. Either leave us and allow me to say it, or I'll get out here as well and speak with her inside."

With one foot out the door, the driver turned to me and made one last plea on Jasmine's behalf. "Miss Fowler is already suffering for her supposed wrongdoings. You can't punish her more than she's punishing herself."

That was good to know, but I needed to see it for myself.

CHAPTER 44

JASMINE

THE DRIVER'S DOOR slammed, and I was alone with Juliet. The lump that had blocked my throat all afternoon dropped to my stomach and swelled like a balloon.

I braced myself for what was coming. I felt I deserved much more than the verbal lashing she had given Simon at the train station, but knowing I deserved it didn't mean I wanted to hear it. Given Juliet's uncanny ability to bring to light and confirm the worst opinions I held of myself, I was terrified of what might be unearthed.

Not wasting any time, she said, "The look of satisfaction on Maggie's face as she watched Elaina die at the end of the film today was the same way you looked at me when you were standing over me in the hall."

I shook my head to disagree, but Juliet was right. I'd noticed the similarity too, but I had hoped I was the only one.

"Was it really that pleasurable to see me in agony?" Juliet's ever-present hint of spite was there, but the least I could do was answer her questions honestly.

I forced my eyes to hers. "I didn't know you were in agony."

Juliet's eyes fluttered away, disbelief flashing across her face. With a deep breath, she recovered her expressionless stare. "You are naive, but you are not that naive."

Lacking Juliet's emotional control, my voice quivered, "I just thought you'd had too much to drink. I didn't know you were in pain. I never—" What was left of my composure broke. "I never would have left you out there if I'd known!"

My breakdown frustrated her and she demanded, "If you'd known what?"

"If I had known you were sick! I never wanted you to be in pain! I would have done anything to help you! I'm so sorry!"

I couldn't understand the words pouring from my mouth, but Juliet made out the word *anything*, if nothing else. Her face looked wet with tears as she leaned toward me.

"And I would have done anything short of dying to avoid coming to you for help." Her message was clear, and she didn't sound like she was crying, which meant my own tears were just creating the illusion of tears on her face.

"Why didn't you tell me you were so bad off?" I didn't mean to be accusatory, but charged emotions squashed levelheaded thought.

"I was barely conscious! I could hardly tell you anything! And what I was able to tell you, you scoffed at! What did you want me to do?"

"I wanted you to tell me that something was wrong and that you knew what it was! I wanted you to let me go into your room and see that something was wrong, but you were adamant that I stay out!"

"Are you blaming me for what happened?"

"No! I blame myself! For everything! I just wish—" I looked away from Juliet, gasping for air and trying to regain control, not wanting to scream my biggest regret at her.

"I wish," I started again, "I had given you reason to feel like you could trust me and tell me. And I don't just mean that night. I mean the whole time I knew you. I'm so sorry." I could barely whisper the inadequate apology.

"I did tell you." Juliet searched my face for acknowledgment that we were both talking about the baby.

She was right. She had told me in a fit of rage at the train station, and then minutes later she had denied it with the same amount of nonchalance as she'd announced it. Choosing not to mention that detail, I nodded my head. "I know."

"And then you told me that I did not deserve a child, that I would ruin it, that a child would be better off with no mother than with me." Juliet sighed and looked me right in the eyes. "You'll be glad to know that no child will ever have to suffer through having me for a mother."

She quickly looked away, but not before I saw one gut-wrenching tear slide down her cheek.

Reduced to whispers and complete disgust with myself, I sobbed, "I'm sorry I was kissing the father of your child when you met me, and I'm sorry for killing your little girl, and I'm sorry for every despicable thing I said to you in between. I'll never forgive myself, and I don't deserve your forgiveness either, so I'm not going to ask for it. But I will be sorry for the rest of my life."

CHAPTER 45

JULIET

So Jasmine not only knew about the baby, but she knew the baby was a girl and thought she was responsible for her death. I had wanted her to feel remorse for leaving me to suffer in the hall, but I had never attributed the loss of the baby to her.

Jasmine was clearly distraught, genuinely repentant, and utterly miserable. I considered releasing her from that prison, telling her it was preposterous to feel responsible for something she knew nothing of until after the fact, but instead I sentenced her further.

"There will be no other child."

Jasmine looked up, sniffling, wiping her eyes with her sleeve. "I'm sure you'll want one someday."

"Even if I want one, there will not be one."

"How do you know that?"

"Because the doctor said conception would be a physical impossibility. The damage was too severe."

Jasmine had reached the plateau of calm that comes when someone has cried uncontrollably for a period of time. Raising her hands in question, she said, "They can't be sure. So long as you still have all your parts."

I did not care to discuss my parts with her. I shrugged my shoulders in response and watched her wipe away a fresh wave of tears.

"So not only did I kill your first baby, but now you'll never be able to have another one because of me?"

"Stop saying that," I muttered.

"What?"

"Kill."

Jasmine's face showed faint hope. "You don't think I killed her?"

I did not answer immediately. When Jasmine was forced to exhale the breath she was holding, I said, "I think you acted negligently."

"Negligent manslaughter," Jasmine agreed, nodding. "That's what I charged myself with."

Apparently she had done her research and learned the proper term for the crime she thought she had committed. I stared out the window, grimacing at her use of the word *manslaughter*, its connotation more offensive to my sensibilities than *kill*.

I felt Jasmine's eyes on my back, wanting to say something more.

"What?" I made sure my tone conveyed the proper amount of enthusiasm I felt in regards to hearing whatever she wished to say.

Jasmine swallowed audibly and meekly asked, "Have you heard from Simon?"

The question pierced my chest like a dagger, with Jasmine twisting the exposed end. The feeling was so real that I fought for a breath. When I turned to face her, Jasmine's face showed hopeful anticipation. Either I masked the trauma well or she was more ignorant than I thought.

"Yes," I answered simply.

Jasmine's chest swelled with relief.

Showing no emotion, I added, "He's dead."

The statement deflated her like a popped balloon. Her face briefly displayed the same lack of surprise that mine had when I learned of Simon's death.

"Are you just saying that? To make me feel more guilty than I already do?" Jasmine creased her eyes, searching for the truth.

I shook my head. "I'm more than satisfied with your present guilt. I had no intention of discussing Simon with you."

Allowing the ignorance she did possess to shine through, Jasmine said, "If he's dead, how did he get in touch with you?"

I sighed. I wanted to tell her to get out of the car, that our conversation was finished, but I also wanted her to feel the weight of Simon's death. I wanted her to know that he was not simply someone with whom I had occasionally shared a bed.

I pulled two envelopes from my handbag and gave one to Jasmine. "I received this a week after you left California."

Jasmine held the corner of the envelope between the tips of her fingers and tried to hand it back to me. "I can see that it's from Simon."

"Read it."

"I did read it. I see his name right there." She nodded toward the return address.

I snatched the envelope from her, removed the letter, and unfolded the paper. Shoving it toward her, I said, "Read what he wrote."

Jasmine recoiled from my advancing hand. "I don't want to read your mail. That's between you and Simon."

"Then I'll read it to you, but you're going to hear it one way or another."

My voice trembled as I began to read. "Juliet. I still believe in destiny, and I still believe you are mine."

I stopped and took a deep breath. Reading Simon's letters was how I punished myself on a daily basis, picking a scab that did not deserve to heal. His words served as a permanent reminder of how undeserving I was of his devotion. I had read each letter countless times, but I had never attempted the excruciating task of reading one aloud.

Jasmine set her hand on the paper, being careful to avoid contact with mine, and gently slid the letter from my grasp. "I'll read the rest to myself."

Her eyes ran across every line more than once. Folding the letter, she quietly asked, "Did you go see him?"

"I went, but Simon never came." I held out a second letter. "His bunkmate delivered this while I was in London."

Jasmine began reading. Knowing every word by heart, I read along with her. I did not see whose tears fell first.

Handing the letter back to me, Jasmine whispered, "He really loved you, and you must've really loved him too, and I ruined it."

I briefly met her eyes before looking away again.

Jasmine dissolved into quiet sobs. She told me she was sorry one last time and left the car.

I thought seeing Jasmine's remorse would ease my own, but she carried a guilt I'd never intended to lay upon her. The cross was not hers to bear, but I simply watched its weight crush her as she walked toward the hotel and turned away when I could stand to see no more.

CHAPTER 46

JASMINE

South Carolina

December

1941

ON GOOD DAYS Daddy made it to the supper table, but on bad days he did not leave the bed. The good days dwindled until I thought he had seen his last one. Daddy wasted away in a bed while I wasted away at a sewing machine, and in the evenings, with our time together increasingly precious, we found ourselves staring at each other with little to say.

Daddy's appetite was still strong, but his arms had gotten so weak that it sometimes took him hours to finish his supper. His pride never let me help him, and after a while it wouldn't even let me watch him. After he excused me at the same time every night for a week, I started excusing myself to save him the trouble.

So when Daddy sat me back down with a flick of his finger as I stood to take my dishes into the kitchen, my heart thumped against my chest as I wondered what could be so important that it was worth bruising his pride.

"There's some notebooks in that top drawer." Daddy's eyes shifted to show me which drawer he was talking about. "Can you get them for me, please?"

An airy whistle accompanied every word, and if I closed my eyes, the voice was Mr. Marshall's high-pitched squeal as he lifted me from the bicycle and hauled me off to jail, giving me a life sentence.

It had taken me years to realize Mr. Marshall simply sped up the inevitable, but at the time, I had been secretly pleased when the greetings from his front porch became a hiss, and then a whisper, and then only a wave, and then one day he hadn't been there at all.

I pulled the notebooks from the drawer and handed them to Daddy, wondering if his voice was going to follow the path of Mr. Marshall's until he too was no longer here at all.

"These was your mama's," he whispered, not because it was all he could manage, but because a whisper caused the least strain on his voice when he had more than a sentence or two to speak. Daddy had always been a man of few words—even less words now that his lungs were full of dust—but after almost twenty years, he told vivid stories about my mama like they happened yesterday.

"She wrote in them since she was in nursery school, before she could even spell a lotta the words she was trying to write. I think she'd want you to have them so you can know where you come from."

Daddy's slender fingers fumbled with the ribbon tied around the notebooks. I wondered if it was him or my mama who had wrapped the two pieces of colorful fabric around the stack and made a bow at the top, making the books look like the present I thought them to be. With great effort, he pried the knot loose and handed me a notebook no bigger than my hand.

The corners of the pink book were worn smooth. A lopsided red paper heart had been pasted on the front cover. Inside the heart, in uppercase letters, a child's unsteady hand had written *LIZAS DYRY*. A line had been drawn through the second word and just below it, in slightly better penmanship, *DIARY* had been written.

Running my fingers across the words like they were written in Braille, I breathed, "Mama wrote this?"

"Yup. Every last word."

My hand trembled with anticipation as I opened the diary to the first page. Time had yellowed the paper and faded the pencil strokes, but after almost twenty years of hearing about my mama, I finally got to hear from her.

Decimbur 25, 1907

   Mama givd me this buk for Crismus today. It don got no wurds so I wil put sum in it.

   Luv,
   Liza Jane Ford

I was lost in Mama's thoughts when Daddy spoke, his voice clearer than it had sounded in months.

"Can you read it to me, Jazzy? I ain't read none of it since you was a little girl."

I turned back to the first page and began, "December 25, 1907. Mama gave me this book today…"

◯ ◯

I READ from Mama's diary every night until Daddy fell asleep. He listened with his eyes closed, seeing her stories in his mind. They were all just stories to me, but five years into the diary entries they became memories for him. As I read about the day he and Mama met, his smile grew wider than I had ever seen it.

August 19, 1912

   Today I started the fifth grade. There's seven other children in my class. They're the same ones I been with since kindergarten except for one. The new one's an ugly tow-headed boy named Cooper. I ain't never known such a mean boy in my life, and I have to sit beside him the whole year because his name's Fowler and my name's Ford. We was talking about our favorite things at school today, and I said mine's flowers because they're so pretty and smell so good. Then that awful Cooper looked right at me and said his favorite thing was rabbits because they eat all the flowers. Everybody laughed except for me and Miss Parker. I hate that rotten Cooper Fowler and I hope he goes right back where he came from.

Two years later in my mama's world and two days later in mine, she changed her tune.

November 16, 1914

I'm gonna marry Cooper Fowler. He don't know it yet, but I am. He's still real mean, but Mama says that's because he likes me. He ain't so ugly no more either. His clothes are always clean and he don't smell like cows. Lucy says our babies will be real pretty if we get married. She says my red hair and his blond hair will make strawberry, and our eyes will make aqua. I don't know if it works quite like that, but we'll find out one day.

Today after lunch I was picking flowers and Cooper was playing baseball with the other boys. I got some courage and told him I was gonna marry him. He pushed me in the dirt and said he'll die before he marries me. If being mean to somebody means you like them, Cooper must love me already.

"You're lucky Mama wanted anything to do with you after the way you treated her," I told Daddy, closing the diary for the night.

Smiling, he whispered, "Well, she was right. I did like her, but I was just a boy. I didn't know the right way to show my feelings. You'll see that I didn't keep treating her so badly, though. Not too long after that I started walking her home from school and picking flowers for her."

Daddy's smile faded. "I've been dreaming about your mama, Jazzy. I ain't done that in a long time."

"Good dreams?" I swallowed hard, not sure I wanted to hear the answer.

"Same dream every time. She's sitting on a swing outside the schoolhouse."

"Just swinging?"

"Not swinging. Just sitting." Daddy took the deepest breath he could hold. "I think she's waiting on me."

I couldn't take a breath at all, deep or otherwise. "Waiting on you?"

"Waiting on me to be with her." Tears glistened in Daddy's eyes. "I don't think she's gonna be waiting much longer, Jazzy."

೦೩ ೮೦

I REFUSED to give my daddy permission to die. I slowed my nightly reading pace, knowing that he would at least hang on to hear the rest of Mama's diary entries. Two weeks passed before I realized just how selfish it was to want him to go on living as his recurring dream came to life in my mama's words.

April 10, 1920

Today is my eighteenth birthday. I thought it was just going to be another day, but that's not how it turned out at all. Cooper left a note on the front porch this morning, asking me to meet him at the schoolhouse tonight. My stomach flipped all day long, wondering why he wanted to meet me there since neither of us had been to school since we were thirteen.

I got there a little early, so I walked across the schoolyard and sat down on one of the swings. A few minutes later, I saw Cooper walking through the field across the road. He looked so handsome, wearing a navy suit, a white button-down shirt, and a light-blue tie. I'd never seen such a big smile on his face, and I didn't think it could get any bigger, but it grew as he got closer.

Cooper stopped in front of me, took my hands in his, and pulled me up from the swing. My heart was pounding so hard that he could probably feel it beating through my hands. He looked right into my eyes and told me he loved me. Then he told me he wanted to love me forever and asked me to marry him. Turns out my twelve-year-old self knew what she was talking about. I'm going to marry Cooper Fowler!

Mama's diary vividly painted the picture my daddy had seen all along. Her red hair and cotton dress blowing in the spring breeze. Daddy walking toward her, young and strong, full of life. Him lifting her off of the swing. Her arms around his neck. His arms around her waist. Both of them crying joyful tears.

I had pictured a little girl when Daddy told me he had been dreaming about my mama on a swing. But Daddy didn't dream about my mama as a child. He didn't even dream about the day they promised to be together forever. He dreamed of the day their promise would be kept.

❈ ❈

WITH great reluctance I turned to the last words my mama ever wrote and read them out loud.

February 4, 1922

I don't think I can do this alone. I pray that I won't have to find out. There's a thin layer of snow on the ground and the sun ain't shone in three days, but the work must be done. Cooper and Daddy left early this morning to go into town to buy supplies. Mama let them drop her off at Sally's house. She's been watching me like a hawk for a month, and we all talked her into taking a break today. I don't think now that was such a good idea.

I got out of bed to see them off, but it was so cold that I got back under the covers and fell asleep. My stomach was cramping when I woke up. It wasn't hurting too bad, and the cramps only came every fifteen minutes or so, so I just stayed under the warmth of the covers until I was desperate to go to the outhouse. As I stepped off the porch, I felt something wet between my legs, and a little puddle formed at my feet. At first I thought I hadn't made it to the toilet in time, but my bladder was still full. I knew losing my waters meant the baby was on its way, but I thought I still had lots of time. I went inside and tried to busy myself with taking care of the house, but the pain got worse and the cramps came more often. Every time my stomach tightened I had to stop what I was doing and grab something nearby. The pain became too much to stand through, so I got back in the bed.

The cramps are coming every five minutes now. Every time I feel one coming, I lay the pen down and squeeze my pillow real tight. It feels better to have something to hold onto. When the next cramp passes, I'm going to pour myself a bath. Hopefully that will slow the pains until Mama gets home. If that don't work, I don't know what I'm going to do. Just pray she gets home soon, I guess. Whatever I have to go through will all be worth it when I'm holding my little Cooper James or Jasmine Rose.

"Nothing's ever worth it when you have to say it'll all be worth it," I murmured, closing the notebook, thinking of what I was putting my mama through as she wrote those last words in her diary.

Daddy's eyes popped open. He leaned toward me, and with great conviction, he said, "You was worth it."

I suddenly understood that Daddy didn't hold on to life to hear my mama's words one last time. He held on so I wouldn't have to read them alone.

"I want you to promise me you'll get outta the mill, Jazzy. Go back to California, do whatever you gotta do, but don't stay here. Promise me."

"I promise I will do everything in my power to get out of here," I said, taking his hand and forcing myself to give him the permission he needed. "I think you and Mama have waited long enough, Daddy. You got me raised and that's what you promised her you'd do. You tell her I love her when you see her, all right?"

"She knows you love her, Jazzy," Daddy wheezed. Reaching under his pillow, he pulled out a newer notebook. "This is what happened after your mama stopped writing. I've been filling the pages every day while you're at work. We don't got no pictures from when you was a baby, and I don't want you feeling like you didn't exist until you started forming your own memories. So I wrote down everything I could remember."

"Will you read it to me?" I wanted to avoid telling Daddy goodnight as long as possible. I also wanted to hear his voice tell me his story, even if it was told in nothing more than a whisper.

Daddy cleared his throat and began reading, his voice hoarse but recognizable.

"The memory feels like a thousand bees stinging my skin, but while it was happening, I felt nothing. I had to get my wife out of the bathtub. Her head rested above the water, but her lips were blue and specks of ice glistened on her eyelashes."

Daddy told me how I came to be in the world and how my mama held me on her chest, as aware of my presence as she could be. He told me how we came to be at the mill and how he immediately regretted the decision but couldn't bring himself to walk in the memory of my mama's footsteps every day.

Summing up my existence, he read, "And just like that, my daughter's world became confined to a property line."

Daddy closed the notebook. He slowly scanned me top to bottom and left to right, like he was reading the last page of his story. After several seconds, he lifted his eyes to mine.

"I love you, Jazzy."

"I love you too, Daddy." I raised the corners of my mouth into what was meant to be a smile but wouldn't quite come to fruition. He weakly returned the gesture and closed his eyes.

I sat with Daddy until he started to softly snore. Kissing his cheek, I lingered against its warmth. No matter what the morning might bring, we had said goodbye.

CB EO

I TOSSED and turned all night. With the first light of morning, I tiptoed to Daddy's door. After I knocked to no answer, I quietly called for him. When there was still no answer, I opened the door a crack and peeked inside.

Daddy was lying on his back. His eyes were closed and the bed covers were pulled up to his neck. He looked like he was asleep, but the blanket didn't rise and fall with the steady breath of a person who's only sleeping.

I had known all night that Daddy wouldn't wake up in the morning, but I couldn't bring myself to confirm what I already knew, so I walked down the street and tapped on Andrew's bedroom window until he stirred. Blinking away a deep sleep, he saw me peering inside and sat up. I thought it was obvious that I wanted him to open the window, but when he just stared at me like he was never going to figure that out on his own, I waved him over. Clearly annoyed, Andrew trudged to the window and lifted it.

Squinting to block the rising sun, he said, "Geez, Jazzy. It's Christmas Eve. Even the rooster's sleeping in today."

"I need you to come check on my daddy."

"What's wrong with him?"

"I think he died during the night."

I must have been in shock. A few hours didn't seem long enough to reach a peaceful acceptance in regards to the death of the person I loved more than anyone in the whole world, but my voice sounded calm and I felt very serene.

Andrew's eyes popped open. "You think he what?!"

He didn't really want an answer, closing the window and rushing out the front door before I could walk around to the porch. I hurried along behind him as he jogged to my house and didn't catch up until his haste hit a wall outside Daddy's closed bedroom door.

Andrew and I stood side by side, staring at the door like we might be able to see through it if we concentrated hard enough. He seemed to wilt the longer we stood there, his shoulder slowly sliding down my upper arm.

"I already looked inside," I quietly offered, trying to lessen his trepidation.

I knew it was inappropriate to ask a sixteen-year-old to check a man for signs of life, but little Andrew Carter had been bigger than me for so long that I tended to forget he was still a boy, and not even a working boy. He was a schoolboy, fortunate enough to still be living out his boyhood.

"What did you see?" His arm shivered against my elbow.

"He looked like he was sleeping."

Andrew's annoyance briefly returned. "Maybe he is, Jazzy. I already told you it's early."

"He looked like he was sleeping, but he didn't look like he was breathing," I elaborated. "If you'll stand here, I'll go check." I felt like I was in a better state than Andrew, and his presence gave me the courage I needed to enter the room.

"No, I'll do it." Andrew took a deep breath and opened the door wide enough to slip inside. A minute that felt like an hour passed before he reappeared, his face pale. "He doesn't have a pulse."

A sudden rush of emotion brought tears to my eyes, but they were not tears of sadness.

"He's with my mama," I whispered. "He's been waiting to see her for twenty years, and he's finally there."

"He's in a place we can't even dream of." Andrew awkwardly draped an arm across my shoulders. It was also not a sixteen-year-old boy's job to comfort the bereaved.

"Shouldn't I feel sad, though?"

"He was real sick, Jazzy, and he wasn't getting any better. Maybe you just know he's better off."

I did know he was better off, but I also knew I had just lost the only person who loved me. Reality was bound to break my heart eventually.

◌◌ ◌◌

I SPENT Christmas Day trying to flatten my crumpled check from California. I spent the day after Christmas convincing a bank it was legitimate.

The teller refused to take my word for it, and I could hardly blame him. My skirt suit did little to mask the fact that I was a dirt-poor mill worker. Had I been the bank teller, I would have laughed in my face when I presented a four-thousand-dollar check from a Hollywood film studio. He was too bewildered to laugh, but he told me he would have to speak with the issuing bank at my expense.

I waited while he was patched through to the bank that issued the check, who was patched through to the person who signed the check, who was patched through to Mr. Green, who was eventually patched through to the man behind the counter in front of me, who slid the telephone receiver underneath the bars that separated us when Mr. Green asked to speak to me.

He wished me a Merry Christmas and then scolded me for not cashing the check sooner. I explained why my Christmas was not merry and told him I needed the money for a proper burial. His tone quickly turned to one of pity, and he asked to speak to the teller again.

After doing a lot of listening and very little talking, the bank teller hung up the telephone. He offered his condolences for my loss and told me the long-distance call wouldn't be at my expense after all as he counted out forty hundred-dollar bills. He banded them together, dropped them into my pocketbook, and handed me a root beer candy stick which I quickly exchanged for a peppermint before I hurried out the door and down the sidewalk to where Andrew waited in his truck.

"I feel like I just robbed the bank," I heaved, showing him the stack of bills inside my bag.

"You're acting like you just robbed the bank, too. Get in before somebody robs *you*. You can't be walking around with that kind of cash, Jazzy."

"Nobody will know how much I've got," I said, climbing onto the passenger seat. I slid one bill out of the pile and pointed toward the men's clothing store down the street. "I need to get a suit."

Andrew drove past the restaurant where Daddy and I had eaten during our one and only trip downtown. I felt the first twinge of loss, but it passed quickly as I busied myself with finding exactly what I was looking for inside the store.

I bought a navy-blue suit, a white dress shirt, a light-blue silk tie, and a pair of navy dress shoes. I knew my daddy's spirit had left his body, leaving his burial attire unimportant, but I wanted him laid to rest exactly as my mama had described him the day he asked her to marry him.

I spent what was left of the first hundred dollars paying for Daddy's body to be released from the hospital morgue. Two hundred more was spent making arrangements with a mortuary to prepare the body and transport the casket.

With thirty-seven-hundred dollars to spare, Andrew, his mama and daddy, and I followed the hearse ninety miles to the cemetery. We gathered around a pre-dug hole beside my mama's grave. All four of my grandparents were buried on either side of Mama's grave and Daddy's hole.

As the mortician lowered Daddy into the ground, I noticed that half of Mama's tombstone was meant for him, already engraved with every detail except his date of death. I scanned the graves of my entire family. They were collectively framed by a rectangle of large white rocks, and there was absolutely no room for me. The only child. The only grandchild.

Maybe they assumed I would have a husband and would want to be buried next to him, but if I never got married, what then? There was no direction the rocks could be moved to make space for another grave.

The irrational anguish over my body decaying alone in death was what sparked the more crushing realization that I was completely alone in life. By the time the last shovel of dirt was thrown on Daddy's grave, grief had a death grip on me.

ଓ ଔ

ONLY BECAUSE Andrew had threatened to jump in after it if I threw what was left of my Hollywood money onto Daddy's casket, I found myself in possession of thirty-seven hundred-dollar bills I wanted to get rid of. I didn't deserve to benefit from what had transpired in California, so swapping the money for something wasn't an option.

I was buying a tin can and a shovel from the company store, being handed change the store owner's wife refused to keep, when she ducked below the counter and came up with a message typed on a slip of paper.

"Telegram came for you the other day. A Mr. Green. Said he'll call you here tomorrow evening at seven o'clock."

"I can call him now," I told her, scanning the paper for a clue as to why he wanted to talk to me. Seeing no explanation, I assumed he just wanted to make sure the bank had given me the money.

"I ain't gonna have you tying up the line that long," she huffed in her usual disgruntled tone. "You wouldn't be able to afford it anyway. It'd cost you a lifetime of local calls."

I asked her how much a lifetime of local calls would cost me, hoping she would say thirty-seven-hundred dollars and save me the trouble of digging a hole in the backyard.

"Could be twenty dollars or more I'd imagine, depending on how long you plan to talk."

I held out a twenty-dollar bill and told her I only planned to thank Mr. Green for his help. She glared at my offering through slits of suspicion before snatching the money from my hand and making quite a show of confirming its authenticity. She was holding the bill in one hand and a magnifying glass in the other, stretching her arms toward a light on the ceiling when the store owner appeared from the back room, set the telephone on top of the counter, and disappeared again without saying a word.

I dialed the operator, and a few minutes later Mr. Green was on the other end of the line. He did not want my thanks. He wanted me to attend the London premiere of my film. I told him I would send the money I didn't spend on the burial back to him if he would be so kind as to let me out of my contract. He said his invitation had nothing to do with my contract; it was simply an offer for extended employment.

I told him I didn't wish to extend my employment. He asked if I was satisfied with my current occupation. I told him my current occupation would keep being my occupation regardless of whether or not I attended the premiere.

He told me Juliet had been traveling around entertaining the troops since the Los Angeles premiere, and he thought it would be nice if I joined her on her travels. I told him I didn't feel much like entertaining right now. He told me I would be more of an assistant than an entertainer.

I told him he would likely lose Juliet as an entertainer if he made me her assistant. He told me that was nonsense. Then he told me he was offering me a break, possibly a permanent one, from the mill.

I thought of my last promise to my daddy. I had vowed to do everything in my power to get away. Surely Juliet hadn't been informed of Mr. Green's plan yet. The minute she learned of it, she would refuse to participate and I would stay at the mill where I belonged.

I kindly thanked Mr. Green for thinking of me and accepted his offer, knowing Juliet's power would override my power, but feeling like I had kept my promise all the same.

CHAPTER 47

JULIET

London

February

1942

WAR-TORN BUT NOT WEARY, Londoners bustled about amid more partially standing structures but fewer piles of rubble than when last I visited. A small reconstruction effort appeared to be underway by men fortunate enough to be wearing civilian attire.

With the Germans focusing their nightly attacks elsewhere, and because I had received no word of my home's demise, my homecoming was not accompanied by the severe apprehension that had surrounded my previous visit.

I twisted the doorknob and was surprised to find the front door locked, having assumed the instruction was futile when I told Genevieve to keep it that way. I knocked on the door, searching for the key in my handbag. There was no answer. I knocked again, more forcefully, and found the key and unlocked the door. The door swung open and revealed bare bookshelves.

"Genevieve!" I demanded, racing up the stairs and finding everything as it should be, but no sign of my house guests.

"Genevieve!" I climbed the second flight of stairs and gave her bedroom door two quick raps before throwing it open. The room, like with the rest of the house, gave no indication of an abrupt or unexpected exit, with nothing missing or out of place aside from the books, Genevieve, and her children.

There was no doubt in my mind that my books had met a fate Genevieve had casually mentioned when she first entered my home.

These books, they'd probly buy foive years' rent where I used ta live, maybe more.

A thief had taken my books and sold them. A thief who used the key she had graciously been given to lock the door behind her as she left.

Livid, I crossed the hall and headed straight to my bedroom closet where the first book Sister Ava gave me, *Peter and Wendy*, was supposed to be. It had never been stored on the shelves with the others. It was tucked away in a box, alongside the little pink dress, the matching hair ribbon, and the glossy Mary Janes I wore to my first play.

I could forgive Genevieve for selling my books, assuming she did so to put food into her children's mouths, but if she had disturbed the contents of my box, I did not care if someone was threatening her life; she would have been better off accepting that person's wrath than living to see mine.

The entire box was gone. Furious tears broke free as I cursed myself for ever making Genevieve aware of my most prized possession in the first place.

I had never intended to show her the box, but as I carried Gabriel around the house during my last visit, making sure everything was as it should be, Genevieve had followed close behind and chatted incessantly, making up for the months I had been away.

She'd stopped talking when I lifted the white gift box off of the closet floor, more interested in the contents of the box than the subject on which she spoke. I had shown her the dress and then the book, and explained the significance of both. When a photograph fell from the book's pages, Genevieve had snatched it mid-air.

"That's you," she had announced without hesitation as she pointed to the little girl. Moving her finger to Sister Ava, she had said, "And who's that? Your mum?"

"My teacher," I had answered, reaching for the photograph and not wishing to share further details with her.

Holding the photograph away from my outstretched hand, Genevieve had flipped it over to read the inscription on the back.

"That's very noice. Whad'ya tear it in 'alf for?"

"What makes you think I tore it?" I had asked defensively.

"Well, I would'n think an accident would chop it roight down the middle loike that. Looks loike ya did'n wanna be 'oldin 'er 'and no more."

I had plucked the photograph from Genevieve's fingers and mumbled something in response as I returned the box to the closet, and Genevieve had picked up her previous topic of conversation right where she left off.

I sat crumpled on the closet floor, grieving the loss of all I had left of Sister Ava, sobbing without abandon as I relived the last twenty years in my mind. A quiet resolve to find Genevieve slowly overtook the tears until I lay on the floor dry-eyed and determined to see to it that my belongings were returned. But first I had a premiere to attend.

CHAPTER 48

JASMINE

THE CAR DOOR OPENED and Juliet stepped out looking like the glamorous movie star the world expected her to be. Brightly blazing eyes met mine, and as desperately as I wanted to look away, I could not. Her behavior was so unusual, I was frozen.

Juliet and I had always gone to great lengths to avoid, ignore, and at times act as though we were invisible to each other. Now she walked toward me with deliberation, maintaining eye contact and bypassing a crowd of eager fans without so much as glancing their direction.

Her behavior grew stranger when the tips of her fingers clasped my coat sleeves. She drew me toward her and her cheek came so close to mine that I thought she might kiss it.

"I've had an absolutely dreadful day," she quickly murmured into my ear. "If you leave me alone, I will leave you alone." Sweeping her face past mine and leaning into the other cheek, her grip tightened ever so slightly. "If you speak to me, I am warning you now that I am likely to destroy you."

Releasing me, Juliet put a smile on her face and dashed back to her waiting admirers, apologizing for the delay.

☙ ❧

I HEEDED Juliet's warning and did as she asked. Until we sat side by side in a car after the premiere. Something about riding beside her in uncomfortable silence always seemed worse than opening my mouth and taking whatever reaction I could get.

"Are you all right?" I asked, bracing myself for the response.

Juliet inhaled and then exhaled with a force reminiscent of our first car exchange, when her head had smacked against the window. That time she had eventually answered me, but this time she did not.

After I gave her what I thought was sufficient time to say yes or no, I said, "You looked like you'd been crying earlier."

She cut her eyes at me but said nothing.

"Is there anything I can do to help?"

"You can stop talking," Juliet muttered, still staring straight ahead.

I honored her request until I felt like I was going to explode if I didn't speak.

"My daddy was sick when I got home from California the first time."

"I don't care."

"He died on Christmas Eve."

Shaking her head with frustration, Juliet turned to face me.

"I know that he's dead. That's the only reason you're here. Gordon felt sorry for you. But I don't feel a bit sorry for you. I think you deserved to lose the only person who cared about you. You wanted to make sure that I knew I was alone, and now you also are completely alone in the world. What goes around comes around, Jasmine Fowler, and like I said before, I do not care."

Juliet turned back to the window, her head still rattling side to side. Her insolence would have been hurtful had I not already known everything she said to be true, but it was her sniffles that filled the silence moments later, not mine.

"I wasn't trying to upset you."

"Yes, you were!" Juliet cried, whipping her head around, her eyes boring into mine. "Otherwise, you would have done the one thing I asked of you! I simply wanted to be left alone, but you pushed me and grated on my nerves like you always do! This is what always happens! You push and push until I erupt!"

"I'm sorry."

Juliet rolled her eyes. A breath of laughter escaped an oddly timed smile. "You're always sorry. Although you're really not, or else your behavior would change. But as long as you say you're sorry, you're the innocent victim and I'm your tormenter, right?"

The car slowed to a stop in front of a row of attached houses. Juliet quickly looked out the window and then back to me.

"If you are truly sorry...for everything," she began, her eyes growing round as she placed strong emphasis on the word *everything*, "you will make certain that this is the last time I see you. You have ruined well over a year of my life. That is long enough." She opened the car door and stepped outside. An exasperated, "Good riddance!" was cut off by the door as she forcefully closed it between us.

I had wondered why Juliet had not adamantly refused my extended employment opportunity. The answer came to me as I watched her disappear inside the house. She had not refused because she hadn't been told. Mr. Green may have informed her of my daddy's death, but he had clearly failed to mention that I was set to meet her bright and early in the morning to begin serving as her constant companion.

CHAPTER 49

JULIET

I SLAMMED THE CAR DOOR for Jasmine's benefit and the house door for mine. I had warned her and she had not listened. Or she had listened and had chosen not to comply. Either way, I was rid of her forever and could move on to more important matters.

I bolted myself inside the house with locks that would render Genevieve's key useless if she were to return. I had been assured it was safe to spend the night in my home, but being safe did not equate to feeling safe.

With the first bump in the night, I barricaded the bedroom door and spread out a map of London on the bed. The goal was simple—find Genevieve. Achieving the goal was an entirely different matter.

She supposedly had last lived within earshot of the bells. I found St. Mary-le-Bow on the map. From there I could have determined the general area where Genevieve was likely to be found, had the bells not been sent crashing to the ground during one of the last strikes on the city.

As it was, I had a map with a circle around the defunct bells, a circle around my house, and a circle around the Underground where I'd first encountered Genevieve. The three points formed a triangle that stretched across a daunting portion of London, and there was no reason to believe she was still within those boundaries.

Realizing my efforts were futile, that I did not know where to begin or end my search, I tossed the map aside and watched it float to the ground, my resolve quickly turning to resignation. Unless Genevieve came to me, I would never see her or my belongings again.

I crawled into bed with a shred of hope that Genevieve had divulged her intentions to one of my neighbors. As I slid my hand underneath the pillow, the tip of my middle finger received what felt like a paper cut. Wincing from the unexpected sting, I turned on a lamp and found a crudely written note.

Dear Juliet,

You never gave me your address in California, so I'll just have to hope you come home and find this. Space has come available for me and the lads at one of the shelters outside the city. I didn't ask how they found room for us. I assume it's because somebody died.

"Just tell me where you are, Genevieve," I muttered.

Anyway, your house is lovely and I would like to stay, but bombs still fall almost every night, and the day may come when we don't have a house to come home to. If we don't take the spot at the shelter now, they'll give it to somebody else and we may find ourselves homeless again.

"Which shelter!"

We'll be leaving in the morning. One day I hope to see you again and thank you for all you did for us.

Your friend,
Genevieve

"We are not friends! Which shelter!" I yelled at the paper a second time as though the answer might magically appear. When I flipped the note over, it did.

P.S. If you noticed your books missing, it's because I remembered you saying they were important to you. I don't want to leave them behind. I've packed them in boxes, and the shelter has agreed to keep them in their library. Not for people to read. I guess just for decoration since it's a library. I have Peter Pan, too. The whole box, not just the book. I'm not giving it to the library. I'll be keeping it with me.

At the bottom of the page, as an obvious afterthought, Genevieve had scribbled an address. I swept the map off of the floor and searched until I found my target.

The shelter was so far outside of London that it barely made the map. Bombs had not been dropped on the city for months, which meant Genevieve's note was written much closer to my last visit than this one. And temporary shelters were just that, making it unlikely she was still at the given address. But all I truly cared about was finding my belongings, so if I was able to find them without finding Genevieve, it would simply be a stroke of long-overdue luck.

CHAPTER 50

JASMINE

IN ORDER TO KEEP my promise to Daddy, I felt like I had to go entertain the troops while it was still within my power to do so. The driver darted through the city streets and maneuvered the outskirts without any trouble, but when he turned onto a road barely wide enough for one car, he slowed down until we were hardly making progress.

The countryside was pretty to look at and painted with more shades of green than I knew existed, but grass was grass, and I had a feeling I would get a second look at it sooner than anyone other than myself expected.

"Sir, I'm supposed to be there soon. Are we getting close?"

"I wasn't expecting the glaze on the road. I should've stayed on the highway."

"The rain?" It had only briefly stopped raining since I got to London. Surely he was used to driving in the rain.

"A good bit of the rain has frozen to ice. Black ice. It's almost impossible to tell what's wet and what's solid."

The car crept along another five minutes I didn't have to spare before the driver made a last-second decision to turn onto a different road.

"You're going to miss your function altogether at that pace," he said as I toppled into the door. "We'll be better off fighting the traffic on the main thoroughfare."

The driver sped down the slightly wider but still deserted road, apparently no longer concerned about black ice. The road looked just as wet and potentially glazed as the last one, but I assumed he'd suddenly gained the ability to distinguish between the two.

I realized he hadn't at the same time he did. The car dipped into a valley, and all four tires became completely useless on a road that was covered by a sheet of ice. The car spun like a top, the momentum plastering me against the door. Round and round we went as the driver tried to regain control of the car and I tried to regain control of my body.

The car's back end finally slid off the road and dropped into a shallow ditch, the abrupt stop throwing me backwards onto the seat. I lay there, my insides still spinning and my heart bouncing around my chest. I was going to throw up as soon as the vomit figured out which direction to go.

"Whew!" The driver exhaled a sigh of relief. "The sun really caused a blind spot right there. Are you all right?"

"I think so," I gagged, the nausea reorienting itself as I tried to answer. I heaved repeatedly into the floorboard, apologizing between coughs.

"It's my fault. I—" The driver stopped talking mid-sentence. His head turned toward a rumbling in the distance that was quickly gaining ground.

"What's that?"

"Sounds like a lorry." Correcting himself, he said, "A truck. Let's hope he can pull us out."

I righted myself as the truck appeared on top of the same hill we had just slid down. Many thoughts ran through my mind as it barreled toward us; hope that the driver could pull us out of the ditch was not one of them.

I had time to think that the position of the sun hadn't shifted enough to reveal to that driver what my driver had been unable to see. I had time to think that a larger vehicle with more wheels to manage would probably have greater difficulty than we did. I had time to think that if my driver lost control in the blind spot, we were probably still in it, possibly leaving the car as invisible as the ice. I had time to decide I should get out of the car. I had time to turn and grab the door handle farthest from the road. I did not have time to follow through.

"He can't bloody see us," the driver muttered a split second before I heard screeching tires, indicating that he did see us, only too late.

I heard the clash of colliding metal, and then I was toppling head over heels, the car falling away from me piece by piece. I was swallowed by something blisteringly cold, and then I was enveloped by a bone-deep warmth, and then the world slipped away.

Part IV
ა ஐ
To Begin Again

CHAPTER 51

JULIET

"Whatever we're waiting for, might we wait on it inside?" My teeth chattered as my lips, having lost all feeling, clumsily formed the request. A whipping wind ripped through my overcoat, chilling portions of my body not normally exposed to such frigid temperatures.

Gordon ignored the question, impatiently lifting the cuff of his sleeve to glance at his watch before looking back to the camp entrance.

"I know I secured clearance for her," he announced to no one in particular.

"Who?" I breathed, the word floating into a clear blue sky. It was a positively beautiful day for anyone fortunate enough to be indoors.

"Jasmine."

"Jasmine? Ugh, I'm going inside. I'd no idea I was subjecting myself to frostbite for her!"

"Wait here," Gordon said distractedly as he started walking toward the entry gate.

"I will not," I huffed and entered a building I did not know if I was approved to enter, but the warmth seeping through the door was worth the risk.

I chewed life back into my frozen upper lip, growing more incensed as I thawed out. Not only was my time with Jasmine not complete, but I had been intentionally kept unaware of our impending future together, leaving me free to make a complete fool of myself in front of her. I'd gone on and on about being rid of her forever, and she had known all the while we were to meet again twelve hours later.

I had agreed to have her attend the premiere, nothing more. Perhaps my great reluctance to agree to the former had led to my being left ignorant of the latter, but if Gordon thought it best to surprise me with Jasmine's continued presence, he was going to see just how quickly my reluctance could become a refusal.

I hoped Jasmine *was* unable to get through security. I hoped she had been detained, preferably indefinitely. The thought of her sitting in a holding room, being asked questions she could not understand and giving answers that could not be understood brought an insuppressible grin to my face.

Gordon found me, his face flushed, not from the cold but from the exertion of walking to the security gate and back. His ample layers of both flesh and clothing left him unaware of how brutal the outside air felt to an average-sized person.

"They haven't seen her." He looked at me and shrugged his shoulders, responding to a question I did not ask or care to have answered. Checking his watch again, he said, "It's nine thirty. I guess we'll go in without her."

"I don't see why you wanted her here at all," I grumbled as Gordon ushered me back out into the elements.

"It was one more day, Juliet. You could've suffered through it."

I could have and I would have, but it seemed as though I would not have to. For the second time in two days, I could hardly believe my luck.

ß ∂

I STOOD in front of the massive wooden doors of the medieval stone monastery, lost in the memory of the day I was abandoned behind an eerily similar facade. All logic told me the building was not the place of my nightmares, but as I banged on the door, my heart rapped at the thought of what lurked on the other side.

The door began its slow reveal, and the emaciated face of the nun who restrained me while my mother walked out of my life peered through the opening. Her bony fingers slid through the crack and reached for my arms. I took a step back as my hands felt her cold, lifeless touch. I took another step backwards as the nun attempted to pull me inside.

I had backed down three steps and my foot was searching for the fourth when a plump, middle-aged woman appeared in the doorway with a shock of curly blond hair surrounding a pleasant face.

Her welcoming smile fell as she hurried to my side. "Are you all right, dearie?"

"I'm not sure." I sank onto the steps, out of breath for no rational reason.

"Shall I go get the nurse?"

I shook my head, taking deliberate breaths to calm my racing heart.

"How about a glass of water?"

I nodded. I did not want water any more than I wanted the nurse, but I could think of no better reason to send the woman away while I collected myself.

She was gone long enough that I was able to accept the half-filled glass with a fairly steady hand and take a sip that did not dribble down my chin.

The woman's smile returned as she said, "Your color's starting to come back. You were white as a sheet there for a minute. If I believed in ghosts, I'd have thought you'd seen one for sure!"

I didn't believe in ghosts either, but I had just been accosted by one. I laughed nervously, thankful my sunglasses had hidden the terror in my eyes when the woman opened the door. She would have likely thought I had escaped the asylum, and at the moment I wasn't so sure I didn't need to be committed. I tried to think of an explanation that wouldn't make me sound completely mad.

"This place reminded me of somewhere I knew as a child. I was overcome by the memory for a moment."

Nodding with understanding, the woman said, "All these old buildings look basically the same on the outside, but we recently remodeled the inside. I don't think it will conjure any memories unless you've stayed here in the last couple of years."

I shook my head, thankful again for the glasses. Apparently when they were paired with a wide-brimmed hat, I resembled a homeless vagabond in need of shelter.

"Then I think you will find the accommodations more than satisfactory. Come inside and take a look."

I stood and followed the woman to the door, the crippling fear having subsided as my heartbeat slowed.

"I'm not here seeking shelter," I clarified as I stepped inside a perfectly unfamiliar entryway. "I'm..." *I'm here to retrieve what was stolen from me.* "I'm here to visit someone."

The woman showed me to a chair inside a large storage closet that was doubling as a small office.

"We don't normally allow visitors unless they're expected," she explained as she situated the backs of her thighs against the edge of a desk. "Is someone expecting you?"

She'd better be.

"I honestly don't know if the person I'm looking for is still here," I answered, instinctively removing my sunglasses and hat inside the dim room lit by a single, buzzing bulb. "I'm not certain that she was ever here, but if she was, she must have arrived sometime last year. She's called Genevieve, and she has two young boys, Michael and Gabriel. I don't know her last name."

It was not until I looked up at the woman, awaiting a response, that I realized my hat and sunglasses were on my lap and not my head. Surprised eyes and parted lips were frozen on a face drained of color.

She regained herself when our eyes met. Fanning her face with her hand, she frenziedly cried, "I told her you would come!" and scurried out the door without inviting me to follow.

I propped my elbows on the desk and applied pressure to the headache I was surely about to acquire. If Genevieve's happy-go-lucky self walked through the door without my box in her hands, she was very quickly going to find out I was not the friend she thought me to be.

CHAPTER 52

SISTER AVA

ANNIE BURST THROUGH the classroom door, bending over to catch her breath. "She's here!"

"Who's here?" I asked as startled nursery schoolers quickly resumed their games, accustomed to the secretary's disruptions.

Annie took the question to be rhetorical, not bothering to answer. "She's here, Ava! In my office! Go to her! I'll stay with the children."

"Who's here?" I asked again, my heart inching toward my throat.

"Only the person you've been praying would come since the moment the box arrived!" Annie placed her hand on the back of my chair. Fearful that she might jolt me to the ground in her excitement, I rose to my feet.

"Juliet's here?" I whispered, unable to breathe.

"Yes!" Nodding toward the shelf where the white gift box sat, she said, "Now get the box and go!"

When I did not move, Annie took it upon herself to retrieve the box. She set it on my desk and removed the lid. With the contents of the box exposed, she took a step back and waited.

Dazed, I slowly moved to within reach of the box and ran my fingers along the child-sized dress that lay inside. Lifting it and holding it out in front of me, I was momentarily inside my cottage at the girls' school—Juliet wearing the dress, admiring herself in the mirror and slipping her baby-soft hand into mine. Her look of pure joy was forever emblazoned on my mind.

The memory compelled me to run to the little girl I so loved, but as I returned the dress to the box, my eyes were drawn to two photographs on my desk—one inside a frame and the other propped against it. Were it not for those photographs and an overly observant street child, Juliet's belongings would've never found their way to me.

Genevieve had noticed the photograph as she dropped Michael off for school one morning. When she told me she had one just like it, I assumed she meant she had a photograph of herself as a young girl, possibly with her mother, wearing similar clothing or standing in front of a similar background. When she returned with a duplicate of my photograph, tucked inside a box filled with items I had given to Juliet, I had almost fallen to my knees.

Genevieve had become certain her purpose in life was to reunite me with Juliet, and when she left for London, she insisted that the box remain in my care. I also believed it was no coincidence that Juliet's house guest had arrived at the shelter with a son who was placed in my class, but I was hesitant to presume the message she was meant to deliver was one of impending reconciliation.

I felt Annie's eyes hurrying me along as I studied the photographs for the thousandth time. They were identical, aside from the fact that one had been split down the middle and then brought back together with such care that the two halves were as close as they could be without allowing my hand to clasp Juliet's as it had originally.

Regardless of whether or not Juliet had been the destroyer and then repairer of the photograph, I was suddenly paralyzed by twelve years of lost time. She was not the five-year-old girl I loved to kiss goodnight and be the first to greet every morning. She was not the child who spent her weekends with me. She was not even the girl who ran across the field, vowing to never see me again.

She was an adult. A successful actress who would have long since forgotten the moments I held so dear. Juliet was not here looking for me. She was simply seeking her belongings.

I slid the altered photograph underneath the dress, closed the lid, and held the box out to Annie. "Here you are."

She did not lift a hand to accept it. "What are you doing?"

"I want you to give her what she came for."

"Ava, this box found its way to you after all these years. It was meant to bring the two of you back together. You must believe that!"

"I...I can't see her." A wave of despair threatened to knock me to the ground, but I believed my words to be true.

Annie pleaded with me to reconsider. "I thought this was what you wanted!"

"I did want it! I do want it!"

The children, surprised by my raised voice, stopped playing as eight pairs of bulging eyes looked at me with concern. I assured them I was all right, and though I wanted to scream, I lowered my voice.

"I have wanted nothing more than to see Juliet since the day I left her. But I left her. I abandoned her after she had already been abandoned by her family. I was all she had, and I walked away and left her with no one."

"But you reached out to her." Annie pointed toward the desk drawer full of returned letters.

"And she returned every letter I sent, unopened, and I don't blame her. I broke her heart, and eventually it became selfish to go on pursuing her. It was not right to reopen wounds that had surely healed. If I truly wanted what was best for her, I had to let her go. I never stopped loving her, but I learned to love her from afar."

"But—"

"There are a million buts," I interrupted. "And I've thought through each and every one, and I always come back to what is least detrimental to Juliet. I did not have her best interest in mind once before. I won't make the same mistake again."

I held the box out to Annie a second time. "Please don't tell her I'm here." The words squeezed my heart as I spoke them.

Annie looked at me with severe disappointment, but with a deep sigh, she accepted the box. Shaking her head, she turned and walked out the door.

CHAPTER 53

JULIET

As I WAITED, I started to daydream, imagining Jasmine inside a military holding cell waiting to be rescued by Gordon. Better yet, perhaps I had successfully used her guilt against her and she was already on a boat, be it floating or flying, headed home to her sewing machine.

Approaching footsteps brought me out of my reverie. I turned and saw my box and no Genevieve. If the box contained all it should, I could not have asked for a more perfect ending to my pursuit.

The woman released the box with downcast eyes and a disheartened sigh that begged for inquiry. Eager to escape while I was able, I pretended not to notice the drastic change in her previously chipper demeanor and hurriedly accounted for my most sentimental items.

As I replaced the lid, I remembered my bare bookshelves.

"Mrs...?"

"Anne Rice, dear."

We exchanged a quick nod of belated greetings. "Are you aware of other books, possibly in a library if you have one?"

Her face twisted with confusion, and I realized the absurdity of my question. Starting again, I said, "Genevieve supposedly also brought boxes filled with my books. She said they were to be stored in a library."

Mrs. Rice scratched her forehead, coaxing a memory to the forefront. "Well, we do have a library, and we did receive a large donation last year. I can't remember the circumstances behind it just now, but I'd be glad to find out for you."

I thanked her and she made for the door. Turning back, her cheery disposition returned as she said, "Won't you walk with me?"

I followed Mrs. Rice down a long hall, receiving a private tour I would have preferred not to be on, being shown this room and that, glancing inside each one with waning interest and hoping I would not find myself face to face with Genevieve.

I wasn't opposed to seeing her. I wished to see her sometime in the future even. I simply did not want to be unexpectedly bombarded as I walked through the shelter.

I could think of no casual way to work the question into the conversation, so when Mrs. Rice paused between thoughts, I interjected, "Does Genevieve still live here?"

"If I remember correctly," she began, pausing and making a sincere effort to remember correctly, "her flat was bombed and then rebuilt late last year. I believe she went home when it was finished."

Seeing as how Genevieve had no flat to bomb, I found it highly unlikely that Mrs. Rice remembered correctly. With my question resulting in more unanswered questions, I decided to ask no others and silently continued the tour.

We turned a corner and Mrs. Rice stopped so abruptly, three years of ballet training were finally put to use as I successfully balanced on the tips of my toes to prevent a collision.

"I need to speak with someone for a moment. Do you mind waiting here?"

I did mind, but I indicated that I did not, shaking my head and smiling politely. Mrs. Rice closed herself inside a classroom labeled *Kindergarten*, and I wandered across the hall to examine the children's art work taped along the wall.

I was crouched in front of a particularly well-drawn picture of a country cottage, thinking that little Emmaline—the artist according to the bottom of the paper—deserved a higher place of distinction on the wall, when I heard the doorknob turn.

A second later, a soft voice spoke my name. The voice did not belong to Mrs. Rice, and it did not belong to Genevieve, but it was familiar.

Suddenly all thoughts slipped away as the voice's owner took vivid shape behind my eyes. I stopped breathing, certain my mind was playing a trick for which I would never forgive it.

Using the wall for support, I slowly rose to my feet and turned around. Golden-brown eyes locked with mine, and the last twelve years shattered into a million pieces.

CHAPTER 54

SISTER AVA

EIGHT CHILDREN were offering hugs of comfort for tears they did not wish to see falling when Annie somberly returned, surely to further convey her disappointment in regards to my missed opportunity.

Clearing a path between the children, she hissed, "She's in the hall. She doesn't know you're here, but she's right outside the door."

My eyes shot to the door's glass as desperation for a glimpse of Juliet competed with a swell of immobilizing fear.

"I saw how she looked at the items inside that box," Annie continued. "They're not simply things to her. They're precious. If she was wounded as deeply as you say, surely she has permanent scars that can still be faded by the only other person who knows they exist."

My legs decided my mind best not be consulted, and I was standing and halfway to the glass before I realized desperation was outweighing fear. I was certain my eyes would recognize her—I had seen recently published photographs—but I was terrified my heart would find a stranger.

I closed my eyes and said a wordless prayer as I stepped in front of the glass. After several seconds passed where I was no longer praying but simply prolonging the apprehension, I warily raised one eyelid.

I couldn't see Juliet's face, but my soul leapt and love welled up from its depths with such power that I thought I must be experiencing what a new mother feels upon first sight of her child. I wanted to throw the door open and envelop her with a love that never faded. I wanted to weep for the years that were lost and rejoice that not one more day would be added to those years. I wanted to never lose her again, but most of all, I wanted to never hurt her again.

I took great care to make no sound as I opened the door and stepped into the hall. With my legs threatening to give way, I gripped the door handle for support and quietly called Juliet's name.

She gave no indication that she heard me. I began to think my suspicion was true, that we were not meant to reunite and I had been given one final chance to turn back and leave her be. But seeing her in person, so close I could reach out and touch her, I could not bring myself to accept such a fate.

I was mustering the courage to say her name again when she began to rise. She slowly turned around, and familiar blue eyes found mine. A self-control I didn't know I possessed was all that kept me from throwing my arms around her and holding on for dear life.

Juliet's blank expression didn't change as I searched her face for acknowledgment that she recognized me. My heart dropped as I realized how foolish it was to think she would know the middle-aged woman standing before her.

I looked away, losing a determined battle not to cry. I had imagined our reunion in almost every possible scenario, both good and bad, but I had never considered that I might have to tell her my name.

Out of the corner of my eye, I saw Juliet's foot leave the ground. She cautiously took one step forward and then another, stopping so close that I could see my reflection dancing in her pupils.

She still displayed no emotion, but her lips parted and she whispered, "Are you real?"

Nodding, I lifted a trembling hand to her cheek. Juliet closed her eyes and placed her hand over mine. She wrapped her fingers around my palm, whispered "I'm so sorry, Sister Ava," and fell into the embrace I had been waiting twelve years to give.

ك ڀ

I DID not expect years of hurt and heartbreak to miraculously dissolve with one spontaneous reunion. Even so, it was difficult to see the undeniable pain on Juliet's face as I released her and held her at arm's length to admire the beautiful young woman she had become. She forced her eyes to mine and smiled, making a convincing attempt to hide her sorrow, but I had known her face long before it became a professional masquerade.

Clasping her wrists, I offered an apology that felt like it was being delivered twelve years too late. "Juliet, you have nothing to be sorry for. My actions leading up to leaving you at the school were deplorable, and my inaction since then is inexcusable. Not a day goes by that I don't wish I had handled it all differently. I cannot adequately put into words how sorry I am for hurting you."

Juliet shook her head. "I have more to be sorry for than you could ever imagine. But I don't want today to be about difficult conversations. There will be time for that."

A genuine smile flashed across her face and then faded as her eyes fell away. "I forgave you long ago for not telling me you were leaving. And I know you didn't choose to leave me behind. The decision was never yours to make. But I'd be lying if I said your absence from my life did not have a detrimental impact that has accompanied me into adulthood. And while I take full responsibility for the choices I've made, I can't help but feel that if you had been there, in any capacity, I would have followed a very different path. So while I understand why you left and could not take me with you, I don't see how one angry outburst was deserving of a punishment as brutal as never hearing from you again."

I felt Juliet's wrists gently break free from my grasp.

"Never hearing from me again? What do you mean?"

"I mean..." Juliet lifted her shoulders as though she should not have to explain what she meant. "I had no way of contacting you. It was solely up to you to see to it that we did not lose touch altogether." Her eyes filled with tears as she quietly asked, "Did you not think enough of me to at least make a small effort?"

"Of course I did," I answered emphatically, feeling like I was failing miserably at never hurting her again. "I thought—think—the world of you. I wanted nothing more than to have you in my life."

Juliet looked toward the ceiling in an effort to confine the tears to their pools. As they rolled down her cheeks one by one, a small voice whimpered, "Then why didn't you?"

I shook my head, confused. Surely she had not forgotten about refusing my letters on a weekly basis for two years.

"Juliet, I sent you my address. I sent you train tickets. I made every effort to keep distance from destroying our relationship. I should have pursued you longer. I should have shown up at your door. I see that now, but what was I supposed to think when every letter was returned, unopened? The only conclusion I came to was that you truly wanted nothing to do with me, and it didn't seem right to force my memory upon you any longer."

Juliet either could not or did not try to hide her skepticism.

"I never so much as received a hello from you, much less a train ticket."

I didn't need to go on trying to convince her when the proof was only feet away. I led her to my desk and opened a drawer brimming with sealed envelopes. I lifted a handful and showed her the postmarks. "Someone received them and returned each and every one unopened."

Juliet took a shaky breath. "The day you left for Scotland, I waited outside your cottage all afternoon and into the evening, certain you would not leave without saying goodbye. I ached for you for so long that I would have given anything for word from you." Throwing her hands into the air with exasperation, she said, "Just two days ago, when I thought all I had left of you had been taken from me, I lay on the floor and wept. I never would have discarded your letters."

Juliet watched me intently, waiting for confirmation that I believed her. I nodded my head, but I was left speechless as her truth brought my own into question. The letters were in my hand, all with the correct address, all with the proper postage, all marked *return to sender*. There was no denying I had sent them, and there was no denying they had been returned. There was also no proof that Juliet had ever received a single one of them.

Juliet's eyes suddenly lost focus. Her chest heaved as she reached the conclusion I could not bring myself to consider.

"*Someone* would have gladly discarded them, though. I'm only surprised she didn't read them and respond as if she were me."

CHAPTER 55

JULIET

I WAS CERTAIN that I had never received one letter from Sister Ava. I was just as certain that I now knew why.

I tore open the envelopes one by one, seething with anger as I found Christmas cards and birthday greetings and unused train tickets. Veronica Adams' behavior had always been detestable, but to go to such great lengths as to intercept my mail, all because her pleasure was derived from my pain—and there was nothing more painful than losing the only person I loved—required more evil than I thought even she possessed.

Furious tears burned my eyes as I realized the far-reaching implications of Veronica's maliciousness. I thought Sister Ava had stopped loving me, so I had stopped loving myself. Because I did not love myself, I could love no one else. Simon was dead because I was incapable of love. My child was dead because I was incapable of love. Jasmine—

The horrifying truth knocked the breath from me. I was Jasmine's Veronica.

CS 80

I WAS told I could find her on the third floor of the hospital. I hurried up the steps, my mind racing with all I wanted to say but unsure of what would actually be said. I questioned whether I should pay her a visit at all, but I was determined to accomplish the first step toward reclaiming my life from Veronica's death grip.

A whirlwind of emotions left me feeling slightly nauseous as I made my way across the room, clutching my handbag so tightly that my fingernails dug into my palms. I stopped at the nursing station and mustered a civility she did not deserve.

"Veronica?"

Rather than immediately looking up from the open magazine hidden within the pages of a medical journal, she raised a finger while she finished reading nothing of importance. Reaching a stopping place, copper-colored ringlets gave way to a pale face stained with freckles. I saw only a slightly older version of the despicable girl I remembered, clothed in the uniform of an occupation her personality was not suited for, and I wasn't sure I could bring myself to deliver the message I intended to impart.

Veronica did not look the least bit surprised to see me. She lowered her gaze to the top of my cheek, and an impish smile slowly crossed her face. Avoiding all forms of greeting, she made a casual observation about her handiwork with a shrill hiss.

"It's such a shame the consequence of your outburst isn't noticeable in the pictures. I'm glad to see that it remains visible in your natural state, though. I was worried that you had nothing to remember me by."

I ran my finger along the slight indentation of a centimeter-long scar below my eye. The blemish was not visible in the pictures because it was intentionally concealed with makeup, but every morning for twelve years it had served as a branding—a permanent reminder of the day my world fell apart.

Proving she was nothing more than an adult version of the child she used to be, Veronica sneered, "I do wish you'd told me you were coming. I would have prepared something poetic for our reunion. I'm a bit out of practice, but if you have a minute, let me see."

Veronica looked toward the ceiling, clearly reveling in my unexpected visit and not at all remorseful for her past behavior.

"Little baby Juli-ette," she slowly began, tapping her fingers against her bottom lip as she attempted to form a hurtful thought that rhymed with my name.

"I don't have a minute," I interrupted. Veronica was pitiful, more pathetic than I remembered, a miserable adult still seeking to wreak havoc. With three words I could forever strip her of her power.

"I came to tell you that I forgive you," I announced with conviction, my feelings not matching my words but my ability to deliver any line convincingly, no matter its absurdity, leaving her stunned.

Veronica's eyes creased as she came out of her momentary stupor. With her life's work suddenly threatened, she became belligerent. "I did not ask for your forgiveness."

"Well, I'm giving it to you whether you want it or not."

"What exactly are you forgiving me for?"

"Everything."

Veronica snorted and rolled her eyes. "You've no idea what everything even involves."

I leaned toward her, aware of hospital staff going about their duties with an ear turned our direction, and swallowed the spite desperate to coat my words. "I know you saw to it that I did not receive word from Sister Ava after she left for Scotland. If I can forgive you for that, I can forgive you for anything."

"How do you know about those letters?" Veronica hissed.

"Sister Ava gave them to me when we were reunited." I left out the fact that we had only been reunited for one day.

Veronica's face furled. She looked like she wanted to wrap her hands around my neck and squeeze with all her might. As I boldly held her gaze, relief washed over me. I was not Veronica. I was not inherently vicious. I had the ability to feel love and joy and empathy. It was not my soul's desire to hurt others. I had lost my way, but I was not lost forever.

☙ ❧

THE TELEPHONE rang soon after I returned home. I answered and a vindictive voice said, "I'm ready to deliver the masterpiece you did not allow me to compose earlier. You're going to wish you had stayed to hear it."

My restraint wavered as I felt compelled to pound the telephone onto its cradle, but I was not going to let Veronica think she had unnerved me, so I said nothing.

After loudly clearing her throat, she recited, "Little baby Juliette, I'll tell you a secret no one knows yet. A girl was found in a field by the side of the road. She lay out there all day, her body so cold. She's lying in a bed in an upstairs room; the doctors say she'll be dead very soon. When asked what happened, she gave only one clue. Before she lost consciousness, the name she gave was you. I suggest you come down here and clear your name, before she goes to her grave leaving you somehow to blame."

"Veronica, what are you talking about?"

Leaving the rhymes behind, she described a scene that did not sound entirely fabricated. There had been a collision involving an articulated lorry and a car along an icy country road. The driver of the lorry had only minor injuries. The driver of the car was found unresponsive near the scene of the accident and was taken to the local hospital. When he regained consciousness, he asked about the state of his passenger. With no one aware of a passenger, a search was conducted in the field where the car had dismantled. She was found hidden within the brush, and with her condition grave, she was brought to the larger hospital in the city with the hope that something could be done to save her, but upon further examination, little could be offered aside from easing her discomfort.

"I've seen patients sustain worse and survive, but she doesn't seem to have much will to live. I suspect she won't make it through the night," Veronica concluded.

Jasmine's name had swirled through my mind as Veronica told her tale, but although she had been unaccounted for since the premiere, I refused to believe she was the passenger Veronica spoke of. Jasmine was on a boat, crossing the Atlantic. I was certain of it. I had guilted her onboard myself.

"Where and what time was the accident?" I asked, hoping to eliminate Jasmine completely.

"Oh, I don't know." Veronica sighed as though my inquiry was bothersome. "But I do know the driver of the car called her Jasmine Fowler and said she was on her way to a military base to meet you."

I only partially heard the rest of Veronica's diatribe.

"She was a bit hard to recognize with all the bruises, but when I looked closely, I knew I had seen her before, standing beside you on a poster for your new picture. I told her you and I were old friends, and that's when she whispered your name in a brief moment of lucidity. It wasn't spoken particularly amicably, but since you are her only known acquaintance, I was told to ring you about contacting her family."

When I did not respond, Veronica's irreverence grew. "Juliet, I don't have all day, and Miss Fowler certainly doesn't. Her family might wish to say goodbye."

"She has no family," I managed to answer, my mind blank aside from an image of Jasmine sitting on the floor with my dresses spread out around her as her fingers meticulously worked to let each one out. I had entertained the memory only once before, at the Los Angeles premiere, as the thought undoubtedly brought a wave of immense gratitude bordering on fondness— emotions I'd never wished to associate with Jasmine.

"Of course she has a family," Veronica retorted. "Everyone has family. Well, everyone except for you. And you had a family. Likely still do. They just want nothing to do with you."

"I'll be there in half an hour," I said, ignoring Veronica's derision.

"There is no need for you to come. Only family is allowed into the room."

"I am the closest person Jasmine has to family." My heart grew heavy as I realized that was likely the truth.

Sharing my sentiment, Veronica chided, "Poor excuse for family you are, then. You weren't even wondering why she never showed up at the military base."

I slammed the telephone onto its hook, no longer concerned with Veronica. Someone had to tell Jasmine to live. She had rescued me once, and the time had come to return the favor.

I RACED up the stairs of the hospital, bypassing the first three floors since Veronica's lyrical taunt had placed Jasmine in an upstairs room. I was prepared to convince whoever needed to be convinced that I was one of her relatives.

I was immediately recognized on the fifth floor, and with no need to convince anyone of anything, I was shown to Jasmine's room. The nurse opened the door and walked to her side while I waited with one foot still in the hall.

A white sheet covered Jasmine's body, leaving only her face visible. I let out a relieved breath to see that she looked like herself aside from a jaggedly stitched chin, a crimson-colored swell on one side of her forehead, and a ruptured lower lip that was swollen and stained with fresh blood.

The nurse talked to Jasmine as if she were awake while she pulled back the sheet and revealed one cast covering her right forearm and another on her left leg, stopping just below the knee. Jasmine's eyes did not open and her face did not change as the nurse poked and prodded her from her toes to the top of her head.

Her assessment complete, the nurse brought the sheet back to Jasmine's neck and walked to where I stood in the doorway. She waited for me to take the final step inside before brushing past me and gently closing the door behind her.

Jasmine's life did not look particularly threatened, and I had prepared nothing to say aside from telling her to live. I stood against the wall, my conscience telling me that she still needed to be told to live, not physically but freely, and that because I was the one who sentenced her, I had to be the one to release her.

I took slow steps toward the bed, each one more languid than the last. My eyes did not leave Jasmine's face and her eyes did not open as I leaned forward, examining her injuries at such close proximity that I felt my breath bouncing off of her cheek.

A twitch of her nose offered about a millisecond of warning that she was going to sneeze. An eruption of saliva and blood spattered my face. Jasmine's eyes sprang open and I recoiled, stumbling backwards and welcoming her back to the land of the living with a flurry of words I'd most certainly not come to say.

CHAPTER 56

JASMINE

THE DOOR OPENED and Juliet's scent filled the room. I almost opened my eyes, but the footsteps approaching the bed were quiet. A nurse's shoes, not Juliet's heels. Her heels had stopped near the door.

The nurse told me the weather was lovely and then described exactly what made it so lovely as I bounced my knees in response to her pinching my toes. Satisfied I hadn't been paralyzed since she last checked, she attempted to crack whichever ribs weren't already broken, tried to dislocate both of my elbows, and finally grabbed my jaw, slinging my face from one side to the other—I guess to make sure my neck still worked. After a quick tap on the top of my head, her footsteps faded away and the door closed.

Juliet's perfume lingered, but I did not imagine she was lingering with it. Truthfully, I didn't expect her to be there at all. I had never doubted she would relay my whereabouts to Mr. Green, but I had been just as sure she wouldn't come to the hospital herself.

I was about to lift an eyelid and assess my surroundings when Juliet's high heels clapped across the floor, coming to a stop beside the bed. As I felt the warmth from her nostrils streaming across my face, I realized that I had waited too long to open my eyes.

Scaring her by popping my eyes open wasn't something I wanted to do. Sneezing all over her was something I wanted to do even less, but before I could begin my gradual awakening, a tickle shot through my nose and a painfully violent sneeze sprayed blood-tinged mucus across Juliet's face.

I opened my eyes to see her backing away in horrified disgust. She covered her face with her hands, too late to protect herself from the sneeze, but just in time to muffle a string of unpleasant words that didn't come together to form a complete sentence.

"I'm sorry," I slurred through my busted lip.

Juliet stood three feet away from me with her face in her hands. Slow heaves turned to quick puffs of air as she started crying uncontrollably. Even though she had never laid a finger on me—in fact, she'd always gone to great lengths to avoid even inadvertently touching me—I thought there was a reasonable chance that being doused with my bodily fluids might finally do her in and started working my good hand out of the bed covers.

As I struggled to free my only line of defense, Juliet slowly slid her hands down her face. Sparkling, dry eyes peered through her fingers. She wasn't crying. She was laughing, through a smile that stayed on her face after her hands were no longer there to hide it.

I had never heard Juliet laugh or even seen a genuine smile. I had no idea what she found so funny, but her amusement was contagious, and though my ribs screamed and my lip split itself wide open again, for the better part of a minute we were lost in shared giggles.

Regaining her composure, but not so much so that her eyes lost their shimmer, Juliet said, "I'd say that about sums up the last two years. Myself an absolute mess and you apologizing for it."

She plucked a handful of tissues from the box beside the bed and quickly wiped her face and hands before taking another one and pressing it against my lip.

"Well, I caused the mess," I mumbled into the tissue.

"Do you really believe that?" Juliet tossed the tissue into the trash can. When she turned back around, her eyes had lost their shine.

I didn't need to think about the question. I had answered it while I lay helpless in a field with nothing to do but think.

"No," I exhaled. "But I know that I said and did things that weren't exactly helpful."

Juliet looked relieved to hear that I didn't blame myself, but I could see that she blamed herself for my having ever blamed myself.

"And you said and did things that weren't helpful either, but neither of us did anything so terrible as killing somebody. Do *you* believe *that?*"

Juliet's eyes met mine for a short second and then fell away. Reaching for another tissue, she nodded her head.

"I know Simon did not die as a direct result of my actions, and I know the baby was lost before I knew I was losing her, but I also know I could have taken greater care in both situations and the result might have been different."

"Or maybe everything happened exactly like it was supposed to."

Juliet didn't say anything, but as she brought the tissue to my lip, she raised her shoulders and lifted her eyebrows in agreement that the possibility did exist and had already crossed her mind. No other words were spoken, but as she continued to dab at a lip that refused to stop bleeding, I didn't feel the need to fill the silence.

಼ ಺

"I KNOW you said you're taking me home, but what exactly do you mean by that?" I asked as Juliet helped me hobble from the hospital wheelchair to the back seat of a taxi.

Sliding in beside me, she said, "Los Angeles. Unless you had somewhere else in mind."

That was where I had in mind, but I was surprised to hear that was also where she had in mind.

"Did you ask Mr. Green if it's okay?"

"I don't need his permission to take a housemate."

"What if he wants your next coworker to stay there?"

Juliet shrugged. "I'll tell him the room is already filled."

"Doesn't he decide who lives in his house?"

"I suppose he does. And I decide who lives in mine." Juliet glanced my way to see if I understood the point she was making.

I did, but I found it hard to believe. "That house is yours? You own it?"

"Yes."

"And it belonged to you when I stayed there before?"

"Yes."

"So you could've thrown me out at any time?"

"Could have and almost did. On more than one occasion."

Juliet smirked, but I knew she was telling the truth.

"But you never even threatened to make me leave or told me it was within your power to do so."

Juliet was quiet for several seconds, possibly searching for the reason herself. Not coming up with one, or at least not coming up with one she was ready to admit, she sighed and said, "Besides, I don't plan on having another coworker for a while. As soon as you're able to walk, we have troops to entertain."

♋ ♌

JULIET LEANED into the sleeve of my jacket as the airplane lifted off the ground. Grinning, she said, "Your suit still smells like my soap. Haven't you washed it since you gave it a bath?"

"Well..." I shrugged. "It's like I got a permanent perfume."

Juliet shook her head, but the smile didn't leave her face.

"No, it's like you've got a permanently ruined suit. I don't know why you did that. That was a terrible idea."

I proceeded to tell her exactly why I did it, both of us laughing until we were crying as I recounted every moment of my extremely unpleasant start to California.

Some memories Juliet and I would never laugh about, but with the ones we could, we laughed all the way home.

Acknowledgments

Thank you, God, for giving me a story to tell.

Thank you, Mom and Dad, for putting up with school changes and career changes, and for being my biggest supporters.

Thank you, Joe Locke, for the cover art and for your patience and guidance during the process.

Thank you, Meredith Higgins, for your copyediting services.

Thank you to everyone who read early drafts of the book and encouraged me to pursue publication.

Thank you to my brother, Nick Holt, for reading the final draft of the book and offering brotherly words of wisdom.

Thank you to my grandparents for telling people I was an author before I was willing to give myself that title.

Thank you to every person who has inspired me throughout my life. You have helped make my dreams come true.

ᘓ ᘔ

 Jessica Holt was born and raised in Spartanburg, South Carolina. She has been living behind her eyes and creating stories for as long as she can remember. She currently lives in Greenville, South Carolina with her dog, Mutt, but hopes to soon be able to say that she spends part of her time in her favorite South Carolina city—Charleston. Please visit Jessica at www.jessicaholtwrites.com.